SHADE OF THE SHADOWLANDS

AMY PROKOPIS

ISBN 979-8-9854601-7-9 (Paperback)

ISBN 979-8-9854601-6-2 (eBook)

Cover image by Lena Yang

Edited by Lucia Ferrara

Published by Amy Prokopis Publishing, LLC

First printing edition May 2023

www.amyprokopis.com

For Malory
You always believed in me and helped me through some of the toughest moments.
This one is for you.

"There is the heat of Love, the pulsing rush of Longing, the lover's whisper, irresistible—magic to make the sanest man go mad."
-*The Iliad* by Homer

CHAPTER I

It would've made more sense if I'd just gotten back from a morning jog, but no. I woke up sweaty with my heart sprinting away from my body every morning since homecoming. I had to leave the bathroom where I was attempting to brush through the damp locks at the nape of my neck to turn off my alarm. This had become enough of a habit that I was contemplating turning off my morning alarms entirely.

The bathroom was already steamy from the shower. I pushed the curtain aside to adjust the water temperature, pausing when I straightened back up and found myself staring out the window. The giant tree in the middle of the yard swayed a little in the breeze. In my dreams, she was always right next to it, just staring up at me in the window with blood cascading down her chest from the slash across her throat.

Alison Rivers was still missing, and the entire town had lost their minds about it. I guess it was understandable for many reasons. First, everyone was concerned by the discovery of what they deemed Super Wolf, a larger-than-ever documented wolf that supposedly prowled the national park not far from Burbrook city limits. It was actually a hellhound sent from the Shadowlands after me and we killed it in the forest, but not until after it attacked and dragged Alison into the trees. Now, everyone was extra scared about the Super Wolf being the possible attacker. No one had asked the truly scary question yet though.

Was Alison Rivers still alive?

No. No, she wasn't. I felt queasy at the memory, but not any worse than the guilt and horror I experienced when I woke up each night from my dreams of her standing outside my bedroom window, watching me. I threw up the first two nights I'd had the dream.

I jumped when someone pounded against the bathroom door.

"Speed things up, honey," Mark said from the hall. "I have to get to the job site early."

I let out a deep breath and turned from the window. "Becky can take me."

"No, she had to show a cabin outside town. She already left."

I groaned. If I had known before it was too late that the Beetle needed a tune-up, yet again, I would've asked Macy or Izzy for a ride to school. "On it," I called back, aware of how annoyed I sounded and not really caring.

I could hear Mark's grumbling as I got undressed.

I didn't bother washing my sweaty hair and the time that saved, along with the messy bun I pulled it all into, seemed to settle Mark enough when I made my appearance downstairs. He was dressed in his work clothes with his lunch cooler in one hand and keys in the other. He started for the truck outside while I grabbed my backpack.

I hadn't been in my uncle's work truck in a long time. Now

that I thought about it, I didn't have my driver's license at the time and the reason for the ride had been summer volleyball practice.

"Woah," I commented as I climbed into the passenger seat. It reeked of cherries and smoke. "Since when do you vape?"

Mark adjusted in his seat, casting me a glance that told me he didn't want to talk about it. After a moment of consideration as he started the engine, he finally decided to explain himself. "Terry smokes that stuff all the time. I guess I just got used to it over the years."

He backed into the street and turned on the radio. Classic rock. Our taste in music was maybe the only thing Mark and I had in common, and it was how he met my Aunt Becky. They used to go to concerts all the time before getting married. Becky used to tell me that he wasn't so uptight then. I couldn't imagine it.

"I need to drop off my application at Beans and Books after school, but I can get a ride with Macy."

"I can take you," Mark said. "We should spend some quality time together anyway."

I wanted to resist. I knew that what he really wanted was to subtly lecture me about hanging around the Quinns and warn me about reckless behavior. The unspoken jab at Jamie and Izzy reminded me about why I was dreading today.

"Shoot," I said. "I have academic team practice after school. We won't be done until four."

"That's fine. I'll pick you up then. Gives me time to talk with Terry about next weekend."

"What's next weekend?" I asked. He barely stopped at the stop sign at the entrance of the neighborhood before pulling onto the main street.

"Terry and I are checking out a new supplier. We'll probably stay overnight in Holston and be back Sunday morning."

He was excited. The business was going well. Some new company just moved their warehouse between Holston and Burbrook and he'd landed several clients wanting to build houses. He told me it helped ease some bills and freed up more money to put in my college account. I was up to two semesters now.

"How about I take you to drop off that application tomorrow morning and we grab lunch afterward?" he asked as we pulled into the school parking lot. The talk hadn't come up on the way to school, but there was still tomorrow.

"Sure," I told him as I swung the door open and hopped out. I didn't give him time to say anything else before grabbing my backpack and shutting the door.

Someone honked three times to the right and I turned to see Izzy's Jeep in the first row, Macy's blonde head in the passenger seat next to her. I went around the back of Mark's truck and went to the Jeep, noticing how Mark slowed to a near stop as I loaded my backpack into the backseat and climbed in. I'd hear about that later.

"Hey," Macy greeted, turning completely around in the front seat to look at me around the headrest.

"Morning guardian lessons?" I asked Izzy. She smiled at me. Since she was still keeping up her charade about shadowing the school athletic trainer for her nonexistent college class, she and Macy were meeting before school to talk about all things guardian. Jamie didn't like the lessons. He thought it would force Macy to wake, which meant she'd discover her powers. He thought it would leave her out of control and unable to manage her newfound powers, but it couldn't have been further from the truth.

"Still nothing," Macy groaned.

"Any day now," Izzy assured her.

"You have fire, and you have your mind thing," Macy said

and pointed to both of us in turn. "I just want to know what I have."

"Paranoia," I said. "That's what you have. Your powers will come in when you need them or when you're mentally ready for them."

Jamie had explained that bit to me early on and it was the argument I gave him the last time we spoke. We couldn't be in the same room without having an argument, so I tried avoiding him as much as I could. He had nagged me for a while about needing to train my powers and train for combat, but after I blew up and told him to make up his mind about if I should be trained or protected, he kept quiet.

"I'm telling Coach I quit today," Macy said with a sly smile.

"I almost forgot," Izzy said.

"Speaking of forgetting things," I said and checked my backpack on the off chance that Becky had packed for me, "I forgot lunch. Looks like it's chicken nuggets for me."

"Oh no," Izzy said, pulling her keys from the ignition as the bell rang. "Let's meet at the back doors of the cafeteria at lunch and I'll drive."

"Bad girls' club. I like it," Macy giggled. She was enjoying the whole immortal, demon-hunting thing more than I had when I first woke.

Izzy left us as soon as we made it inside, continuing down the hall for the gym while Macy and I went to chemistry class. Mr. Puck had been keeping suspicious eyes on all of us since homecoming, especially Izzy after the accusations they tossed back and forth at the drink table. Izzy still wasn't convinced he was totally innocent, but she's stopped her investigating now that he'd caught on.

I didn't look at the back of the room when I joined Macy at her table. Mr. Puck didn't like my request for a new group, but everything he'd said about me being careless since hanging around Jamie seemed to change his mind. It was a Friday after a lab week, which meant we had to analyze our data from the experiment and finish the report. I had already done that the last day we conducted the experiment, so it meant the rest of our group was already busy on their laptops with other things. I handed in our finished report before Puck could reprimand us.

The rest of the school day was just as uneventful, aside from sneaking out with Izzy and Macy for lunch. It was almost relaxing, like things were going back to normal until I noticed the poster outside of Mrs. McKellen's English classroom on my way to academic team practice. Alison's homecoming photo took up most of the page with the phone number for the local police printed in bold letters underneath and the plea to call with any information. I recognized the gold bracelet around her left wrist as the very one she'd stolen off me at the home-coming game. A gold pendant hung around her neck to match.

"Everyone gather around," McKellen called out, "Tori, come on in."

I pulled my gaze away from the poster to enter the room, not noticing the boxes on the front table until now. There were two; cheap fabrics mixed together in one and plastic props in the other. Sitting in a neat stack on the corner of the table were the flyers for the annual Fall Festival, a local Halloween event that happened at the same time as Fall Break at a local farm.

"Before we go over our study packets," Mrs. McKellen said as she moved to her computer, "we need to talk about the Fall Festival duties for this year."

She handed me the flyers and I took one before handing them to Jessica, noticing it was two pages and not one. Black jack-o'-lanterns boarded the first page with the details about the event and the various groups sponsoring it. The second page was a map of the farm with the academic team listed as working the haunted corn maze. We were listed as "scare actors," which meant the box of fabric was likely full of costumes we'd have to wear.

"You can take your seats. I'll just pull up the Facebook page," McKellen said, abandoning the table for her desktop. This would take a while.

I turned toward my usual seat but stopped when I remembered it was next to Jamie. We'd been practicing at the table in the order we sat in during matches, so I hadn't been back to my seat since homecoming. Our eyes met and I felt like they'd punched a hole in my chest.

Jamie had on a leather jacket; the same one he wore on the days he rode his bike to school. He had a deep green T-shirt underneath. He held my gaze for a long moment before lifting his backpack from my seat and setting it on the floor, never once taking his eyes off me. His expression was full of apology, for what I don't know. I was the one who had rejected him. I was the one who turned my head when he'd leaned in for that kiss, making it very clear to him that I wasn't interested. Only, I knew the truth.

I sucked in a deep breath as I remembered the vision the ferryman showed me of us kissing in the forest, matching, and then Jamie face down in the lake. I could feel the pendant the ferryman gave me as it shifted under my shirt, warm against my skin.

I was the last to sit, slipping into a seat at the front. Hayden Porter smiled at me as I hurried to pull my study packet from my bag, dropping it in the process. He leaned over to pick it up before I could.

"Thanks," I told him.

"I think Green Day over there was saving you a seat," he said.

"I'm not interested."

He snorted, shaking his head in disbelief as he said, "Sure looked like you were last week."

I ignored him as McKellen turned off the lights. "Monster Mash" boomed through the speakers as the video panned a crowd of people passing the sign for the Gillard Family Farms. There were kids in a bounce house, taking turns doing flips and flopping onto the cushioned floor of the inflatable haunted house. Macy smiled up at the camera from the face-painting booth, wearing all black with cat ears, whiskers painted over her cheeks. The video went through the haunted corn maze in double-time, speeding past the waving horror creatures that hid in the stalks. The video ended with the entertainment tent, one section lined with picnic tables and the other an open space where families danced. The live band was composed of retired men, all of them dressed as characters from Ghost-busters.

"This year, the Gillards have opened a zipline and they are donating all of the ticket sales from that to the Find Alison Fund," McKellen said over the ending of the song. After finally pausing the video, she bent behind her desk and appeared seconds later with a plastic pumpkin bucket. "We are running the haunted maze like we always do," she said, setting the bucket aside and going back to the computer. She changed the screen so that a map of the maze appeared. The stations for jump scares were numbered along the paths.

"Jamie was the first one here today, so he can pick his station first," she said, walking to the far side of the room. Jamie reached into the bucket and pulled out a strip of paper, unfolding it and reading aloud.

"Three," he said. I looked to the map; station three was noted near the last dead-end of the maze. It was a large circular space with a wooden platform in the center labeled "SC."

"You got lucky," Mrs. McKellen said. "Station three is a two-person area. One person is the scarecrow, and the other is a Grim Reaper that chases people toward the exit. Jamie, pick someone to work with you." I felt my stomach sink when he looked at me.

"Tori Johnson," he said, offering me a smug smile. I wished I had sat next to him after all, just for a chance to smack the satisfaction off his face.

"Great," McKellen said. "Tori, why don't you just move over here then. You two can go ahead and start deciding who will do what." I didn't bother picking up my bag as I crossed the room, simply dragging it by one strap. Jamie smiled wider the closer I came.

"You won't like me if I get a scythe in my hands," I told him as I sank into the chair next to him.

"Okay, then I'll be the reaper. You can be the scarecrow," he said, "I hope you aren't afraid of heights."

"Why did you pick me?" I asked him.

Jamie shrugged. "I wasn't aware that we had stopped being friends," he said.

"Did I miss anyone?" McKellen asked, cutting me off before I could utter a word of insult. "So, I do have a box of last year's costumes. The only new one they requested is a zombie, so you are on your own with that one, Connor."

Connor Taylor made a groaning sound and zombie-walked toward his seat again. McKellen moved a large box to the front table, a puff of dust rising into the air when she dropped it.

"There's no way that werewolf costume is going to fit me. Jake wore it last year and he's six-foot," Jessica said, holding a hand above her head in measurement. Jamie went for the costumes when I didn't budge, coming back with both arms full of clothing.

"At least you won't freeze," he told me, handing me a pair

of thick overalls. My costume was in three parts. The overalls were a size too big, but I could adjust the straps and roll up the ankles. The blood-stained plaid shirt had pieces of synthetic straw sewn into the cuffs, already itchy to the touch before I'd even slipped my arms in the sleeves. A piece of wheat was tucked into the band around the brown hat.

"Nice dress," I told him. I couldn't help but smile as he slipped the robe on. The sleeves were made extra-long and tapered, almost like wings when he held them out. The headpiece had a dark mesh over the face, making it hard to see him behind it until you were close enough. "This is actually good quality," I said, stepping closer to him. The fabric was thicker than it looked. It was soft under my fingers. Jamie adjusted the hood, so it flared out around the mesh. I reached out to feel the mesh, my face heating when I felt his jaw underneath and caught sight of his dark eyes peering back at me.

"Perfect fit," I said, stepping back and focusing on folding my costume.

"McKellen said she had the scythe in her car," Jamie said, pulling the robe over his head. I looked anywhere but at him. The rest of the team were pulling their costumes off as well and stuffing them into backpacks. I sat down as Mrs. McKellen struggled with the computer again, switching the screen to our review packet. I tugged my notes from my bag and began scanning the first page of the packet, rechecking the math section in my head.

"Let's start from the beginning," McKellen said, signaling for all of us to review our work. We checked our answers in silence, everything about academic club rankings on the honor system. I was almost surprised when I hadn't missed a question by the end of it, not having put too much work into studying this week.

"All right, raise your hand if you got a perfect score," McKellen said. Hayden snorted as if it was impossible. I raised my hand, looking Jamie full in the face when I noticed he hadn't raised his. Anger flared within me hot, and I hoped he could see it. I wanted to rip through the pages of his packet just to catch him in the lie. There was no way Jamie Quinn, who'd been through more school than any of us, had missed a question.

"Great work, Tori," Mrs. McKellen said. She was the first to clap her hands, the rest of the room following suit. She waited until the sound died down to continue. "As always, the student with the least missed questions gets to choose the discussion topic from this week's list." She said. She scrolled further down the document to reveal a short list of events from the past week. Most of them were political. There were a few pop culture items listed such as a controversy between two popular YouTubers and another about Kim Kardashian. I swear she's always in the news. I scanned past them all when I noticed something about music near the bottom, a link to an article about a lawsuit between two rappers over the ownership of some song I'd never heard.

"The rapper lawsuit," I said.

"Of course, she picks the law one," Jessica said.

"I think we are ready to move on," Mrs. McKellen said, her cheeks tinged pink. She never was good with confrontation. Whenever the class got a little rowdy, she usually tried to quiet us with a lecture about grades being important. "So, if you follow the link on the board, you can read up on the case and prepare to discuss."

The room filled with the sound of zippers as we all pulled out our laptops. I sat mine down a little harder than intended, still thinking about Jamie standing up for me. His was already turned on and ready to go, but instead of being open to the article, he had a blank Google Doc open with just a single sentence.

Want to talk about it afterward?

I slid his laptop back to him and focused on getting mine started up. I typed the link from the board into the browser and a picture of the rappers at the concert appeared. One was tall and thin with so many gold chains around his neck that it was a wonder they didn't buckle his scrawny frame. The other was covered in tattoos, all different colors and patterns like you'd find on a patchwork quilt. Jamie pushed his laptop toward me again, accidentally making me click an ad for teeth whitening.

I want to talk about it.

I exited out of the ad and pulled his laptop toward me so I could type as Mrs. McKellen changed the Smart Board so that a timer was counting down from five minutes.

I shoved his laptop back, the rubber on the bottom vibrating under my fingers on the tabletop. Jamie gave it one look and let out a sigh. His jaw tightened the same way it always did when he was stressed.

"I just want to know why you're so angry with me," he said.

"I'm not mad at you. I'm just..." I paused to think of the right word. Jamie had lost almost everything he'd allowed himself to have and as soon as he decided to take a chance on something real again, I shot him down. So, why was I the one pissed off in all of this? "I'm frustrated," I finished.

"I just want to understand why," Jamie said, his tone so gentle it nearly broke my resolve. No wonder I was pissed off. It was a lot easier to lash out than it was to be civil. Maybe he'd leave me alone if I was cruel enough.

"It doesn't matter," I said. "Just leave me alone."

He did. Neither of us spoke as we did our research. I noticed I'd scrolled to the bottom of the article without reading any of it. I glanced down at Jamie's notes to see that he hadn't written a word. His laptop was still open to the Google Doc, the cursor blinking on a new line as if he wanted to write more.

"Okay. It's time to discuss our thoughts on the lawsuit. Who would like to start?" Mrs. McKellen said, just barely pulling me back to reality.

CHAPTER 2

I woke up earlier than usual. This time, I did go on a jog.

It felt freeing not only to be in the crisp morning air but to run until my heart was racing of my own accord. I liked the burning I felt in my hamstrings as I ran hard up the incline toward Burbrook Mountain, practically coasting on the way back down. I kept going in the opposite direction, crossing the main road when I saw Mr. Puck drinking from a squeeze bottle at the corner.

He noticed me as I slowed to a stop. I could tell why all the girls at school used to gush about seeing him on runs now. He was young and in shape, but it wasn't just that. He wasn't even sweating but was dressed in just a pair of Nike shorts as if on a run in Texas and not Colorado in the middle of the fall. My image of the stuffy, academic teacher I knew him as was shattered the longer I looked at him.

His left forearm was wrapped with the black ink of a tattoo along with his right bicep. He had a large tattoo that stretched from his left shoulder to his chest, but he was too far away to make out what it was. He raised a hand and waved at me before jogging ahead toward the old train station.

I took that as my cue to head home and jogged the entire stretch back, showering before anyone else was up. I was reviewing my job application for Beans and Books with a cup of coffee at the kitchen table when Mark came down.

"Is Becky still asleep?" I asked. He let out a sigh and rubbed his temple.

"She's up," he said, his tone telling me everything I needed to know. I rose from the table, eager to leave the house before Becky and Mark would be in the same room.

"Meet me in the car," I told him, setting my mug on the counter and going for the front door. He called for me to wait, but I ignored him. I took his keys from the ring next to the door and headed for the truck in the driveway. I sat my phone in the cupholder when I got in the passenger seat. My phone didn't sink all the way in and fell into my lap. There was a vape pen in the cup holder.

He said he didn't vape. *Sure.*

I moved the pen to the center console and found a tube of lipstick there. I pulled the cap off to reveal the almost new red stick. Becky never wore more than a little mascara unless it was a special event. The last time I could remember her wearing lipstick at all was when she and Mark had gone to a Christmas party years ago. I was a freshman then.

The door opened and Mark froze, eyes going from the lipstick to me. His expression fell and he climbed into the truck. We sat in silence.

"I remember Becky wore red lipstick at that Christmas party," I said.

Mark exhaled. "Yup."

"When's the last time you two went out on a date, like, not

sitting at home watching Netflix while you both ignore each other and play games on your phones?"

He turned the key in the ignition and backed out of the driveway as he said, "Since she left that lipstick in here. Put it back in the console, will you?"

"With your vape pen?" I teased.

He tapped the breaks a little harder than intended as he put the car in drive.

"So, Beans and Books," he said. "Why the sudden motivation to get a job?"

I picked the easiest answer. "I decided to save for college." It was a mix, really. I needed tuition money, if I even went to college at all, but I also needed a distraction. I wasn't spending time at the Moore Estate anymore and the extra free time meant more time to think about the dreams and Jamie. Mark liked that answer. He was nodding, clearly impressed.

"It's good character building to earn something yourself," he said. It was quiet again until we made it to the main road, and I saw a banner for the Fall Festival strung between two posts in the median.

"The academic team is in charge of the corn maze at the Fall Festival," I started as we passed the sign.

"Sounds like good volunteer hours for your college application."

"True, and I get to be a bloody scarecrow in the very middle of the maze. The people will come in and I'll scare them, and the Grim Reaper chases them toward the exit. It keeps people from just hanging out in the maze."

"Oh, I remember that maze. We used to call it Make-out Maze," Mark said with a smirk. "Who gets to be the reaper?"

The silence that followed was deafening. I could feel Mark's eyes on me as we pulled to the stoplight. I could see the sign for Beans and Books—it was just halfway down the block.

"Jamie Quinn," I said. Thankfully, Mark didn't say anything right away, giving me a chance to ask the real question. "The maze is pretty involved, and we have to set up all the scare zones before and help decorate... The whole team is going after school every day this week to help the Gillards set up the farm."

"No," Mark blurted.

"I haven't even asked yet."

"They won't need all those people every single day. You can go Monday until dinner time and then be there early Friday before the festival starts." Mark muttered an insult under his breath when the car in front of us didn't go as soon as the light turned green.

"This is all because Jamie's going to be there, isn't it?" I asked.

"Not just that," Mark said. "You've been in trouble at school this year and you've broken curfew just about every time you've gone out."

"I called Becky both times and there were reasons beyond my control."

"Becky thought you getting drunk homecoming night and being sick the next day was punishment enough, but if it were up to me, you'd still be grounded for that. So, I say no. You can't spend every night this week at that farm between the corn-stalks with that boy."

"We aren't even together!" I yelled. "I avoid him at all costs, and I don't talk to him. I barely talk to Izzy. Macy and I don't spend enough time together and you're smothering me all because of a couple of mistakes It's the first time I've ever really been in trouble at all."

"And it better be the last time," Mark said under his breath as he slowed the truck and scanned the street for parking.

"It's a school event. I can't be the only one who doesn't

help out." I eased my grip on my application so it didn't crease any more than it already had.

"You can go Monday after school and as long as you're home by dinner, you can go early Friday." He waited as a blue Subaru backed out of a spot in front of the coffee shop. "I'll drive you."

He'll drive me? "It's just a few miles from the school. Macy will be there with the student council. It would be easier for her to take me than you."

Mark let out a deep breath and turned his glare at me. "We're done discussing it and if you bring it up again you won't be goin at all."

I unbuckled my seatbelt and opened the car door before he could pull into the parking spot. I slammed the door and started toward the front door of Beans and Books, pausing in the entryway to calm myself.

The shop was small. You couldn't really consider it a coffee shop the way Starbucks was, farther down the street, or consider it a bookshop like The Quill, a bookshop in Holston. There were barstools along a narrow table pressed against the large front window. Two small round tables sat in front of the four bookshelves that made up the bookstore section of the shop. At the very back were the register and a counter where you could order from the small chalkboard easel of coffee options.

"Victoria Johnson," Willow Jackson said as she came out the swinging double doors that led to the back of the shop. Her long hair was mostly gray now, tangling with her beaded earrings that brushed her shoulders. She was dressed casually for being a business owner, always did. She had a pair of loose jeans on and a purple tie-dyed T-shirt with a baying wolf on the front. She pulled me into a tight hug and before I could even hand her my application, she was leading me behind the counter.

"Is it just you today?" I asked. I knew she was short-staffed. Her niece told me as much when I picked up the application.

"Sam started back at college this week, so it has been just me around here," she said as she rummaged through a basket under the counter. "She told me you stopped in for an application though and I had another boy apply earlier this week. He starts tomorrow. Can you work after school and most weekends?"

"Well, for the most part, yes," I said as she pulled out two name badges. It took her a few tries to pull off the names printed there.

"When can you start?" she asked, picking up the label maker next.

"I am supposed to help set up for the Fall Festival after school all of this week and then the festival is Friday and Saturday, but I can be here after school instead if you want me, Mrs. Jackson." At this point, I didn't care about missing the festival set-up after school. I just wanted to be anywhere but home under Mark's scrutiny and his and Becky's bickering.

"Oh, call me Willow," she said as a new label slid from the bottom of the machine. She pulled the backing from the label and carefully pressed it to the name badge. My co-worker's name was Angel.

"Okay, um, Willow," I started as she picked up the label maker again, "I am helping set up for the festival Monday, but I can be here after school the rest of the week except Friday. This would be my first job, but I'm second in my class at school and I take advanced classes. If you want me to come in before Tuesday for training, I can do that."

Willow waved a hand in dismissal at me, "Angel can show

you the ropes. Do you prefer to have Victoria or Tori on your tag?"

"Tori's fine."

She typed in my name, and I watched her label my new tag while she explained the basics. She told me about the punch card system her niece helped her set up the store. The coffee assortment was limited to a light roast and a dark roast and a single espresso machine on the back counter. Cappuccino. Mocha. Latte. Americano. That was about it for coffee, but there were many options for tea, all coming from individual Twining's packages.

The storeroom consisted of just three wire shelves filled with packages of coffee beans and extra supplies. A refrigerator sat in a corner, designated for all the creamer and milk options. The broken walk-in built into the back wall was stuffed with books.

"I won't be here when you start on Tuesday, but Angel can help you. He's worked in a few coffee shops much busier and larger than this one," Willow said as she handed me a key to the shop and left me at the door.

I waited at the truck for Mark to come back. When he did, he had a sandwich for each of us from Subway. He still looked a little irritated with me as we got back into the truck.

"Let's just go home, I guess," he said after a moment. I ate the jalapeño chips on the way home, glad our bonding moment was over.

CHAPTER 3

The dream was different this time. Longer. It started like normal with me getting up in the morning and going into the bathroom, stopping in front of the window to look down at Alison standing next to the tree in the backyard. Her dress was coated in blood from the gash across her neck. It was at this point that I normally woke up. Instead, she started to walk toward the house. I lost sight of her from the window and as I leaned closer to the glass, I heard the whisper of a girl as if she stood right next to me.

The lake.

The bathroom door banged open behind me and that's when I woke up. I sat straight up in my room, my gasp so loud that I half expected Becky to come to check on me. I could hear Becky and Mark talking in their room, arguing about Mark's work trip next weekend.

"Who does business on Halloween like that?" she asked.

"This guy does, and Terry and I have to go for the weekend if we want to get the contract, so I'm going. You'll have to find a friend to go to the festival with."

"You should've told me sooner. How long have you known about this trip? You and I made plans for Saturday and now I have to be the bad guy and explain why we can't go."

I tried to ignore them, my heart still racing, as I dressed for my run. I didn't bother going to the bathroom, finding an old hair tie on my desk that would suffice for as long as I was out. I had taken two steps from my room when I heard Mark ask me where I was going.

I turned to face their room, Becky joining him in the doorway with a forced smile.

"Off for a run?" she asked. Mark looked questioningly at her.

"I've been going the last few mornings before school. I won't be gone long," I told him. Mark considered the words for a moment.

"Do you have your phone?" he asked.

Nope. I left it still plugged in in my rush. I went back into my room for it and my air pods, showing them to him on my way to the stairs.

I ran the same route I had all week, running uphill toward Burbrook mountain and then back again until I was at the entrance to our neighborhood. I crossed the main road, feeling a little less out of breath than during the last run. I turned down the road where I saw Mr. Puck stretching the day before. It was a long stretch of concrete that led to one of the nicer apartment complexes in town. I started running the outer loop of the tall buildings.

Did this mean that Mr. Puck lived here? It shouldn't surprise me, but somehow it did. He wore some of the nicest dress clothes for a man who lived in one of these small apartments, but he was also single and young. He probably didn't need a lot of room.

I slowed my pace a little as my legs began to tire. I was

heading back to the front of the complex, which meant I had a little over a mile left to make it back home. I made it past the main gate when the last of the song I was listening to ended. This was the farthest I'd run all week and my playlist must not be long enough, because silence followed along with the rhythmic sound of feet running behind me.

I glanced back and it felt like a new kind of energy flooded my body. There was a man following me, gaining on me. I burst into a sprint, not looking back until I was close to the end of the stretch of road.

The man looked off—not quite running the way a normal human did. I looked back again, the man close enough now that I could make out the orange glow of his eyes, the sharp points of his teeth, and the claws growing from the ends of his fingers.

I should have screamed. I should have, but my mind shut down any other thoughts than running as fast as I could. This wasn't just some man though; this was some kind of demon. I had trained with Jamie for weeks, but I'd never actually faced a demon and I wasn't sure if I could do it alone. The corner was approaching fast and when the concrete switched to gravel, I turned in the opposite direction from home.

The last thing I needed was a demon knowing where I lived. I ran toward the abandoned train station. There were so many places to hide there and maybe old materials I could use as a weapon against this thing. I cursed Jamie Quinn under my breath for not letting me have a demon blade. Damn him. Killing this thing would be easier with one, especially if it was a demon and not something like a vampire or werewolf. I glanced behind me again to check, and the man looked different than before. The same orange eyes stared back at me from a dangerous few yards away, but the claws were longer now, and his face had taken a new shape. It was long and I saw the shape of wings growing from his back.

I forced my legs to move quicker, feeling a little unsteady like I might collapse. I needed to get under something, or at least around something that would make it hard for this monster to swoop down on me from the sky.

I ran for the train station. My heart sank as the door held firm. I threw my weight against it, but it didn't budge. I turned to look at the man and screamed as he ran at me. I moved away from the door just far enough that the monster went crashing through it and into the station. I ran back toward the main road, my feet numb as they pounded against the gravel. I heard a voice yelling behind me, only spurring me to run faster.

The main road wasn't busy. There were a few cars coming from both sides, but maybe I was moving quickly enough. Maybe I could cross before they reached me. I was just a few feet from the road when someone grabbed the back of my shirt.

"Tori!" he yelled as I let out a shriek. My toe caught the ground and we both went down, skidding across the gravel and stopping feet from the road. One of the cars honked in warning as it whizzed past. I rolled to my back and had a punch ready to fly when I realized who had stopped me.

Mr. Puck was dressed much more weather appropriate this time, two hands poking out of a black long sleeve reaching out to cup both sides of my face. I let out a deep breath and felt my own hands shaking now as I brushed his away.

"There was a man following me," I said, breathlessly. He nodded his head but didn't say anything right away. He looked back toward the train station and then back at me.

"Come on," he said as he helped me up. "I'll run with you home."

I was spent from the chase, so we didn't run home as much as we walked.

"Are you helping with the Fall Festival?" Puck asked as we walked across the main road, waving to the old lady who stopped the oncoming traffic for us.

"Yeah. The academic team is in charge of the corn maze."

"Student council is kind of spread out across the farm, so that makes things a bit more complicated this year," Puck said. I forgot that he was in charge of STUCO.

Once we crossed the road to the entrance of the neighborhood Puck set the pace. It was a quicker jog than my average, but he acted like it was slow for him.

"You should coach the cross-country team," I said, a little out of breath from just the couple yards we'd gone.

"No." His tone was firm enough that it caught my attention. He slowed a little and relaxed his expression.

"I was asked a couple of times," he explained after a beat, "but I run for a different reason. Coaching would take the fun out of it for me. Does that make sense at all? The athletic director thought I was being a little ..."

I remembered my middle school volleyball days. At first, it was just fun being with Macy and then, playing made me feel good. I thought about how I was always the last one in the gym, mostly because Becky or Mark were always the last ones there to pick me up, but I used the time to perfect my serving. It was more than just that now that I thought about it. I would serve the ball into the wall as hard as I could, focusing more on how loud the pounding of leather on drywall could get. That sound, the way my arm would ache after a few rounds of it, that was what I remembered most about those practices.

Why was I so angry? It was a kind of therapy, hitting volleyballs until my hand was red and numb. The only thing that was different now was that I didn't have volleyball anymore. Mark and Becky were just as dysfunctional as before, probably a little more so now thanks to me, but I always felt better after volleyball. Maybe it was never about the sport or the teammates at all.

"I get it," I told him. "Volleyball wasn't worth it anymore with everything that comes with senior year."

"You should join cross country," he said. "You're out here before the sun, which is more than most of your classmates can say. You're a decent runner too."

I nearly gave him the same answer he'd given me. *It would take all the fun out of it.* It wasn't fun I was looking for though. I was chasing that feeling I'd get when I pounded volleyballs into the gym wall.

"This one's me," I said, increasing the pace a little as we got closer to my house. I stopped in the driveway, Mr. Puck standing at the end as though our jog here had been the easiest warmup he'd ever done.

"Hey, Tori," he said as I started for the front door. He shifted from one foot to the other. He looked like he was still deciding what to say. "Is that your normal route?"

"Yes."

He paused a moment before he said with a look of warning, "I run that area every day at the same time."

I nodded. "Thank you."

Mr. Puck waved and started his fast-paced jog toward Burbrook Mountain.

Becky convinced Mark to let me hitch a ride with Macy to school. It was an argument, but I convinced him to let Macy take me to Fall Festival set-up after school instead of waiting on him to pick me up.

"So, what was it that attacked you?" she asked me as she parked in our usual spot.

"I don't know," I said as I watched Izzy hop out of her Jeep and walk toward us. "I was going to ask Izzy."

We waited until Izzy joined us. I retold the whole story, giving as many details about the demon as I could.

"Sounds like the same kind of demon Jamie hunted down a few nights ago," she said.

"Hunted down?" I asked. "He's been hunting and not telling anyone?"

Izzy shrugged. She let out an annoyed sigh and nodded. "He goes on these hunting ventures when he's in one of his moods. He says it makes him feel like he's doing something productive, but I know it's not about demons or the gate." She directed her gaze at me.

"I've been wanting to ask since homecoming ..." Macy started.

"All you guys need to know is that we had a fight. It wouldn't have worked out with us—we just don't get along. Izzy, can you get me a demon blade?"

The change in conversation put an end to Jamie's and my past. Izzy looked back at me in shock, mouth parted.

"What's a demon blade?" Macy asked.

"It's a kind of knife guardians can use. It makes killing demons a whole lot easier. Just a scratch from the blade and the demon is sent back to the Shadowlands," I explained. Izzy sat forward in the backseat, so her shoulders were between both headrests.

"It only works on demons though, not other kinds of monsters like vampires or shapeshifters. I thought Jamie gave you one. He said he had one for you."

Of course, he did.

"No. I don't have one and I'd say after what happened yesterday I should."

"You're right," Izzy said. The bell for first period rang, but she put a hand on Macy's shoulder to keep us from leaving. She leaned down toward her right shoe and when she straightened up again, she had the hilt of a dagger in one hand. There was a soft click and a silver blade shot out the end. Macy let out a small scream and I jumped.

"Damn it. You scared me," Macy said with a hand over her heart.

Izzy turned the blade, so the sunlight caught it. Just like our tattoos winding up our forearms, Latin words were inscribed along one side of the blade. It was probably what gave it its power, what made it such a force against demons. She clicked the button again and the blade retracted back into the hilt.

"Take it. I'll make Jamie give me yours. We can swap some other time," she said and got out of the car. Macy and I both scrambled to get our backpacks from the trunk. There was a small clip on the hilt of the dagger that I used to stow it under the waistband of my jeans as we made our way into the building.

The detention Macy and I got for being late to Mr. Puck's class only added to my relief about getting out of Mark picking me up. Macy and I were late getting to the Gillard Family Farm and it looked like all the students had already been given their duties. Mr. Puck pulled onto the grass across the road from us.

"That's not awkward at all," Macy said under her breath as we got out of the car the same time he got out of his.

"Sucks for you," I told her. "You're with STUCO, not me." She groaned and started to ask Puck where she needed to go, but he wasn't looking at us anymore. His jaw tightened and he lowered his clipboard as he stopped next to Macy's car, looking at Izzy who was walking toward us from the big red barn.

"Howdy, Teach," she called out.

"I didn't know volunteering at a school fundraiser counted as college credit," Puck said back to her.

"I'm going to find Mrs. McKellen," I told Macy, leaving her as a buffer between whatever strange competition this was between Mr. Puck and Izzy.

Thankfully, our first duty was decorating the maze with signs. It took the entire time and meant that I got to walk the maze mostly alone, never once seeing Jamie aside from the moment we all picked up stacks of signs to get started.

When the entire team gathered at the entrance of the maze to review what else there was left to do, I let them know I had to work the rest of the week. No one seemed to care, but Jamie did seem a little irked, probably because he hadn't heard about my new position at Beans and Books.

I met Macy at her station; same as last year, face painting. I knew that when Mark got here to pick me up, I didn't want Jamie to be anywhere in his sight. I had just gotten to her tent when Mr. Puck called me over to the ticket booth where he'd be working. He sat down the nail gun he was using to tack the sign with ticket prices to the booth. He had that same expression as when he'd jogged home with me, like that looked as though he was trying to avoid talking to me at all.

"I know that you spent a lot of time with the Quinns," he started, keeping his voice low so only I could hear. "I wondered if you had Izzy's phone number. I … well, I said some things I shouldn't have, and I think she deserves an apology."

"Oh, um, sure."

Izzy's number was easy to find. I stored our whole circle under "emergency" but I stopped reading her number aloud and just handed my phone to Puck instead. He held a finger up to me to give him a moment and started walking away from the barn and toward an empty stretch of field.

"What's that about?" Macy asked, stopping next to me.

"He wanted to apologize to Izzy," I said with a laugh of surprise.

"God," Macy groaned. "The two of them stood here passive-aggressively arguing about the nerdiest shit I've ever heard for like twenty minutes. Do you think he's really up to something like Izzy thinks?"

I wasn't sure anymore. He acted like he knew something.

Mr. Puck came striding back to me a moment later and Macy wandered back to her station as nonchalantly as she could. He looked dejected and I wasn't surprised. Izzy had wrath I hoped to never be on the receiving end of.

"Thanks," Puck said and handed me my phone. "Your uncle called as we were wrapping up."

"He's probably here to get me," I answered and looked over the line of cars on the side of the gravel road. I spotted Mark's truck stopped in the middle of the road. I gave Macy a wave goodbye and hurried to meet him.

The truck reeked of cherries, but I didn't say a word. Mark was in a good mood, so I let him tell me all about his day on the way home. It filled all our time together and meant I didn't have to explain the tardiness or the detention or the knife that weighed heavy in my pocket.

CHAPTER 4

Beans and Books was deserted when I got there after school on my first day. The old-timey bell above the door tinkled when I walked inside. A moment later, Angel appeared in the doorway to the storeroom, not finishing the standard "welcome to Beans and Books" greeting when he saw me.

"You must be Tori," he said. For some reason, I expected Angel to be older. He looked eighteen or nineteen, but that wasn't the only thing about him that captivated my gaze. He wasn't just good-looking, he was beautiful. He was a six-foot-two lean-muscled man that only existed on the runways of Paris and Milan, not dressed in a black apron with a topknot to keep his dark hair out of his face while he made lattes in Burbrook.

"Yeah. Victoria Johnson, but you can call me Tori," I answered. He let the door swing shut as he rounded the counter. He lifted a black apron from a hook in the corner and tossed it to me. I caught it and began pulling it over my head as he held out a name badge.

"I'm Angel Martínez," he said. "Someone likes to make good impressions. Willow told me you wouldn't be here until four-thirty. What do you want to learn how to make first?" He walked behind the counter again, turning the easel so I could see the short menu. My usual coffee order was the most boring thing in the world, so I didn't know much about it. I remembered the way Jamie teased me about it the day we threw an old McDonald's breakfast sandwich at Macy's car.

Drink hot coffee in the winter, iced in the spring and summer, and lattes and mochas in the fall.

"Pumpkin Spice Latte," I said. I ignored the memory of Jamie from that day by focusing on Angel's forearms, sleeves rolled up to his elbows in a way I never could without potentially exposing myself to any demon or monster in the room. For once, a normal boy.

"Heads up, this won't taste like that stuff from Starbucks," Angel said and pulled a white mug from the shelves along the wall. I went behind the bar to watch him work. He didn't explain a thing, just making sure I could see everything he grabbed and every button he pressed. When he finished, he slid the mug to me.

"Oh, I don't actually really like those," I said.

He smirked. "Okay. Tell me how you take your coffee and I'll teach you how to make it."

"Black."

I don't know why it was embarrassing, but it was. Maybe it was because we were in a coffee shop with the fancy machine, and he'd worked in so many according to Willow. He could make any cup with pretty foam art on top and I just wanted a plain cup of black coffee.

"Finally," Angel said and poured a cup of the dark roast into a mug. "Someone who likes the coffee more than the cream."

"What do you like?"

"Blondes."

I could feel the heat rush to my cheeks and a little bit of hot coffee dribbled down my chin. I sat the cup aside as the coffee dripped onto my apron. Angel said something in Spanish, probably about how ridiculous I was based on the way he smiled at me.

"For the record, I do have a thing for blondes, so you're not really my type anyway." He shrugged and wiped the spill off the counter with a rag.

"And I just ended things with this guy, and I was being rude by staring at you like some..."

Angel acted like he hadn't just heard my embarrassing tangent, thank God. It gave me a chance to get a grip before he led me to the storeroom to explain the organizational method.

It only took about an hour and three customers before working alongside Angel felt so natural that you'd think we'd both worked at Beans and Books together much longer. Angel was the pro at making the more complicated coffees, so he took command of those orders. I knew my way around the bookshelves, anyone would after just a few minutes, so I helped the few customers that came in to look.

I didn't see a sign of anything supernatural on my runs since being chased down by that demon. I did see Mr. Puck every morning though, both of us giving polite waves, or in my case a breathless nod when our routes would cross near the main road. I felt a little less paranoid by Friday after taking some time that week to run the old railroad and get familiar with it. I always stopped at the main station to take a breather, always tempted to go inside and imagine Jamie sitting at a piano there but never actually going in.

The dreams still had me jolting awake in the morning, slick with sweat, but Friday morning was different. I didn't hear the voice until I woke up and was standing in the bathroom.

The lake.

I looked at the shower as if someone were hiding behind the curtain, but it was just me. When I looked up at the window, I thought I saw Alison River's bloody body standing beside the tree like I'd seen her every night before.

I went back to my bedroom when I heard my alarm chiming, surprised to find a text from Macy. It was a link to an article. Alison's homecoming picture was at the very top just under the headline, "The Police Have a Lead in Missing Person's Case."

The article was brief, starting with details about the homecoming dance, and that Alison was last seen with friends at the dance before leaving. Macy had reported to the police station to give a statement since she was the last person who'd seen her alive. Jamie, Izzy, and I told her exactly what to say. She admitted they'd been drinking and that they left the dance after Sean Peterson broke things off with Macy. She told them they were hanging out in the parking lot. The story was that Macy decided to go back into the dance and that Alison was going to join her after getting rid of the liquor bottle.

The article said everything we already knew. Police were still investigating the stories. They were still searching the camping areas. The new pieces of information were that they'd found evidence to suggest that Alison was likely dead. I was surprised the article was as graphic as it was. Police found dried blood all over the field where we had killed the hellhound, tested it, and confirmed that it was mostly Alison's.

The rest of it was animal, the only part of the mess we'd been unable to clean up.

When Jamie went back after the attack, he said Alison was nowhere to be found. We assumed something had dragged her away after we left, and the article made the same assumption. They said Alison was likely mauled there and dragged half a mile away where the team of police found human tissue and tendon samples that matched Alison's medical records.

I walked back to the bathroom as I felt my stomach twisting to the point of nausea, getting there in time to drop to my knees before the toilet.

"Are you okay? Are you sick?" Becky asked from the doorway. I sat back on my heels and held the phone toward her. She didn't take it, her somber expression telling me that she'd already seen it herself.

"I'm fine. It was just ... gross."

"I know. They didn't have to give us all the details," she said, pulling a washcloth from the cabinet and running it under the faucet. I flushed the toilet and sat on the lid, taking the cool cloth from her as she sat on the edge of the tub.

"Can you drop me off at the farm in a few hours instead of Mark?" I asked. Today was the first day of Fall Break, which was barely a break at all. We had today and Monday off from school.

"He's trying to do better. You know, understand you and be more trusting."

"He's punishing me is what he's doing," I told her.

Becky didn't correct me, shrugging when I sent her my challenging look.

"What's with everything this year anyway? Is it because of Jamie?" she asked.

"Not everything is about Jamie. Why are you and Mark both so hung up on him?"

"Your mom acted like this when she met your dad," Becky answered. The words were cooler than the washcloth against my cheek. Becky looked back at me like she'd just revealed my entire plan. There was no way she knew everything though.

"I made it clear to Jamie that I wasn't interested," I told her, thinking hard for something to change the subject. "There is this cute boy at work though."

"New boy?" Becky asked. "What grade?"

"Older boy," I said, practically hearing Mark's chiding as I spoke, "Okay. I know what you're thinking, but I'm not interested in him either. He's just really hot is all."

Becky laughed and stood up from the tub. I finished getting ready for my run, taking the normal route plus an extra loop around our block before looking at my neglected English homework. I had an essay due Tuesday when we got back to school, and I hadn't even started the research for it yet.

I worked until it was time to put on my itchy scarecrow costume. I pulled my curls into low pigtails and kept the makeup simple before going to remind Mark about dropping me off. He was finishing packing his suitcase for his work trip with Terry tomorrow.

He reminded me of his rules before letting me get out of the truck. The festival lasted until eleven. The corn maze didn't open until eight when the entire farm went from the fun kid-friendly trick-or-treating event to the terror-filled Halloween party that everyone at school would talk about until Thanksgiving Break. The whole academic team would help pass out candy to kids until then. Mark told me that I had to call him, not text, before starting my shift in the maze.

"If I don't get a call from you, then I'm coming to pick you up."

"Why do I have to call you at all? You know where I'll be," I said.

The questioning was bold even for me and the surprise on his face was almost funny. Mark let out a deep breath. He pulled the truck into the grass on the side of the road. A bounce house was slowly being inflated to one side of the barn. I saw Mr. Puck helping a woman set up a photo station where little kids could stick their faces out of a hole cut into a piece of board painted like a giant pumpkin.

"Tori, I know that I've come down hard on you recently, maybe a little too much," Mark started, pulling my attention back to him. He kept his eyes on the farm and his hands on the steering wheel. "When your teacher called us about you, I didn't think too much about it. I always thought it was weird how much you liked studying and all that, so I thought you were just being a kid when you went to that party. When the next call came and then breaking curfew and the drinking ..."

"I'm sorry, Mark. I was just trying to figure some things out," I said. I hadn't worn my leather jacket or the studded cuff in ages. I didn't want to try anything new anytime soon. For once, I was happy with being plain old Tori.

He nodded that he understood and turned a little in his seat to look at me.

"You don't have to call me. I won't pick you up either unless you need me to. Macy can drop you off at home after the festival ends, which I know is at 11:30 with clean-up. I read the flyer," The warning was there in his tone.

"Thank you," I said, the relief like a shot of espresso. I leaned over and pressed a kiss to his cheek before promising that he could trust me. I hopped out of the truck and did an awkward half-walk, half-jog toward the red barn.

"Tori," Mrs. McKellen greeted, checking off my name on her clipboard. "You can join any of the Burbrook High tents to help pass out candy. You need to be in your station in the maze by seven-thirty to make sure everything is set up before anyone goes in."

I wasn't surprised at all to find Izzy at the tent next to Macy's face-painting station. Each tent had either a game set up for kids to play or an adult in a costume to pass out candy. Izzy looked like she usually did, wearing knee-high boots with a tight pair of pants tucked into them and a black T-shirt on. The only thing identifying her costume was the pair of black wolf ears on top of her head that she'd saved from the homecoming dance.

"You really went all out, didn't you?" I teased when I joined her.

"Well, well," she said and gave a wolf whistle. "Are you supposed to be scaring the crows off or attracting them?" She tugged at my pigtails and looked over my costume. I had been too preoccupied with how itchy the straw sewn into the wrists and ankles was to notice the elastic around the waist that gave me more of an hourglass figure than I really had.

"Have you talked to Jamie at all about giving me a demon blade?" I whispered to her. She let out a dramatic groan and went to the folding table at the back of the tent where two plastic cauldrons full of candy sat.

"No," she said and handed one to me. "And don't think it's because I didn't want to. He hasn't been home."

"What do you mean he hasn't been home?" I asked.

Macy looked up from her spread of makeup at her station to listen. She stood up with a compact of pressed powder and a brush I knew she'd been prepared to take to my cheeks before Izzy dropped this revelation.

"I don't mean that literally. He's been home. He's got dirty clothes in a corner of his room and stuff, so he's coming home. But he's getting home late and leaving early. I haven't seen him since we talked about your demon."

"So, you were right about him needing to be in charge," Macy said. "He really does always have to take the lead on what our circle does."

I was hot with anger, and I was about to launch into a rant about all his faults, but Macy's hand on my face stopped me. I kept my mouth shut as she started doing my makeup.

"Speak of the devil," Izzy said. I whipped around to face her. She smiled and pointed at a freshman boy who was dressed in red with devil horns on his head. Izzy and Macy both laughed.

"That's not funny," I told them.

"Calm down," Izzy said. "I'm just messing with you. You are just as bad as Jamie is, you know. He's directing his frustration into hunting demons and you're directing your new job and avoiding him."

"Izzy," Mr. Puck said. He came from the back of our tent, setting his clipboard on the table. He shook a candy box in his hand before handing it to Izzy who looked a little confused. "I meant what I said on the phone. I didn't mean to, well, I didn't mean to insult you. I hope you can accept me trying to be the bigger person. I just assumed you knew." It was obvious he was trying to hide his smile. He picked up his clipboard and brushed past Izzy on the way to check more tents.

"What's that?" I asked her. She stopped turning the box between her hands, stopping with the front facing up. It was a box of black licorice candy, all shaped like gumdrops. A cartoon crow stood on top of one of the gumdrops with a top hat on. The word "Crows" was printed across the top of the box.

"What was that for?" Macy asked. Izzy's cheeks were turning pink. She didn't look at either of us, staring tightlipped after Mr. Puck.

"Wait," I said as it dawned on me. "Did he just tell you to eat crow?"

She was red in the face now. "I may have been mistaken when I tried proving to him that I knew more about the medical field than he did. Stupid," she said under her breath.

"Oh my god," I said, my turn to laugh now. "He put you in your place, didn't he?"

Izzy turned on me now, tossing the candy onto the folding table as she said, "Victoria Johnson, that's the most sexist thing I've ever heard. I can do whatever I want."

Macy and I laughed as she stormed off, weaving around families of trick-or-treaters arriving for the festival.

CHAPTER 5

We were so busy with trick-or-treaters that I forgot all about getting to my position—until Jamie interrupted Macy and me He was in his Grim Reaper costume without the hood, a plastic scythe held in his right hand.

"We should go get ready. I had to rig your scarecrow stand when you weren't here to try it and I want to make sure it's not too tall for you to climb onto," he said.

I cast my annoyed gaze on Macy, who just rolled her eyes at me. I sat the cauldron of candy on the table and followed him toward the back of the farm. The fun was more spread out back here. There was an outdoor dance floor currently being set up behind the barn to our left, twinkling lights strung above it that nearly lit the way to the maze.

Almost.

The only light in the corn maze was from the jack-o-lanterns with battery-powered tealights inside that were scattered throughout the maze. Otherwise, the only light potential guests were allowed came from the flashlights Mrs. McKellen would pass out at the entrance and collect at the exit. Her post was empty for now aside from a basket of flashlights and another empty one for the collection.

"Looks like we're first," Jamie said as we approached the entrance. It was dark, but not as dark as it would be when the farm switched from fun Halloween to scary Halloween. Still, I snagged a flashlight as we entered and tucked it into the pocket over my chest just in case.

It was quiet as we walked. I was so focused on avoiding a conversation with Jamie that I just now realized that I didn't remember the way to our post.

"Do you …" I was cut off when a flock of black birds took off from the stalks next to me. I jumped, nearly tripping over Jamie. He helped steady me and started laughing.

"Already playing the part of the scarecrow," he said.

I wanted to keep a straight face, but it was a little funny.

"Do you remember the way? The last time I was in here was Monday," I told him.

"Kind of," Jamie said. "I decorated our entire area myself. I walked this path enough times you'd think I could do it with my eyes closed."

"I'm sorry I couldn't help."

He shrugged.

I heard something rush through the corn stalks behind us and I gasped, turning to see the last of the dark shape disappear into one of the side paths.

"Hayden's in a vampire costume, remember?" Jamie said.

I took a deep breath and turned to face him. The small smile on his face made my chest hurt. It must've been obvious because it faded to a sad frown a moment later.

"I know you don't want to talk about it, Tori, and I won't make you …" He let the words hang in the air. I felt the urge to run. I wanted to replace his words in my brain with the thundering of my feet on the pavement, except we had a whole night ahead of us and I didn't know where I was in this damn maze.

"Izzy said you haven't been coming home," I said, watching the confusion set in on his face.

"I've been home."

"After you've been out all night hunting monsters?" I asked.

He snorted in disbelief.

"I'm just protecting the gate."

"Stop saying that like you're the only one doing the job," I said, pointing a finger at him and then toward the stalks as I continued. "Izzy and I are both working to get stronger and we're still looking for reasons why the Shadowlands need my blood. Then there's Macy who still doesn't know her powers. She needs us to help her and you're not even around to see her."

"Don't pull that shit about being there for people," he said, tossing the scythe on the dirt.

"Well, where have you been the whole time you're not home?"

"Where have you been any time, I've tried talking to you, Tori? Every time you even see me you turn the other way."

The lake.

The voice sent shivers up my skin and left me paralyzed. I heard something rustle the stalks to the left again and I started down the path before Jamie could do anything but follow.

"Tori. Stop running away and just talk to me," he said.

A shadowy figure shot across the path where it met the next one. It was too quick for me to get a good look at it, and too quick to be Hayden or any other human in a costume. The dagger was in my hand and the blade shot out the end with a click.

"What are you doing?" Jamie asked, stopping behind me. "And where did you get that?"

"Izzy," I answered, keeping my eyes on the end of the path. "You would've known if you ever went home and talked to her."

"I've tracked every demon that's come out of the gate since the ferryman. Why would you even need a demon blade?"

"Does an orange-eyed demon with wings ring a bell?" I asked, turning to face him. We were inches apart. I could hear the shock as he exhaled.

"Tori," he said, voice low. "What happened?"

"That demon chased me down when I was on a run last week," I told him.

"You should've told me."

"I told everyone in our circle but you and not because I didn't want you to know."

Instead of the anger I'd expected, hurt painted Jamie's face.

"I'm sorry," I whispered.

"No. It's not your fault," he said, taking another step forward so he could reach out and twirl the ends of my pigtails. "I've been watching the lake. I thought I could protect you if I got rid of every demon that got out of that gate. I can't even kill demons right anymore."

"I can take care of myself," I reminded him, putting my hands to his chest with the intention of pushing him away. Instead, my fists tightened around the dark fabric.

"I know you can but," he said. "But I don't want you to have to. I don't want anything to ever get near you again. When I even think about it, I feel sick."

I pulled him to my chest, letting my head rest against his left shoulder so my nose brushed his neck. He smelled like fresh pine with a subtle hint of something deeper. I didn't get a chance to decide what that was. He was too distracting. His hands slipped into the back of my overalls, fingers sliding down my back so the tense muscles melted under his skin. I pulled him tighter to my chest as his fingers found the lacy band of my underwear, slipping just under the band but going no farther.

"You told me once that my past didn't leave me broken forever," he said in my ear. "Tori, I want this. I know you feel it too and if it's at all what I think ..."

The lake.

The voice reminded me of the images I'd been running from. Jamie facedown in the lake. The ferryman bursting into flames. The three figures on the wall of the castle. We got rid of the ferryman, but there were still two others.

I raised my head and I saw her again. Alison Rivers stood for a moment at the opposite end of the path, blood sliding down her chest and over the front of her dress. With a blink a dark figure replaced her. It hung in the air like mist, humanoid in shape, with red eyes staring back at me.

"Jamie," I warned, but it was too late. The shadow sped toward us. I pulled Jamie to the ground as it reached us. He let out a cry of pain and the fabric across his back split, holding on by a few inches at his lower back. When he sat up, the costume fell away from him and pooled at his feet. The white T-shirt he had on under the robe was less damaged, but the back of it was coated in red from the gash down his back.

"Let's go," I said, pulling him to his feet and leading the way down a new path.

"Where is it?" he asked, blade gleaming in his hand. He was struggling to manage the pain, that much was clear in his clenched jaw.

"This way," I said and darted farther toward the middle of the maze, chasing the dark mist as I caught it whipping around corners and vanishing in the stalks.

"Tori, we don't know what this is," Jamie said behind me. "Let's call for help."

"Too late," I said as we ran into the center of the maze. It was our station, a large circle cut into the cornstalks with several paths branching out from all sides. There was a short patch of stalks left in the center where the scarecrow stand was mounted. I was supposed to stand with my back against the board at the top and pretend I was tethered there. Instead, a shadowy figure stood there peering down at us with red eyes. I saw a glint of teeth in the middle of its face, a smile spreading wider and wider until it was pulled past what would be humanly possible.

"Two more," Jamie said and took his place next to me. Another shadow slowly glided from a path at the back. I looked up just in time to see the third charge from the left. I turned to swing my dagger at it but was too slow. The demon tackled me around the middle, and we went flying into Jamie. I caught his horrified gaze just as I felt the demon grip the straps of my overalls.

I screamed as it dragged me across the dirt, through the wall of the maze, and into the air. I used the dagger to cut one of the straps. My weight shifted enough that I slipped from its grasp and went crashing back to the ground, my feet pulsating from the impact.

"I can't touch it!" Jamie yelled.

The shadow cut through the stalks before me, appearing halfway down the path ahead. It cocked its head, that eerie smile spreading across its face. It didn't open its mouth, but I could understand it. I could hear the deep snarl of a voice in my head and understood who it belonged to.

Blood. Give or take?

I let out a war cry and charged straight at it, seeing the fear set in its red eyes seconds before I slammed into its body. We skidded across the dirt, a plume going up and mingling with the black mist that started to swirl around us.

"Face me!" I yelled, scrambling to my feet as the demon vanished like smoke. A sound behind me drew my attention.

There she was.

Alison Rivers stood at the end of the path, dressed the same as she was every night in my dream. She smiled an evil half-smirk that chilled my exposed skin. Before I could move, the demon smashed into me from the right. I crashed through the wall and back into our circle. The demon had one of my arms in his hands, razor-like talons cutting into my forearm.

I screamed when my back smashed into the scarecrow stand, taking out the vertical bar and leaving a splintered spear pointing toward the moon. I tightened my grip on the dagger and pulled on the hand holding me, screaming as the talons tore into my flesh. I drove the dagger into the dark mass, feeling it sink into the demon. It let out a horrible screech like a giant bird and I fell.

The demon vanished in a plume of smoke; the scream cut off no sooner than it pierced the air. All the air whooshed from my lungs when my back smashed into the ground and the only thing that kept me in the battle was Jamie's scream.

I rolled to my back, bleeding arm cradled in my lap. Jamie was still facing both demons. One flew at him, passing through his body and leaving behind a knife in Jamie's right thigh. He staggered to the side, knocked off balance as the second one sped past him.

I pointed a hand at the second one and the power easily burst from me. The shadow went flying through the wall of the maze with a shriek. I turned toward the other demon that stood just behind Jamie, but something new raced past me so fast that the cool wind through my hair startled me. I turned to face it just as Jamie let out a yell.

"I'll catch you!" I yelled to Jamie as the demon rose into the air, carrying Jamie with it. Before I gathered my strength, the second demon was back. It slammed into my side, and I went rolling into an adjacent path.

Once I'd stopped sliding and struggled to get to my feet, I saw both demons in the air with Jamie between them. The horrified scream escaped me before I realized it. One cast an evil smile my way as they lowered Jamie onto the remnants of the scarecrow stand, a nauseating punch echoing through my ears as they impaled him.

"Hold them," a new voice yelled to me from behind. Whatever it was, it was a blur of color as it ran the perimeter of the circle, adding "in the middle" as it passed before me again.

I raised both my hands and the demons were forced back-to-back by my power. The figure racing around the stand moved faster than before, a ring of color that sent gusts of wind pushing against me as I stood my ground. Jamie's cries of pain were cut off and I saw him raise a hand to his throat. The demons floating above him both dropped to the ground, backs arched and long fingers clawing at their throats, suffocating.

The speeding figure rushed at one of the demons and it vanished in a puff of smoke. The figure rushed past me again, this time stopping on a dime with the last demon held against its chest. A demon dagger sank into the black mass, and it vanished, leaving behind Mr. Puck.

"No," I breathed as he looked back at me. We both stowed our daggers and ran for the scarecrow stand where Jamie was groaning.

"He'll heal," I said, more for my own comfort than for Mr. Puck's.

"Not until we get him off this thing," he replied.

"Kill me first, would you?" Jamie groaned as Puck and I both took an arm. Thankfully, the post was just three feet off the podium, so while it sounded like hell for Jamie as we lifted him off, we were able to do it quickly. We laid him flat on the podium. His head lolled back, and he let out a loud string of curses before Mr. Puck clapped a hand over his mouth.

"There's still a festival going," he warned us, "and the maze is supposed to open in twenty minutes." I looked at the surrounding paths in case anyone was watching, half-expecting to see a blood-covered blonde Barbie smirking back.

Mr. Puck lowered his hand from Jamie's mouth and went to the blood-soaked half of his shirt. It stuck to Jamie's stomach as he lifted it to get a look at the puncture underneath. Jamie groaned into his elbow until Puck stopped touching him.

"Are you okay?" Puck asked me.

"Y-yeah. I'm fine," I said. "Just got my arm." I looked down at my tattooed forearm, the inked flesh slowly knitting back together where the claw marks were under the torn shirt. I looked up from the grisly sight. Mr. Puck was completely unharmed.

"So, you're super-fast?" I asked.

He nodded and pointed to me. "Mind control?"

"Not really," I shrugged. "Telekinesis. I can move things."

Jamie groaned again.

"And him?" Puck asked.

"Strength."

"Why. Are. You. Here?" Jamie said the words between pained breaths.

Puck let out a sigh. He pushed back his left sleeve to reveal the black ink swirling around his forearm. We already knew he was a guardian. That was obvious. I wasn't prepared for what came next.

He held out his arm so Jamie and I could both read the

Latin wrapped around his wrist. I'd studied my own tattoo for so long that I already knew the meaning.

Guardian of the sixth gate. Complete the circle. Find your match.

Mr. Puck pushed his sleeve down again.

"We should talk."

CHAPTER 6

I rode with Izzy to the Moore Estate, listening to her rant about how she was right that Mr. Puck was more than a simple high school science teacher. Izzy's red Challenger was parked in the driveway behind Jamie's motorcycle. As soon as we got out of her Jeep, Izzy still talking about how she was going to tell off Jamie for second-guessing her, Mr. Puck parked behind us.

"You teachers and your 2018 Camry's," Izzy said as he tucked the keys into his pocket. He paused for a minute, smiling back at her as though she'd just challenged him to a game of poker.

"You trust fund kids and your fleet of sports cars," he said with a laugh and walked past us for the open garage door.

I elbowed Izzy as her jaw tightened.

"I'm going to set his hair on fire," she said and strode after him.

I followed Izzy into the house, past the wall of diplomas and concert photos, and into a den. I'd never been in this room before, not the downstairs den anyway. It was almost identical to the upstairs den with the same built-in bookshelves along one wall and windows along another. Instead of looking over the front lawn, these windows looked over the backyard. There was a large patio just underneath with stairs that led down to the pool with color-changing lights under the clear water that sent a relaxing glow over the area.

Jamie went to a well-stocked bar in the corner and took down two glasses. He poured amber liquid from a crystal decanter into one and handed it to Macy who was sitting on the leather couch with her legs folded under her. She immediately took a long drink and grimaced.

"Hold on," Puck said, pointing at Jamie as he poured a second glass. "If you weren't a guardian, how old would you be?"

His disapproving tone clearly rubbed Jamie the wrong way. He turned from the bar with the glass in hand and a smirk on his face.

"I stopped keeping track when I hit ninety," Jamie said and drained the glass without so much as a grimace.

Macy bit her lip and sat her glass on the side table next to her, adjusting in her seat as though trying to hide the glass.

"How old are you, Mr. Puck?" Jamie asked. He refilled his glass and moved to the side of the couch. Before he could take a sip, Izzy plucked it from his grasp.

"You're a nightmare when you're drunk and angry," she explained and sat next to Macy. Jamie opened his mouth to argue, but Puck cut him off.

"Twenty-three," he said. "And you can call me Will. I think we're going to be co-workers of sorts anyway after tonight."

"How old would you be if you weren't a guardian?" Izzy asked. She'd done enough digging on him that I was sure she already had a solid guess. Will Puck took a seat in one of the armchairs.

"Twenty-six," he answered, glancing at Jamie as though sensing his satisfaction.

"There's quite the age gap in this circle," Macy said. "Tori and I just woke this year."

Puck's eyes went to Izzy, looking her over her and smiling.

"I run a business that started before you were born," she told him and took a drink.

Puck snorted. "I've read the records on this house, and I made some connections of my own. I'm not wrong in saying that you two have been here before as a different generation of Quinns."

"I think we need to know a little more about you, Will," Jamie said, taking a seat between Izzy and Macy. I sat down in the last armchair as Puck adjusted in his.

"That's a long story," he said.

Izzy thrust a hand toward the fireplace to my left and the flames erupted among the logs, sending a whoosh of warmth over us. I used my powers to levitate the decanter and an empty tumbler over the couch and onto the coffee table.

"We have some time," I said. Technically, I had until eleven-thirty.

Puck poured himself a glass and let the liquid swirl in the bottom for a moment.

"How did you wake?" Macy asked. She never was good with awkward silence.

"Hit-and-run," he said as though it was a simple answer, "I had just moved here. I was on a long run during the peak of my marathon training. I was running past the national park where the road gets a little windy. There's a pretty big shoulder there, but the driver took a wider turn than he should've. When I woke up, I was covered in blood. There were muddy tire tracks on my chest, and I was lying in the ditch."

"Who was it?" Macy asked with the tumbler of whiskey in her hands again. Puck shrugged.

"No idea," he said. "But no one ever came looking for me either, so I don't think it matters."

"You said you did research on us. You knew we were guardians, and you didn't let us know you were one. Why?" Jamie asked.

"I knew you and Izzy were guardians. I guessed that Tori was after the story about the drunk driving accident the first week of school."

"Jake wasn't drunk. Noah turned the wheel—it wasn't Jake's fault," I said, the words tumbling out. I don't know if I'd ever let go of the guilt of everyone thinking Jake was at fault.

"Terrible. That must've been pretty scary," he told me and then looked to Macy. "I didn't know you were a member of the circle. Seeing you here when I came in was a shock."

"I overdosed at homecoming," Macy explained, her expression falling a little after she said the words aloud. She'd never told us about what happened that night. We knew her cause of death. It had been obvious, but we didn't dwell on the night past the relief we shared about the ferryman's death.

"What about the Moores who were killed in the railroad explosion?" Puck asked Jamie and Izzy.

"Our parents," Jamie said. "They were guardians at the time, and they'd matched. Mortal again. Izzy and I woke that night."

"Are any of you matched?" Puck asked. His eyes went from Izzy and Jamie on the couch to me and I knew what he was asking. I shook my head and the crackle from the fire filled the silence.

"You still haven't explained why you didn't join us when you found out who we were," Izzy said, finishing the last of her glass and reaching for a refill. Puck did the same and held his glass out to her. She sent him an annoyed look before filling it.

"I'd say we were doing a good job keeping the demon population down on our own," he said and took a sip. "I didn't know about you two until a year ago. I realized the demons that did come into town all avoided the Burbrook Mountain area. I chased a werewolf up the mountain about a mile and then it changed directions like a dog with a shock collar. There aren't many rich families living up here and yours was the only one with a history that caught my attention."

"Still," Izzy said, "three is better than two." She said it as an insult.

"I thought you said you could handle yourself?" he shot back.

"Have you hunted anything like those demons tonight?" I asked before the two of them could start another one of their contests.

Jamie picked up the circle guide from his side table and sat it on the coffee table. "I looked through our guide and none of our predecessors wrote about them." He said.

"I've never seen anything like it," Puck said, sliding the guide toward him.

"They're more dangerous than what we're used to," Jamie said, looking at Izzy and Macy who hadn't seen the disaster of a fight. "The demon blade works on them and so did Will's and Tori's powers. I couldn't touch it to use mine. My hands would just go through them like shadows."

"I could touch it," I said.

The entire room stopped. They all stared back at me in awe for a moment.

"It has to do with your blood," Izzy said, launching into what had happened since I woke. Puck looked more frustrated as she told him about the ferryman and all the demons that were after my blood.

"Why Tori? What's so different about her?" Puck asked.

"Nothing that we can tell," Jamie said.

"I need to tell you guys something," I said, watching every frown deepen. I felt my stomach tighten. I told them about the recurring dreams, about seeing Alison in the maze. I told them how she was there one minute and gone another. I was just about to tell them about the voices and how I heard the demon speak to me when Macy interrupted.

"God, Tori, you're shaking," she said.

I shoved my trembling hands underneath my thighs for a moment.

"I think those dreams are ..." Jamie started, his concerned expression sending me over the edge.

"I'm not traumatized," I blurted. Was I? In just a few months I'd died, seen death, and been to Hell and back when it would've killed most people. No. This wasn't my mind playing games.

"I should start keeping watch again," Jamie muttered.

"I don't want you there," I told him. "I don't need anyone protecting me."

"But Tori," Macy said, turning her glass in a circle between her fingers, "if the Shadowlands really needs your blood and you're scared, you shouldn't have to worry about watching your back also. Maybe the dreams will go away if you have someone there."

I groaned as Izzy and Jamie nodded in agreement.

"Just to be on the safe side ..." Puck started.

I groaned and reached for the decanter. Puck lifted it before I could grasp it and poured what was left into his glass.

"That's a heavy pour for someone who's due to chaperone

a bunch of teenagers later," Izzy said, taking the empty bottle back to the bar.

Puck stood up and took a swig from his glass.

"Is that pool table just for show?" he asked her.

She turned from the bar with a bottle of Jameson in her right hand.

"I've never played in all my ninety years," she replied and walked toward the table on the other side of the room. "Grab a cue and bring your glass."

"Hope you can shoot straight with your arthritis," Puck said and followed her.

"Oh boy," Macy said and downed the last of her glass.

I left the den and walked into the first room I found, the estate's library. The room was as large as the school library but much prettier. Everything was made of polished mahogany, the moonlight casting soft green, red, and blue lights across the concrete floor from the stained glass at one end of the room. I turned from a shelf of very old copies of Shakespeare when I heard a pair of feet coming toward me.

"I just want to be alone," I said, enunciating the words a little stronger than I would've if I'd seen who it was. I relaxed and turned back to the shelves.

"I know," Macy said. "You thought I was Jamie. What's going on with that anyway?"

I brushed the dust off the spine of *Macbeth* and turned to face her again. She held a bottle of red wine to me and said, "My mom always told me dirty secrets are best told over glasses of red."

"There's nothing to explain," I said and took the bottle by the neck. "I thought maybe we could be a couple and now I don't want to."

"That's not true. You so want to."

"It wouldn't work."

"Why not?"

Macy and I had taken a life-long journey together. We weren't best friends until middle school volleyball, but we'd gone to school together forever. She knew me better than anyone. I didn't know if the ferryman's secret was safe with anyone but me though. It didn't matter what I felt or what she would say about it. If Jamie and I matched, he would die. I just needed to wait it out. We would figure out the thing about my blood, kill off the demons that were after me ... The words wrapped around my arm were proof though.

Guardian of the sixth gate. Complete the circle. Find your match.

Those were the instructions. To seal the gate, we all needed to match.

I took another drink, more like a gulp, and told Macy about all the things I found so annoying about Jamie. He was over-protective, which Macy countered was kind of cute. I hated his protectiveness, but I still got butterflies thinking about what he'd said in the maze.

"Just drink with me, will you?" I asked and passed the bottle off to my giggling friend. We sat in the corner of the room where Chaucer met Christie, propped up by the shelves on the floor as we drank until the bottle was empty and there was nothing to do but listen to Izzy and Puck from the other room send competitive insults at each other.

Macy slipped to the floor when I started awake from my dream. It was still dark in the library. My heart raced for a new reason.

"What time is it?" Macy grumbled.

"Eleven-forty," I said, reading the numbers from my phone screen. There wasn't a single text or call from Becky or Mark. Maybe I could get home and go unnoticed or at least be close enough to curfew to beg forgiveness.

"I live down the street, so I'm going to stay here," Macy said and pulled a thick anthology under her head. I knocked over the bottle of wine as I stood up, grabbing it before it could make any more noise.

It was quiet in the house. I went across the hall to the den. A half-empty bottle of Jameson sat on the pool table along with the remainder of their game. I left the wine bottle at the bar and went back to the hallway but stopped when I realized I wasn't the only one awake.

Puck froze a few feet from my left, looking just as surprised to see me as I was him. He was shirtless and close enough that I could see that the tattoo that covered his chest was of a raven mid-flight. I felt my cheeks flame when I saw the towel hanging low on his hips. He looked down at it now that I'd noticed, probably wishing he didn't have a glass of water in each hand so he could better cover himself.

"Bring Aspirin," I heard Izzy say down the hall. I looked her way just as she appeared at the top of the stairs in her under-wear. Her eyes went wide, and her mouth formed a round shape.

"Oh," she said, the sound stretching on as we all stood frozen, exchanging awkward looks. She raised her hands to her messy hair, and I noticed her tattoo. There was more of it than I remembered, at least more than what I had. It was the same style, a few additions in the mix and it swirled up her forearm and around her elbow. I looked at Puck and saw that his was identical.

Jesus H. Christ.

"Um, someone tell Jamie that I need a ride home," I said

and moved to the entryway. I kept my eyes on the front door as I heard Puck's bare feet pad across the tile. I stood there for long enough that I was starting to get nervous before he came down.

"I thought you left with Macy," Jamie said, pulling on his motorcycle jacket.

"No, and she's using one of Izzy's medical anthologies as a pillow in your library," I said, already on the front porch. He shut the door and led the way to his bike. I almost asked him if we could take one of their cars, but I was in too much of a rush. I tossed a leg over the back of the bike and wrapped my arms around his waist.

We didn't see a single car as we flew down the mountain. He parked the bike a block away like normal and ran behind me across the neighbor's yard. I carefully undid the latch to the back gate and skirted the side of the yard to avoid the flood-lights. There wasn't a single light on. Maybe Mark was attempting to do better by trusting me. Some niece I was.

"Help me climb up," I told Jamie.

"Through the window?" he hissed. Before he could ask, I told him that I never locked it anymore and could slide it open. Our eyes met for a moment as he realized why it was unlocked to begin with.

"Here," he said and laced his fingers together. I put my right foot in his palm, and he raised me toward the second floor quicker than I anticipated. I leaned against the siding and slid the glass upward, wincing at the tiny squeak it gave before opening all the way. I wiggled myself in, wondering now how Jamie made the act look so graceful. Once inside, I turned to whisper down to him, but he was propped up on the sill by his forearms.

"Tori, I know that you can protect yourself," he started. "I know you're strong and you don't need me to protect you or anyone else for that matter. I just ... I hate not knowing if you're safe. You heard everyone back there. I think we all need to do a better job checking in."

Maybe it was the alcohol. It was *definitely* the alcohol. I wanted him to climb in and lie against me all night. The butterflies in my stomach made me think about another couple testing boundaries right now.

"I think you need to go home and check in with your sister," I told him and nudged his arms. He let go and lightly landed on the ground below, looking up at me.

"Izzy's been alone all week and never said it bothered her."

"Well, she's not alone tonight," I whispered. "Macy wasn't the only one who had a sleepover."

"What?" Jamie said, eyes wide.

I shut the window on him and got ready for bed.

CHAPTER 7

I didn't sleep well, waking up again with the same nightmare, but the upside was that Mark and Becky didn't seem any the wiser about how my night went. Mark was long gone, probably already in Holston with Terry by now, and Becky sat alone in the kitchen with a mug of coffee and her laptop.

"Do you have any plans for the weekend?" Becky asked me.

"No, why?" I asked as I poured myself a mug.

She shrugged and turned the laptop so I could see the home page of the University of Colorado Boulder. A smile spread across her face.

"You haven't applied to any college, and I was getting nervous. So," she said and started clicking tabs, "I thought we could schedule a tour for Thanksgiving Break."

I sank into the seat next to her and blurted, "I have applied to colleges."

"Really? Which ones?"

The truth was I hadn't applied to any schools yet and I tried not to think about the subject of college and my future. I was doing good to keep my grades where they were and to stay out of trouble thanks to all the guardian stuff.

"CU Boulder," I said and took a sip of coffee, nearly burning my tongue in the process.

"Is that all?"

Maybe sticking as close to the truth as I could afford was the best bet.

"Just CU Boulder, but I'm looking at some other programs," I said as Becky shook her head with an amused smile.

"You are so picky," she said and continued to type. "You're top of the class."

"Number two," I corrected. "Jamie is valedictorian, which doesn't seem to make a difference to Mark."

"Fine. Number two. But your SAT score is high, and you'll get a few academic scholarships. You don't need to worry about being picky. You can go anywhere you want."

I know Becky was just being nice. Mark had told her enough times that they couldn't afford to help me and that it was too expensive for me to take loans. I knew that. Let's not even mention any school outside of the state. I'd be paying them for most of whatever kind of career I got and at this point, it didn't seem worth the mess anyway.

"I'm not even sure I want to go there," I said, pointing to the screen. She finished typing and turned the screen so we could both look. She'd filled out the entire form requesting a tour aside from selecting from the calendar of dates at the bottom.

"That's why we're going to explore the campus," she said. "Sometimes, you have to be there and smell the air to know if you belong."

I tried thinking of an excuse but couldn't find one. "The first weekend would work. Macy and Izzy want to take a girl's night in Holston the next."

"That's your birthday," she said with a gasp. I knew what would come next. Becky had a thing about birthdays. If you didn't blow out a candle and make a wish on your birthday, it set a bad precedent for the year. That's what she thought anyway.

"We can do a candle on Friday dinner," I told her.

"No, it has to be on the day of your birthday."

"Saturday breakfast then."

"It has to be a birthday cake," she said, submitting the form and shutting her laptop. "I'll send a candle with you. Order a piece when you girls get dinner."

I shook my head at her corny tradition, but that didn't keep me from smiling.

"What are you doing this weekend?" I asked her.

She pointed to the pantry door.

"I am going to clean every floor in this entire house and if I can't make the grout in the master bathroom tile white again, I might just rip it out myself."

I laughed. "Sounds like a great Saturday."

"You kid, but the grout is yellowing. It's gross and I want to remodel the bathroom anyway. It might be easier to just take it out than clean it," she said with a grimace. She was probably wrong, but I understood. She wanted to remodel most of the house and already had plans for how she would do each room. She had even stashed aside some of their savings to pay for it, but Mark didn't want a remodel. He didn't like her idea of colorful accent walls.

My phone buzzed on the table. It was a text in our guardian group chat. I noticed that a new number was listed at the top of the chain, probably Puck's.

Meet me at the estate? I found something on shadow demons.

I replied to Jamie's text at the same time Puck and Izzy did. Thankfully, Macy texted that she could pick me up. I couldn't wait for the Beetle to be finished at the shop.

"I'm going for coffee with Macy," I said.

Becky glanced from my face to the steaming mug in my hand.

"Okay," she said, her tone indicating that she didn't believe me at all. That was the thing I liked about Becky. She didn't ask too many questions. "I want to have dinner with you tonight though."

"I'll be here," I promised. "Don't slip in the mop water."

"Ha. Funny," she called back as I made my way upstairs to finish getting ready.

Macy honked from the driveway as I finished pulling on my shoes. I could hear the music blaring from her speakers when I shut the front door. She didn't object when I turned the volume down as I got in.

"Did you know Puck stayed over?" she asked before I even shut the door.

"God, I'm trying to forget it," I blurted.

Macy looked back at me with her mouth open and eyes alight. No one liked gossip like Macy and she didn't stop ogling me until I promised to gush when she started driving.

"It's really none of our business," I told her.

"No, you aren't keeping this secret!" she yelled, "What did you see?"

"*Ugh*. Don't make me say it," I groaned, turning on the AC as I felt my body warm.

"Spill your guts or else it will be more awkward when we're all together. Come on," she urged. It would be awkward either way. I don't think I could look Mr. Puck in the face ever again.

"I think Puck and Izzy matched last night," I said the words carefully, but their meaning got a squeal out of Macy anyway.

"Oh my god! They hooked up?" she asked with a gasp. "I knew it."

"I think we all did, but I don't want to think about it. I'm trying to get the image out of my brain."

"You didn't walk in on them, did you?" Macy laughed.

"No. Well, not walk in on…" I pointed out the stop sign out of fear that Macy was too excited to see it. "He was getting water for the two of them and he was in a towel. Their tattoos were bigger, so they definitely matched."

"Their tattoos?" Macy asked as we approached the gated driveway of the Moore Estate. I explained the lore to her. For a guardian couple to match, they had to be intimate past holding hands. Jamie told me a kiss would do it. A match made the circle stronger, strengthening the powers of the couple, and it meant the couple became mortal again.

"Just where he left it," Macy said as she parked next to Puck's Camry in the driveway. We walked in the front door and were greeted with the sound of laughter from the living room. Izzy stood in the middle with a hand laced in Mr. Puck's. Both were dressed in swimsuits. Izzy let go of Puck to hurry toward us, grabbing Macy and me by the arms and pulling us toward the backdoor Puck had just gone out.

"You realize it's like fifty degrees outside, right?" Macy asked her. I shivered as we went out and onto the back patio.

"Wait until I show you," Izzy said and led the way down the steps. "You'll both want to borrow suits when you see this."

Puck stepped onto the top stair of the pool, so the water reached just above his ankle. Izzy kicked off a flip-flop and dipped her toes into the water. At first, I thought she was just testing the icy water, but I started to see steam coming off the surface. A moment later, and I could feel the warmth from the pool. Puck let out a gasp and stepped back onto the concrete, the water bubbling.

"A little too hot," he told Izzy, leaning over to press his lips to her temple. She smiled back at us.

"It used to take most of my energy to boil a pot of water," she said, the excitement in her voice infectious.

"Does that mean you got faster?" I asked Puck.

He shrugged. "Something like that. I ran home for a pair of trunks to test out my speed. I'm a little faster, but I noticed I can go a lot farther without getting remotely tired. I took the country roads, and I ran just outside the city limits."

"He went all the way around Burbrook and made it back here in ten minutes," Izzy said.

Puck smirked, trying to mask his pride as he said, "I don't know that it was ten minutes."

"Where's Jamie?" I asked.

They both looked back to the house. I wondered how he was handling the news about Izzy and Puck.

"Your powers got stronger, and I still don't know what mine even is," Macy said. Izzy started assuring her that she'd find hers any day now while Puck told me he'd go get Jamie. I watched him go to the house as Izzy and Macy moved to a pair of lounge chairs to the right of a fire pit.

"Tori," Macy called to me, patting the end of her lounge chair. I joined them as Izzy told us about last night, how they played two games of pool, each winning one, and were onto a tie-breaker game when Puck kissed her. She said it felt like something slipped into place. It was the best kiss she'd had in her entire life.

"I could say all the cheesy things you hear about in movies and romance novels, but ..." Izzy let out a sigh and bit her lip. "Even the sex was competitive."

"Gross," I groaned.

"Oh my god," Macy squealed. "You didn't have to tell us." The way she said it made it clear that she wanted to hear every detail. I was glad that Jamie and Puck started down the patio steps at that moment, so I didn't have to sit through the account.

"Here," Puck said, tossing a pair of sweats to Izzy. He'd changed back into his jeans and sweater from last night.

Jamie was dressed similarly. He held the circle guide in one hand and a leatherbound book in the other.

"I thought I looked through everything when we did research on the hellhounds," he said and sat down on the edge of the stone fire pit, "but I forgot about Dad's hutch."

"Hutch?" I asked.

"Our dad built a safe room in the house. It's hidden behind the hutch in the kitchen," Izzy explained. "He stored some of the more important things in there. That's where we found that book and a few others that might help explain some things about you."

"Sounds like homework," Macy said.

"We should all take a book and report anything interesting we find," I said, looking at each concerned face in turn.

"We will, but in the meantime, I found something in this book about shadow demons," Jamie said, flipping the book open to a page he'd marked with a piece of paper. He looked at us once before starting to read from the section. "Shadows aren't demons, but dark entities that can be controlled by a powerful demon. Because they are merely shadows of their former human selves, they can't be touched or fought the same way any other demon can. Guardian powers and weapons work the same against them as they do against any demon or creature from the Shadowlands. The difficult part isn't defeating a shadow but defeating the demon that controls it.

Only the most powerful forces can summon and use shadow demons to do their work."

Jamie looked up, lowering the book to his lap.

"So, someone from the Shadowlands is after Tori's blood," Macy said. "Again."

"What kind of dark force would be strong enough to use not just one shadow demon, but several at a time?" Izzy asked, holding out a hand out for the book. With an annoyed sigh, Jamie handed it to her.

"The Shadow Mistress is the one who wants her blood. Maybe she's acting alone this time," he said.

I remembered the dark castle where I'd been held. I was set to meet the Shadow Mistress then, but I'd escaped, and I saw a tapestry on the way out that showed the kind of higher-ranking forces the book talked about.

"Hand me that paper," I said and tugged it from Jamie's hand before he could object. "Anyone have a pen?" I asked, looking around for anything that might work. My eyes settled on the fire pit. I joined Jamie at the edge and dipped my finger in the ashes. I drew the ferryman on the blank paper the best I could with my finger. I tried making the body of the second figure hourglass the way I remembered her, with long hair nearly falling to her knees around her. The Shadow Mistress was the hardest to draw and her crown looked more like sticks coming out of her skull than the antlers I saw on the tapestry.

"Tori, what is that?" Izzy asked nervously.

I turned to face them, holding the paper between my hands.

"When we were dress shopping and the ferryman dropped me into the Shadowlands, I saw a tapestry in the Shadow Mistress's castle. She's the one on the right. She has a crown of antlers. The ferryman serves her. He's bound to her like a slave. He doesn't have a choice and he's always a guardian who died and was denied passage through the Shadowlands to the afterlife," I said, making sure to add that the tapestry showed me all of this before they could ask how I knew so much about the ferryman.

"What about the middle one?" Puck asked, pointing out the long-haired figure.

"I-I'm not sure," I said. "But she was on the same part of the tapestry as the Shadow Mistress. It was a battle scene with the Shadow Mistress on top of all the dead. This other woman was portrayed on the battlefield. I think she's some kind of warrior."

"Like an assassin?" Izzy asked, laughing in disbelief.

"Maybe," I admitted, noticing how Jamie was watching me now.

"We have to get rid of her," he said, setting the book aside and standing up.

"We don't even know what she is," I said. "And until we do, we should be focused on better defending ourselves against these shadow demons she's sending our way."

"The shadow demons are probably a distraction," Puck interrupted. "This higher power could still be stuck in the Shadowlands for now."

I remembered the voices calling me to the lake. What if they were trying to lure me to it instead of coming after me the way the ferryman had? I could go on my own. I didn't need to be matched to go into the Shadowlands and I would still be immortal.

"We need to be sure," Jamie said.

"How?" Izzy asked.

"Shouldn't we be focused on figuring out why Tori's blood is important to them?" Macy asked. She wasn't wrong, but things moved fast around here, and we'd already searched the whole library for answers to that question.

We didn't look everywhere though.

"Where's this hutch?" I asked.

Jamie led the way. The kitchen was just off the patio. I remember it from my first night as a guardian. Jamie and Izzy argued about how much I should be shown right away. Izzy snuck me a spoon from a drawer that I practiced bending at night.

The hutch held polished silver and enough fancy plates for a whole Thanksgiving party. Jamie's power enabled him to move the entire hutch from the wall without so much as rattling a few plates on the shelves. A hole was cut in the wall that went to a room the size of a closet. It was just large enough for the small desk in the center, bookshelves stuffed with books pressed to every wall.

Jamie went into the room ahead of me, brushing his fingers along the dusty desktop as he went around it. He stopped once he reached the other side and looked up, holding my gaze.

My heart skipped.

Something about the tight room flooded my mind with images. I imagined pressing Jamie's back to the bookshelf behind him. I wanted to tangle my fingers in his dark hair. He'd push me back from my hips until I felt the desk. He'd lift me onto the top. It would be so easy for him, and my stomach would fill with butterflies when he moved between my knees and kissed me.

"So, we each grab a few and look for anything about Tori's blood or the shadow demons?" Puck asked, interrupting my dreaming as he passed me to look over the shelves.

"And anything about that warrior woman," Izzy added, joining him.

Macy waited with me outside the room as they searched, giving me questioning looks whenever I looked her way. I knew she wanted to ask, but it never came up. We were too busy researching. The rest of the group took their books and moved to the den to read. I told them I wanted to stay behind and read alone, which I did for a long time before checking my phone.

Becky texted me twice, once four hours ago and another coming just thirty minutes ago.

Be careful when you come back. The floors are super slick.

Come home early. You need to clean your room before we get dinner.

Clean my room? My room was always clean. I thought about the morning. Now that I remembered, I hadn't made my bed. At least, I didn't remember making my bed. That was usually the last thing I did before I left for my morning run, which I hadn't gone on this morning.

I opened the group chat and told the rest of the circle that I was heading home. Macy agreed to drop me off. I sat my phone next to the book I'd been reading and went to the shelf to look for another. I could probably skim through the last of the book I had plus another before we met again. I picked a clothbound book without a title on the cover and when I sat it on the desk, I noticed Jamie's response.

I know you'll want to come to do more research. The garage code is 1931.

A second look at the message told me it wasn't from the group message like I thought.

I picked up the books and took a step toward the hutch before deciding to leave the clothbound book behind. I'd come back for it later.

CHAPTER 8

The floor wasn't slick when I got back home, but the house did reek of lemon varnish. Becky had done more than just clean the floors. I could tell that she'd dusted every surface. The living room had been rearraigned so that the entertainment center was against a different wall and a bucket of paint sat on the floor where the entertainment center used to be.

"Becky," I called out. A moment later, she appeared at the top of the stairs with a full trash bag in one hand. "What's going on here?"

"I'm taking care of the house, because no one else seems to care that we're living in the eighties around here." She said and hurried down the stairs as she continued, "Mark still acts like it's the eighties and doesn't plan on joining to our century anytime soon, but that doesn't mean I can't bring this house up to speed."

Silence hung between us for a moment. She blushed as she caught my gaze.

"Are you ... Did something happen?" I asked.

"The problem is what didn't happen," she said under her breath.

"What's with the paint?" I asked, going to inspect the can and noticing that she'd taped off the back wall. The paint was new, just purchased today based on the sticker. The swatch sitting on top of the lid was a shade of pink between bubblegum and coral.

"I thought making that wall pink would make ..." Becky let out a long sigh after a moment before turning to me. "Go clean your room."

She said the words in defeat, like I'd tried arguing something with her and she'd given up. I wasn't sure what to do or what she'd let me do, so I just went to my room like she asked.

Just like I thought, the bed was unmade, but there was more out of place than I remembered. My homework on my desk was shifted, my laptop sitting on top of my calculus book instead of the other way around like I usually stacked it. My backpack was against the wall and empty, the contents lying on my mattress. I went to the bed, noticing that my pillowcases were at the foot of the bed and the bare pillows lying near the closet door.

Something grabbed my ankles and before I could scream, my feet were pulled from under me and I was lying spread-eagle on the floor. The dark shape flew over me and I rolled to my knees to catch it, a little surprised when my hand tightened around the ankle of the shadow demon.

I tugged it back to the ground, but it rolled out of my reach before I could get the demon blade from my waist. The shadow demon ran at the wall, passing through it.

"Don't scuff the floor. I just polished it," Becky's voice called from downstairs as I ran from my room and into the bathroom next door. The shadow demon stood in the middle of the room and dodged my first attempt at stabbing it through the middle. It hopped into the tub and with a smile that made my skin crawl and pulled the white curtain shut.

I ripped it back, but it wasn't standing in the shower. The skin prickling at the back of my neck had me spinning around, finding the demon just inches away with jagged teeth open wide. I raised my hands and took a step back as it lunged. We fell over the edge of the tub, the shower curtain ripping free from the metal rings and billowing under us as we landed in the hard porcelain.

The demon gasped in my ear and then it was gone, the point of my dagger where the dark mass had just been. I rubbed the back of my head where it hit the tile wall. Concussion or not, it would heal in seconds. The bathroom wouldn't.

"Are you okay?" Becky asked. I stowed the demon blade at my waste again before her footsteps reached the top stair. Her eyes went wide when she saw me sitting in the tub under the curtain.

"I fell," I explained, pulling myself out of the tub and looking back at the mess. Thankfully, the damage was limited to the shower curtain. I looked back at Becky who was still staring in stunned silence.

"Well, we'll just get another," she said slowly and went back to the hall.

Unless your plans for a nice dinner out included fast-food tacos, McDonald's, or a forty-dollar steak entrée, Jackie's was where you went to eat. It was a diner frequented by every teenage couple looking for a cheap date and every biker club that stopped in town after a drive through the mountains. I always ordered the Jackie Cheese, which was really just your average cheeseburger with a side of French fries.

The food was okay, better than the fast-food chains in town and a fraction of the cost you'd spend at the steakhouse. What you really went to Jackie's for wasn't the dinner, but the dessert afterward. I knew Becky was having a rough day, but it wasn't until she'd ordered an old-fashioned sundae for herself rather than splitting one with me that I decided to ask.

"How much have you heard?" she asked cautiously.

"About?" I wasn't going to jump to conclusions. Becky spun her spoon around the outside of her half-eaten dish. I twisted the cherry stem between my fingers as she fidgeted.

"It's a small house, Tori," Becky said and looked up.

"Maybe you and Mark need to go out together. You're both always so tense about work and stuff and that's not helping," I told her.

She eyed me for a moment before speaking.

"Did he say something to you when you two were out?"

"Well ..." I wanted to point out that she hadn't been in his truck since the Christmas party almost four years ago but bringing up the lipstick seemed to just further point out how far apart they were right now. "Mark is a workaholic," I said.

Becky snorted. "I already know that."

"Yes, but he kind of hinted that he wants to go back to how things used to be—with you I mean." He hadn't said it, but the look in his eyes seemed sad enough when I mentioned the lipstick. They used to go out all the time like that; not just work events but dancing in Holston and weekends in Denver.

She stirred her mostly melted ice cream a little longer, before deciding it was time to leave. She told me to go ahead to the car while she paid and used the bathroom but forgot to give me the keys.

I leaned against the front of the car, watching Becky in the window as she stopped to talk to one of the waitresses on her way to the bathroom. It could be a while.

It was cold; cold enough that I could see my breath. I pulled my phone from my pocket and opened it to the message Jamie sent me earlier. I backed out and opened the group message for our circle. I really should tell them about the shadow demon being in my house, but I wasn't ready for protection mode yet.

The tinkle of a bell drew my attention a little farther down the sidewalk where Angel was stepping out of Beans and Books. He didn't seem bothered by the cold; his sleeves still pushed up to his elbows as he locked up the shop.

I looked down at my phone when he noticed me and typed out the message I dreaded sending. It was just a short sentence.

I killed a shadow demon.

Macy was the first to text back, asking where I found it. I groaned as I typed the words.

At my house.

No sooner had I hit send, Jamie's name appeared at the top of my screen as the phone buzzed wildly in my hand. I almost ignored the call.

"Are you okay?' he asked.

"I'm fine. I can't talk right now. I'm at dinner with Becky," I said. The line was quiet for a long moment.

"You're fine," Jamie echoed.

"Yes," I said. "I'll talk to you Monday." I hung up before he could ask any more questions. When I looked up from the sidewalk, I noticed Angel watching me from the shadows.

"I didn't want to interrupt," he said. "It seemed …"

"Complicated," I told him.

Angel stopped next to the car. I looked through the diner window and saw that Becky was still talking with the same waitress.

"Sounds a little like you're putting up with bullshit," he said.

I snorted and said, "We're not together, so I'm not putting up with anything."

Becky finally gave the waitress a wave goodbye and went to the bathroom. When I looked at him, Angel was smiling as if I'd just said something funny.

"What?" I asked.

He shook his head, stilling wearing that smug smile like he knew something I didn't. It made me blush. It was also a little irritating.

"I get it," he said. "It's complicated."

I didn't reply. Becky came out the front door of the diner, looking from me to Angel and then at me again.

"This is my aunt, Becky Greenwood," I said. "Becky, this is Angel Martínez. He works at Beans and Books with me."

"Good to meet you," Becky said and shook Angel's hand. "So, are you here on a gap year?"

I elbowed her for the comment. Angel laughed.

"I'm going to NYU next fall," he said. "I'm just saving up some money."

"Well, we should probably go," I said, already kicking myself for how awkwardly I waved at him now. "I'll see you Monday after school," I said and tried the passenger door. I pulled twice before Becky got it unlocked and I could slip into the seat. Thankfully, Angel went back to the sidewalk, checking his phone.

"He's cute," Becky said as she clicked her seatbelt in place.

"He's older. He probably thinks I'm some annoying high school girl. We live in two different worlds," I said, wishing she'd just back out and start down the road toward home.

"He's starting at NYU next year, so he's just nineteen or twenty. You'll be eighteen in a few weeks. Believe me, you're still a dumb teenager until you're like twenty-five at least."

"Fine. He's a dumb teenager with a job that pays his rent and puts gas in his car. My car can barely make it across town. I'd hardly say we're the same," I told her. Why were we even talking about this? I didn't like Angel that way. I barely knew him.

"Mark is four years older than me," she said and backed into the street.

"He's ... a painting. That's it," I said with a laugh.

"A painting?" she asked.

"Just for looks," I explained.

"Not for touching?" Becky said with a wild laugh.

I felt my cheeks burn.

"God, I don't like him. He's just the cute guy I work with. Leave me alone." I couldn't keep from laughing.

Becky and I stayed up late watching movies on Netflix and planning our day touring CU Boulder. I didn't change the subject until she started talking about majors and what I could do with a law degree. It felt like a loss already and left an empty feeling in my gut.

I checked my whole room before changing for bed. No demons.

CHAPTER 9

Mr. Puck and I ran part of our routes together each morning. I ran up Burbrook Mountain, back down, across the main road, and then we looped the apartment complex and around the railroad station together. We always ran at my pace, though he pushed me to move a little quicker than I normally would each time.

"Got to get in shape for demon hunting," he told me when we stopped for a break.

"I didn't know I was out of shape," I replied with my hands folded on top of my head.

Will Puck joining our circle didn't change anything about him at school. Jamie even commented that he seemed to expect more out of him in class now that he knew Jamie had been through high school so many times.

"It's costume return day," Jessica told me as we walked into Mrs. McKellen's class for academic team practice. I felt my stomach clench. I'd left my costume at home, which probably didn't make a difference considering that the shadow demons had ripped it. At least it wasn't entirely damaged. Jamie's had been ripped in half.

"I forgot. I'll have to bring it next time," I told her.

"Forgetting seems to be your thing," I heard her mutter before taking her seat.

I paused at the front of the room to decide if I wanted to sit next to Hayden, who had been staring at me all day like I got dressed in the dark, or if I wanted to just suck it up and sit next to Jamie.

"Tori and Jamie," McKellen said from the door. I looked away from Jamie at her. She motioned for us to follow her. I could hear Jessica Harper whispering to Tasha James behind me.

Mrs. McKellen was just outside the door in the deserted hallway. The only sound was the distant whistle of basketball practice. I could tell from her somber expression that we were in trouble. I should've known before now that our disappearance from the maze would be noticed.

"Close the door," she told Jamie as we walked out of the room. He kicked the doorstop. Jamie and I stood quietly side-by-side while she waited for the wooden door to slowly swing shut, the classroom dead silent. I was sure nosy Jessica would be listening in for the lecture.

"Are you two sure you want to be a part of this team?" Mrs. McKellen asked.

"Yes," I said, looking to Jamie who nodded in agreement.

"Well, neither of you are putting in the work to prove that," she answered.

"Excuse me, Mrs. McKellen, but Tori and I have the highest

scores on the team," Jamie said. "We have the highest average correct answers, and we buzz in more than anyone else."

"Yes, well, this isn't basketball," she said and rubbed her temple. She let out a long sigh.

"We can go apologize to the Gillards personally," I offered.

"That would be a good start. Since no one was at the scarecrow post, someone destroyed the pedestal and the cornstalks around it," McKellen said, still rubbing her temple. I exchanged surprised looks with Jamie. So, we would get away with that part at least.

"We haven't missed a practice since we joined the team," Jamie said.

"Why did you miss the festival?" McKellen asked. "You both checked in with me at the beginning of the night. You worked the trick-or-treating tents. Why did you leave?"

I resisted the urge to look at Jamie, so I looked at the brick wall behind our teacher instead. I couldn't think of a lie that would keep us from more trouble or that wouldn't lead to a call home.

"Halloween party," Jamie said quietly.

Mrs. McKellen looked at each of us in disapproval. My stomach sank into my shoes.

"We're sorry," I said.

"It's more than just the maze. The festival attendees seemed to enjoy the experience without your parts, but this is about integrity," she said. "You signed the team's code of conduct, which included attending the very short list of outside events. The Fall Festival is one of three fundraisers for our program."

"We didn't mean to sabotage the team's fundraiser," Jamie said, the annoyance thick in his tone.

"We received money for our volunteer hours, so that's not an issue. What is an issue is that every member of this team is required to participate in three fundraisers for the calendar year. We always do community events, and we only have two more this year. If you both want to continue with this team, you'll have to make up your time in another way."

"How?" I asked.

"I will let you know when I have something arranged," Mrs. McKellen said. After a moment, she walked to the classroom door and held it open for us.

Mrs. McKellen's alternative fundraiser ended up being a project. Burbrook High School celebrated Thanksgiving with a lunch of cafeteria turkey, stuffing, and mashed potatoes. There was a mural made of paper turkeys on which students would write what they were thankful for on and tape to a forest scene along one wall of the cafeteria. It was a tradition the student council kept going. Macy and her fellow officers were in charge of making the mural. Each day closer to Thanksgiving Break, more décor was put up around the main gathering areas. Three weeks out, pumpkins and garlands of orange leaves appeared on every round table in the cafeteria. Two weeks out, brown butcher paper covered the largest wall. Monday before break, trees were painted over the paper with orange, red, and yellow leaves made of student handprints.

Jamie and I had to have enough orange turkeys cut out by the Friday before the break for the school-wide Thanksgiving lunch. Close to four hundred turkeys and Jamie and I had just a week to complete the task, which was why he showed up at Beans and Books near the end of my shift with a grocery bag of materials.

"Welcome to Beans and Books," Angel said while I was

gathering more coffee and filters for the next day. "How can I help you?"

"I'm here for Tori." Jamie's words sent me back through the door and to the counter with an armful of supplies.

"Did you schedule a date an hour before your shift ends?" Angel asked me, amusement on his face.

"No," I said, glaring at Jamie. I could tell from the paper he sat on one of the round tables and the scissors he pulled out of the bag why he was here. I had been promising to help him cut those turkeys for days. The free time I did have between school, academic team, and work I spent at the estate doing research behind the hutch.

We were still finding shadow demons in and around Burbrook. I'd killed another that I caught spying on me after work in the parking lot. Jamie was still out late actively hunting them, so he'd killed more than all of us put together. Thankfully, no one in the circle pushed to add more protection around me after I handled the first demon at my house. I knew Jamie was probably keeping an eye out for any activity near me during his hunting sessions, but I chose to keep that thought in the back of my mind.

"She's been avoiding doing a school project with me," Jamie said and held up the template he'd created from a piece of cardboard. The turkey was shaped as if he'd traced his hand and decided not to cut the fingers apart, the scalloped edges the entire reason I dreaded the assignment. It would take forever to cut that kind of detail.

"I'm not avoiding it," I said, spraying the countertop down and rubbing at it with a rag.

"I figured you wouldn't be busy. Who comes in for coffee at six anyway?" Jamie said, flashing me a smile.

"Just you," Angel said, pulling a mug from the shelf. "What are you drinking?"

"Pumpkin spice latte, if you can make it," Jamie replied.

Angel smirked at me knowingly and held out the mug. "Pumpkin spice latte?"

I knew he wasn't asking if I knew how to make it. It was the first drink he had taught me how to make and he'd teased me ever since I told him I didn't like them. I'm sure he was drawing all kinds of connections now.

"It's not …" I started, getting cut off as he placed the mug in my hand.

"I know," Angel said and took the rag from me. "It's complicated."

I only knew how to make two drinks well. Pumpkin spice lattes and caramel mochas and I only knew the recipe for the latter because Mr. Tennison, who owned a store down the street, always gave me a two-dollar tip with the same advice of "a dollar to spend and a dollar to save."

I finished the mug with a mediocre swirl of whipped cream before walking it to Jamie. He had covered the tiny table with supplies. I glanced into the brown bag sitting next to him on the floor to see that he already had a good stash of turkeys cut out.

"You didn't come here just to cut turkeys," I said, moving the stack of construction paper aside to make a spot for his coffee. I glanced at the counter as Angel went into the back room. I extended a hand toward the next table, and it groaned as I pulled it toward us. Jamie frowned.

"Say it," I dared him.

Angel sat a stack of books on the counter and went to the storeroom for another.

"Why have you been acting like this?" Jamie asked, his tone curious instead of accusatory like I had expected. He picked up the template and a marker.

"Like what?" I asked. "I'm just being myself and trying to

avoid your stupid big-brother mood swings whenever something you don't like happens." I glanced to see if Angel was listening in as he returned with another stack of books.

"You're acting like a bitch," Jamie said. He traced the outline of a turkey on the paper and sat it in front of me. "It's either that, or I did something I'm not aware of. I promise that I didn't mean to hurt your feelings if that's—"

"You didn't hurt my feelings," I snapped as he started tracing another turkey.

"Okay. Then ..." He let the words hang in the air.

I adjusted in my seat, my eyes burning. Maybe I was being childish. I was just trying to avoid him at first, but maybe I had been a little more abrasive than he deserved. I mean, he hadn't really done anything but finally be honest about his feelings. He'd opened up for the first time and I rejected him and have not said a word to him about it since.

Angel approached us with a mug in his hand. He sat it down in front of me. I looked down at the dark liquid, able to see my reflection on the surface.

"I thought I threw out the pot," I said.

"It's a pour over," he said and placed a hand on my shoulder. "Dark roast, the way you like it." He gave my shoulder a gentle squeeze, fingers lingering where the fabric of my V-neck shirt met my collarbone. The moment lasted just a couple of seconds, but it was long enough for Jamie to notice. He watched as Angel went to the counter and picked up a stack of books to take to the shelves.

"I've been a bitch and I'm sorry," I said. "But I don't want anything more than what we are right now." I wanted to look at him so he could see that I meant the words, but I didn't mean them, and I couldn't look up from the mug.

"Then why did you pull me closer in the maze?" Jamie asked.

I looked up. His expression was pleading for an answer. I don't remember pulling him to my chest, but I know that I had wanted to. I liked how his hands felt against the bare skin of my back. When I thought about it, I could still smell the pine on his neck.

I took a sip of hot coffee and then shifted the paper on the table until I found the scissors. I focused on cutting the turkeys from the paper and after I'd moved on to the second one, I heard the marker pull across the construction paper again.

"It's eight," Angel said, breaking our focus.

Jamie and I worked like a machine. He traced the template and I cut. We'd worked in silence the entire time, not realizing how much time had passed.

"I haven't done the floors yet," I said and got up from the table with my mug. Angel stopped me, holding a hand out for the mug. I handed it to him, and he downed the last of the coffee.

"I got it," he said and nodded toward the storeroom, "Grab your stuff and go. It's a school night."

I hurried through the back doors. I pulled my apron over my head and draped it over my arm. I didn't bother hanging it up by the counter. I planned on sneaking out the back door to avoid Jamie. Angel came in for the mop in the corner when I slung my backpack over my shoulder and fished my keys from the side pocket.

"Tori," Angel started, making me pause at the back door.

"I know. I owe you one big time," I said.

He shook his head with a slight smile.

"Do you like that guy or not?" he asked.

I wasn't sure how to answer, so I just nodded and let the door shut behind me before the tears could fall.

CHAPTER 10

I was glad to have the Beetle back, but I would've liked the help that getting a ride to school provided. Monday morning, while it was raining of course, I hurried into the school early with Ziploc bags of paper turkeys tucked carefully in my backpack. I had stayed up late the night before to finish cutting out the last of the turkeys.

"Wow," Macy said when I got to our table in chemistry. "You look like hell."

"I was up late finishing the turkeys for today and I woke up early with the nightmare." I hadn't told anyone about the nightmare and only realized after seeing the look Macy sent me that it had slipped out. I groaned and began tugging out my binder from my backpack, a Ziploc bag of turkeys flying out and sliding under the table behind us.

"*The* nightmare? What nightmare? Have you been having it for a while?"

I ignored her and ducked under the table for the bag before Sean could step on it. After tucking it back in my backpack and sitting up, I could tell she wasn't going to let this go.

"Fine," I told her. "I've been having nightmares since homecoming."

"Nightmares or *a* nightmare?" she asked with an accusing tone. I looked toward the front of the room, hoping Mr. Puck would come swooping in to start class and save me. No luck. We still had two minutes until the bell.

"It's always the same nightmare," I said with a sigh. "Over time, it's gotten longer though. It's like reading a few pages further into a book each time I close my eyes."

"What's it about?"

I lowered my voice to say her name. "Alison."

Macy nodded and said, "I've had a few dreams where she walks back into school covered in blood like it's the most normal thing ever. I've also had a few where they find her body, and everyone cries."

"Yeah. Well, mine is always the same and it's starting to mess with my head." I didn't want to tell her I was hearing voices. Who in their right mind would admit that? Being an immortal guardian and knowing monsters and demons were real was strange enough. Something told me that hearing voices wasn't normal even for guardians and I didn't need to give anyone another reason to worry about me.

"I don't understand why they haven't found her yet. We know where she was," Macy whispered, her voice barely audible as she opened her binder to a blank page for notes. My stomach turned as I thought about it.

"Something probably dragged her away," I said, ignoring the sick feeling.

"Like a bear or ..." Macy shuddered.

I imagined the day that they would find Alison's body as a relief, but it probably wouldn't be. The same tragic discussions would spread like crazy just the way they did when Noah and

Jacob died. People still slid notes into their lockers to pay tribute. Alison's locker had her poster plastered across it.

Jamie came in just as the bell rang, locking eyes with me for a moment before moving to the back of the room. Mr. Puck shut the door behind him and went to the desk. I finished setting up my desk while he took roll, noticing on the last page of my notes that today's date was listed as a lab day. I closed my notes and tucked them in my backpack. When I looked up, I noticed Mr. Puck was looking at me. His expression changed. It was like he was sending me a silent apology. My stomach sank.

"Tori," he started, "since we are doing labs today, I'm going to need you to move back to your original table with Jamie, please."

He knew it was a lab day and he knew what had happened between Jamie and me. Izzy told him pretty much everything now that they were matched. She didn't sneeze without him appearing at her side with a tissue now. He could've asked me in private or at least called me to the hallway to talk.

"Mr. Puck," I started.

"Now, Tori," he said before I could argue. The apology was still there in his eyes, but it was clear in his posture that he wasn't budging. He was going to use his teacher authority, if I forced him to. I wanted to tell him off, but I knew I'd never get away with it now. Maybe later.

"Do you need my notes? I won't need them," I told Macy as I packed the last of my things in my backpack.

"No, sorry." She shrugged.

I pulled my bag over one shoulder and walked to that quiet table at the back of the room.

Jamie didn't utter a word as Mr. Puck got us started with instructions. We set up our equipment in silence as Puck went from one table to the next to hand out materials. He stopped at ours, not handing me the plastic bag right away.

"You two are acting like children," he said.

"I've been through high school more times than you've taught it," Jamie said.

"Save it," Puck snapped at him, his voice low enough not to distract the rest of the class from their experiments. "You're not ninety years old, you've just been seventeen for that long and you're doing a pretty damn good job of acting that way."

"I've been running a multi-billion-dollar company for most of those years," Jamie said.

I elbowed him as he started to raise his voice.

"Bullshit," Puck said under his breath. He let out a huff and shook his head before speaking again, his eyes on Jamie. "I know for a fact that your sister handles most of the business, not you. And even at that, there are enough people in the mix that she barely has to interact with them. They wouldn't know who either of you are if you walked right into their boardroom. So, stop talking like you're some bigshot with a lot to show for it. You are a seventeen-year-old who has happened to be seventeen for a very long time. That's it."

"Now that we've established that ..." I said and reached for the bag of materials. Mr. Puck held it out of reach. Instead, he reached into his back pocket and pulled out a piece of green plastic the size of a small notebook. The hall pass.

"All this between the two of you has really messed up the whole circle. Neither of you talk to each other. Both of you are alienating yourselves from the rest of us."

"I'm not avoiding you guys," I said. Puck raised his eyebrows at me in disbelief. Well, I wasn't meaning to avoid anyone. I hadn't talked to Macy much in the last few weeks, but it wasn't because I didn't want to.

"Izzy's been trying to get you two to fix this, but you're

never home to talk to her," Puck said and pointed at Jamie. He pointed at me next and said, "And you look so miserable every time she sees you that she's not even sure how to bring it up."

"People are starting to notice," I whispered. Macy had been checking on us since I'd moved, but Sean was starting to stare along with both his annoying cronies.

"Good. That means you both don't have a choice," he said. He flashed a devious smile and held up the hall pass.

"You'd really pull the teacher card? You're not even going to play fair?" Jamie asked. Mr. Puck acted like he hadn't even heard. He tossed the hall pass onto the table so that it landed with a loud clap that startled a few students in the room. They were all looking our way now and Mr. Puck wasn't smiling anymore. He looked angry. If the man decided to quit teaching, he'd have a successful acting career ahead of him.

"Both of you," he told us, motioning for us to stand. I was on my feet immediately, dreading the talk that would spread through the whole senior class by lunch. Jamie hesitated before standing up with the pass in hand.

Mr. Puck led us through the silent classroom and to the door. He went into the hall, holding the door open so we could join him. He closed it just a fraction to give us a little privacy as he finished his lecture.

"No one in our circle cares that you two are mad at each other or whatever it is," he said. "But the three of us all agree that it's making it hard to work as a team and that's a problem. We can't figure out the thing with Tori's blood or these shadow demons if we're so focused on if you two can be mature enough to be in the same room together. So, you two are going to talk out here and figure it out. Learn how to grow up. Deal with your business now or I will pull the teacher card and assign you both detention for later."

"Tori's uncle has been on her ass since school started. You

call him and we'll down a guardian for as long as he locks her away," Jamie said. He wasn't wrong. Mark was trying to trust me. I didn't want to be under his microscope any longer.

"Then you'll figure it out now," Puck said with a shrug. "Up to you."

"You and Izzy really are a match," Jamie said with an annoyed huff. "You both fight dirty."

Mr. Puck smiled. "You have the class period to talk it out, but you still have a lab to do or make up if you use the whole period. Come back in when you're done," he said and shut the door behind him.

I expected the quiet of the hall to stretch on much longer than it did. A moment after Mr. Puck left, Jamie turned around to face me.

"I was trying to avoid you … before. Everything that happened before homecoming, I spent so much time trying to not like you, Tori. I thought it would be easier if I could just avoid my feelings in case things didn't work out. I don't want to date just anyone. I want to be with whoever that person for me is, but I can't stop feeling more whenever you're around. So, I stopped being around you until that maze."

"Jamie, it's not what you think," I said, feeling the tears coming.

"You say that, but you pulled me closer in that maze and when you look at me …"

"Jamie," I started. I bit my lower lip as it began to wobble. *I can't cry. I can't cry.* I repeated the words in my head until I felt like I had pulled myself together only to say the words I knew would shatter me again. "I love you, Jamie. I do, but it's not …"

"Then let's try," he said and moved closer to me. "You were right about me being so guarded because of my past and I'm done missing out on what might be out there. Life as a guardian is too long to spend cut off from life."

"What you feel for me is different. It's not what you think," I said, stepping back from him. This was all too much. I wanted him to go away as much as I wanted him pressed against me. I kept my focus on the vision the ferryman showed me.

"I love you too, Tori," Jamie said. "I wasn't sure until I saw you in that dress at homecoming and I knew as soon as I crushed that hellhound that I wanted to make sure nothing could ever stand between us."

"Jamie, you may want to be with me, but you don't love me," I said, still struggling to find the words that would make the right impact, finally putting things back the way they were before he decided to lift the protective veil.

"I want you, Tori. I want to see where this goes, and I know you do too. You say you don't, but you look at me like I've already broken your heart."

"Because you have," I blurted.

He took a step back as though I'd shoved him, staring back at me with a stunned expression. I took a deep breath and continued before he could melt me with soft words more than he already had. "You want me, fine, but you don't love me."

"How do you know?" he shot back.

"Because you're still in love with Emily!" I yelled. I was surprised no one came out of the surrounding classrooms to tell us off. I almost wish someone had. It would've distracted from the shock on Jamie's face. He didn't speak, opening his mouth like he wanted to before closing it again.

"See," I said and pointed at him. "You aren't over her, but you want to be. You want to forget all about her and you're doing whatever you can to do that, especially since our circle includes more than just you and Izzy now."

"And what? You're just a pretty distraction?"

"Yes," I said. "Like Puck said, you're over ninety, but you're still in the body of a seventeen-year-old with all those hormones. You told me that you and Emily were together, and you weren't a match, but that didn't matter. You loved her and you still do."

Jamie kept his eyes on the floor. He adjusted the sleeves of his shirt, so they were covering most of his hands. His hands lingered at the watch strap wrapped around his wrist. After running his thumb across the leather a few times, he looked up at me and his expression was much more neutral.

"If you could choose, who would it be?" I asked.

"Tori, she's not even... There's no choice to make. It doesn't matter."

"I think you know," I said and let the silence fill the hall.

He fidgeted more. He picked at the edge of the hall pass where the room number was etched into the plastic until he accidentally snapped off the corner. He picked it up off the floor and let out a sigh.

"Okay," he said with a nod. "I've missed you."

"I've missed you too," I whispered.

"It'll be like before, or as close to that as we can," Jamie promised. "I'm sorry for everything I've put you through. I never meant to hurt you."

"I know," I said. "And things will be better. No more cold-shoulder, bitchy Tori," I said and blinked away the tears.

He smiled. "No more running away,"

Jamie had barely opened his arms before I wrapped mine around him. I told myself it was the last time I'd let myself think about how he felt and how he smelled. I let out a deep breath and stepped away before I was ready to.

"Well, we should go finish the lab," he said, pocketing the broken piece of the hall pass.

"Have you done this one before?" I asked.

"Have I done this one?" he laughed and pulled the door open.

"Fine. I know," I said with an eyeroll at the unspoken joke.

CHAPTER II

"I can't believe I haven't thought to ask you all week," I said as I stood up on a chair to reach the last available space on the mural to place a paper turkey. "What are you thankful for?"

Jamie handed me a piece of tape and I stuck the turkey to the spot. "A lot."

"Like?" I climbed down from the chair. He considered the question for a moment as he picked up another turkey to hang.

"You," he said with a small smile. "I don't mean to make things weird again, but sitting next to you the first day and getting to know you better after you woke... It was kind of like setting a glass of lemonade under the sun and watching the ice melt."

"Weird analogy, but okay," I said with an awkward laugh.

"No, I mean that you're the sun and I was frozen in time until you came along and told me that I wasn't defined by my past. I don't feel like I'm just a part of life anymore. I feel like I'm living again."

Again. He was living the way he felt when he was with

Emily. I thought about our argument in the hallway on Monday. I hadn't expected my stab in the dark to stick with me this long and I didn't expect it to work so well on Jamie.

"Well," I said, drawing out the word as I looked over our mural. There was such little amount of space that Jamie and I already talked about pulling down some of the paper and green handprints that made one of the trees in the scene. "I am thankful for ..."

It was my attempt to change the subject, but the truth was I hadn't thought about what I was thankful for. Obviously, there was my health and my family, as dysfunctional as it was right now. I didn't care for the immortality of being a guardian. I didn't even care about telekinesis.

"I'm glad I have you too," I told him.

He smiled and sat the tape aside.

"I think it's time we dismantle that tree," he said and pointed to the smaller of the three trees in the mural.

By the end of lunch, we took down two trees in the mural and still had to tape turkeys onto the trunk of the largest. The student council thanked us for helping with the event and Mrs. McKellen assured us that we would be credited for a fundraiser even though no money was raised at all for the turkeys.

We met in Mr. Puck's classroom at the end of the day to make plan for Thanksgiving Break. We had the whole of the next week off from school. We needed to coordinate who would be around to research in the hutch at the estate and who would be in town in case a demon was located.

"I think we should start with what everyone's plans are for break and see what we can and can't work around," Macy suggested. I wasn't surprised that the idea was hers. She always traveled on vacation. "I'm going to be in Florida the whole week with my mom. We leave tomorrow. My aunt is flying in from France. We're staying in this lake house right on the beach. It's going to be so fun!"

"I have a college visit at CU Boulder tomorrow with Becky," I said before anyone could ask. "I'll be here the whole week otherwise."

"You better, because Macy gets back Saturday and we are going out in Holston for your birthday," Izzy told me as she sat on top of the first table in the classroom. Puck leaned against it next to her as we all dropped our bags on the floor and took seats.

"You get back Saturday?" I asked, looking to Macy who was busy redoing her ponytail of blonde curls. "Isn't that a long day?"

"I'll sleep on the plane." She shrugged and dropped her hands from her hair. "It's your eighteenth birthday! I have to be there to celebrate."

I missed that part of Macy and me. She'd been there for the last six of my birthday parties, usually just us, doing the most girly and sometimes embarrassing things. The idea of a guardian-free night out with my favorite people set me at ease and actually had me a little excited for break.

"Izzy and I will be here all week," Jamie said. "I want to keep doing night hunts."

Izzy rolled her eyes. She thought his late nights were unnecessary. Sure, he had sent more demons back to the Shadowlands than any of us because of the long hours, but she didn't think it was doing anything good for him and I agreed.

"Izzy and I have a few dates planned, but nothing that will take us far from the area," Puck said. The way Izzy smiled, the most girly look I've ever seen on her face, was enough to make me blush.

"Well, I plan on being at the estate to research as much as I can after my visit tomorrow," I told them.

Macy let out a laugh.

"Have you not read every book in that hutch yet?" she asked.

"Not all of them," I mumbled. I had read most of one wall though.

"We will keep in touch through the group chat, of course," Puck said. "I think Tori should spend most of her time researching instead of hunting. Her analytical skills are better than any of ours and she'll be safter that way."

Ugh. I internally groaned every time someone brought up my safety.

"Agree," Jamie said, casting me a look as if he thought I'd push back against the idea. "So, let's start there. I take nights. Tori does the bulk of the research in the hutch. Izzy and Puck can be in charge of the daytime hunts when they are needed. Macy can reconnect with us next weekend, nice and tanned."

"Hopefully," Macy quipped.

"You can call me Will, by the way," Mr. Puck told us, which made everyone but Izzy snicker.

"No way," I said. "It's too ..."

"Talk about blurred lines," Macy said, taking her phone out and opening an app.

"You can't threaten us with detention and then turn around and talk like you're our friend," Jamie said and showed me the time on his watch. I had a shift at Beans and Books at four-thirty and it was getting a little close to time to leave. "It makes it hard to take you seriously," he added with a devious smirk. I elbowed him.

"I have to get to work, but I will see all of you after my college visit tomorrow," I said and pulled my backpack over my shoulder. I gave Macy a hug and wished her a good trip to Florida. She promised to bring me back something good. Puck told me to let him know tomorrow if I felt up for a

Sunday morning run or not. With a kiss on the cheek from Izzy and a wave from Jamie, I left to start my Thanksgiving Break.

Becky, a CU Boulder graduate herself, dressed in gold and black for the day. It was a few hours' drive, and she spent the entire time detailing the campus and reliving some of her favorite memories from college. I acted as enthusiastic as I could, but the entire time I was plagued with what-ifs. What if I didn't go to college? What if I *couldn't* go to college and be a guardian? What if I did?

"Are you okay? You seem distracted," she said as we did a slow drive-by the campus on Broadway.

"I'm fine, just thinking is all," I told her as she finally pulled into a parking lot. It was a cold day, the kind of Colorado day that had you planning for snowfall at any moment. The trees on campus were all a burnt orange color, giving off a very Halloween vibe with all the black and gold flags draped on every light pole.

Becky joined me outside the car, pulling her coat on. "Is it Jamie?"

"What? No," I said a little too quickly. I hadn't been thinking about him at all, but now I was. I was thinking about our circle. What would happen to all of us if I did go to college? I hadn't talked with Macy about the whole college thing yet because I didn't want to burst her bubble the way mine was.

"Don't pretend like you don't like him. I know you're upset that it's not working out."

"It won't work out, Becky. It was my call not to pursue things anyway."

"Okay," she said and led us toward the front of the lot, "Doesn't mean you can't feel crappy about it."

I didn't push the subject, asking her instead how things looked different than when she was a student here. That kept her busy as we walked.

Our break lined up with the college's break, so the campus was pretty vacant. The only people walking around the campus looked like they were touring, just like we were. A small group of parents and students were gathering near the Center for Academic Success and Engagement, or the CASE building as Becky told me when we joined them.

When we checked in for our tour, I got a swag bag with University of Colorado Boulder pencils, pens, brochures, and a T-shirt with the CU buffalo on the front. Becky encouraged me to put it on, but I used the time of the tour as an excuse and slipped it in the bag instead.

The tour wasn't that in-depth, and I found out as I went that we would've been better off if Becky had just given me the tour herself. After the tour ended, we ate lunch on campus and walked past the building again as we talked about how nice the campus was.

"We should hike Chautauqua Park before we drive all that way home. It would be nice to stretch our legs before we're cramped in the car," Becky said as we left the area around the football stadium where most of the tour group had gone to explore. "Or we could at least walk Pearl Street. I did that with some sorority friends on my twenty-first birthday ..." She let the words hang in the air, but the smile on her face told me that the night had been very eventful.

"I don't know. I kind of want to get back early to work on a project for history," I told her. She let out a dramatic groan. Maybe coming back to her old stomping ground was making her revert to that twenty-something that did walk of shames on Pearl Street and went skinny dipping in lakes on camping trips. Allegedly, anyway.

"Let's go in a few buildings anyway. Maybe we can find a professor to question or some students to give us more details."

"I'm sure they'll love that," I said, not able to contain my laugh. She handed me her map of the campus.

"We have to check out Wolf Law Building at least," Becky said, steering us in that direction before I could get a word in.

The interior of the building was filled with wood, gold lettering labeling each room. We peeked in both mock courtrooms before going to the second floor. We walked in silence for a while until Becky stopped outside of a café. I looked back at her as she looked over the mostly empty tables and chairs.

"Tori, would you feel better if you did a little exploring of your own?" she asked. I didn't respond. I'd tried so hard to seem interested. I was interested, but I didn't want to be in case college was put on hold.

"I'll be in the café. Text me when you're ready to go and we'll meet up," Becky said with a smile. She ducked into the café and left me in the hallway alone. I stood for a long time before I continued to wander the building without any real objective. I passed several empty sitting areas and passed murals and class photos, quickening my pace. I would walk the building and then leave it for the fresh air. That way, I could tell Becky I'd done it.

I found myself at the entrance to the William A. Wise Law Library when I started to calm down a little. Libraries were always a good distraction. I started to walk the shelves, looking over the titles of the books and feeling my heart rate steady. I rounded a shelf for another aisle and stood just feet from a blonde girl I recognized as one of the tour guides. She turned from the shelf to look at me, a MacBook with a CU Boulder Law sticker over the Apple logo.

"Hey," she said, clearly recognizing me. "Future law student?"

I felt my breath catch in my chest and no matter how deeply I tried to breath, I couldn't quite fill my lungs. Her kind expression changed to concern as she looked over me. I could feel my eyes burn now, threatening to send fat tears rolling down my cheeks and toward my wobbly knees. Before that could happen, I turned and ran.

I ignored her call to stop and ran through the aisles until I remembered the way out. I didn't stop when I left the library. I rushed down the stairs to the bottom floor and then back out into the courtyard. I slowed my pace to a quick walk and kept going, swiping the tears that had started to fall at some point during my escape. I focused on taking deep breaths, my heart slowing the more I focused. I could feel my body tightening again when I thought about Becky waiting on me back in the café, but a new sound distracted me.

"I am king of the underworld," a man yelled, his voice echoing off the surrounding buildings as the laughter of a few girls drowned him out.

"Jonas," a girl called out in laughter.

I followed the sound, passing a sign for the Mary Rippon Outdoor Theater. It took a minute to figure out how to see into the venue, but eventually I managed to figure out a way in without anyone stopping me.

A group of students were on stage, all of them holding notebooks. A girl with braids piled on top of her head sat next to a blonde with a pixie cut, both laughing as a boy waved his arms at the edge of the stage.

"Just imagined for a moment," he told the two girls before getting back into character, "that I, Odysseus, have defeated

Hades and now command the underworld. Odysseus, King of the Underworld."

"Jonas," a girl behind him on stage complained as the two girls laughed again.

"You think that's enough of a riff on the original for Professor K?" Jonas asked, looking at the rest of his group on stage.

"I think the only thing you're king of is getting drunk before the pregame ends," the girl with the braids said, getting a laugh out of everyone there and a glare from Jonas.

One of the girls on stage told him, "The assignment isn't to change the scene. It's to perform it with our own words and direction. We can't change the outcome or vary the story too much."

Jonas made a gagging gesture at his friends in the audience before turning to his group.

"I'm just using my imagination," he told them.

"Well, use your imagination to help us write some new lines," a boy said. "Let's start at the bit where Odysseus summons the shades."

"Shades?" Jonas asked.

"The ghost people," the boy said in annoyance. "The shades are the ghosts of the dead. In this case, the shades come to Odysseus in the forms of Elpenor, Teiresias, and his mom, Anticlea."

Jonas nodded as if suddenly remembering the story. I only remembered it vaguely from a reading it a few years ago in Mrs. McKellen's class, but all the books from the epic reminded me of the Shadowlands. The Mistress was a little like Hades. There was the ferryman, who was kind of like Charon who brought the souls of the dead across the river Styx. The Shadowlands wasn't Greek by any means, but all these life-after-death stories and mythologies were similar. Maybe what I was looking for wasn't in the hutch; maybe other mythologies could point me in the right direction.

"So, can we hit pause and talk about the motivations of the shades again?" one of the girls asked.

The boy threw his hands into the air, placing his notebook on his head and bending it over his hair like a hat.

"Did any of you read *The Odyssey* like we were supposed to?" he asked.

"Honestly, I haven't gotten this far in the book yet," the girl said.

"It's not a book. It's ..." The boy stopped mid-rant to move to the far left of the stage. For a moment, I thought he'd see me standing in the last aisle, but he was too focused on the brick-like book sitting on the stage. He lifted it and opened it to one of the many tabs sticking from the top. The front cover was black with the gilded outline of Odysseus tied to the mast of a ship.

Go to the lake.

The voice was so loud in my brain that I flinched and looked behind me, half-expecting to see whoever had been whispering the words to me since homecoming. The only other time I heard a voice like this was in the Shadowlands, but the voice was from a different person. It told me to obey the Shadow Mistress and the voice alone was enough to paralyze me in my tracks and nearly got me stopped when I tried passing the gate to the dock again.

I remember the strange figures there and being stopped, suddenly remembering why the student's discussion about the shades in the poem seemed so familiar. When I escaped from the Shadowlands, I walked right past the guards at the dock gate because they thought I was someone else. They said the mistress was sending someone.

"Bow before the noble lady," the gatewoman called, *"The Shade of the Shadowlands."*

I turned around and hurried back to the campus pathway and started walking back toward the law building. I pulled my phone out and opened it to the circle's group message but paused. Macy wasn't around, so it wasn't worth bothering her with this. Izzy and Puck were in Burbrook, but this wasn't the kind of news to drop everything for. This was something we needed to investigate more, something Jamie was probably doing right now. Researching.

I exited the message and started one to Jamie instead.

The other figure is a shade. The Shade of the Shadowlands. That's her title.

I kept walking until I felt my phone buzz like crazy, looking down to see Jamie's name pop up on the screen. I answered and put the phone to my ear as I noticed Becky walking toward me.

"Are you sure? How do you know that's her title?" he asked.

"When I left the Shadowlands, there were guards at the gate and they thought I was her. That's what they called her, the Shade of the Shadowlands, and said the mistress sent her."

"I don't even know what a shade is," Jamie said.

Becky held up two to-go cups of coffee, attempting to wave at me with one in her hand.

"Um, I might, but I have to go," I told him. "We're heading home. Meet me in my bedroom in a few hours?"

"Just like old times," Jamie said before I hung up.

"Wow. You went far. Thank God for Find My Friends," Becky said and handed one of the cups to me. She led the way back to the car, not questioning me when I asked to go home.

CHAPTER 12

"What is he ..." Becky let the words hang in the air as we pulled into our driveway. Mark was loading a suitcase into the bed of his truck, looking a little exhausted as he waited on us to get out like he already saw the lecture coming.

"What are you doing?" Becky asked.

I gathered my backpack and the swag bag from the backseat, eager to put some distance between myself and whatever fight was about to ensue.

"I have to get to Holston with Terry. We're negotiating a deal with that company tomorrow morning."

"I thought you already negotiated that."

"Well, yeah, but we think he's going to sign with us tomorrow and it's a big deal, Becky."

"When will you be back?" she asked, putting her hands on her hips.

Mark shrugged. "Sunday?"

I shut the front door behind me and went straight upstairs where I couldn't hear them anymore. I worked on my history essay that wasn't due for another three weeks. After I had written a few pages, Becky came in with a plate of spaghetti and a forced smile on her face.

"I'm sorry you have to be in the middle of all the fighting," she said. I was a little surprised she was addressing it. Mark and Becky acted like the fighting was normal. It was like I didn't exist when they were arguing and when it was over, it was like I hadn't witnessed anything at all.

"It's okay," I said and took the plate from her.

She sat down on my bed, prompting me to close my laptop and turn from my desk to face her.

"No," she said. "It's really not okay."

"So ..." I said slowly, "Are things with you and Mark okay?"

She stared at my bedspread for a long moment, running a finger along one of the seams quilted into the pattern.

"No, they aren't," she finally said. "But he said we will talk when he gets back from Holston."

She sat for a moment and then left to finish some laundry. I tried going back to my essay but couldn't focus on it enough. I started looking up information about shades, finding lots of references in Greek mythology. I kept working, opening my window once I heard Mark and Becky getting ready for bed.

Jamie appeared in the windowsill just after ten. He wasn't dressed in his usual biker jacket, but a Burbrook High School sweatshirt and a pair of joggers.

"No bike?" I asked as he straightened up.

He gave me a curious look.

"When's the last time you looked outside?" he asked, moving aside so I could see out. I knew it had gotten cold. I was wearing a long-sleeve shirt and one of those fluffy hoodies that went to my knees. I guess, I'd just been so distracted lately that I hadn't realized how far into the semester it was.

It looked like it started snowing well over an hour ago. A

layer of white had gathered on the back lawn. Of course, he drove the Audi here.

"So, what have you found out?" I asked him and shut the window.

He glanced at my laptop on the desk with an embarrassing number of tabs open, all a variation of the question: *What is a shade?*

"The same things you know by the look of it," he said and turned to face me. "Shades are basically ghosts in mythology. They are incorporeal, which explained why I couldn't touch the shadow demons in the maze."

"But that doesn't explain why I could though," I added. He nodded silently. "Puck's powers worked on them though. Your strength is so dependent on touch, so maybe it's not about *our* powers. The shadow demons can't be touched physically. So, are we thinking that they are shades and not demons?"

Jamie shook his head. He went back to the window where he sat his backpack on the floor and pulled out the circle guide. "We have notes about the shadow demons. It's too perfect a match for them to be anything else. They're like shades though. They aren't exactly …"

"Acting of their own accord," I finished.

"Right. The circle guide said they're acting on behalf of someone else who has a large amount of power. The guide compared that kind of being to a guardian, someone with authority in the Shadowlands. The other figure, the shade, is the one sending the demons after you."

"That's what's confusing though," I pointed out, pulling up the tab on my laptop with the image search for "shade." Most of the photos looked like the Grim Reaper, a few specific video game characters, and others the Greek depiction from *The Odyssey*.

"Why doesn't the shade just come here herself?" Jamie

said, more a confirmation than a question.

The silence fell and gave me time to glance over all my tabs. I had thought about everything I'd experienced since becoming a guardian and what I had learned. There were rules about who could pass through the gate. Even guardians couldn't pass through the gate without their match and survive. At least, all guardians but me.

"I have a working theory," I said.

"Okay. Try me." Jamie sat on the edge of my bed. I sat on the desk chair and gathered my thoughts for a moment. It wasn't much to go off, but it was a likely scenario given what I knew about the gate.

"It's weird, but the not-as-powerful beings like demons, vampires, you know …"

"Lesser forces," Jamie chimed in.

I nodded.

"The lesser forces can leave the gate as they please. The stronger beings have power that only works within their homes. We aren't strong in the Shadowlands unless we are with a match—we die there without our match. The ferryman had power here, but he couldn't get here himself. Maybe that's the key piece. The shade can't come here without doing something."

"Maybe the shadow demons aren't here to hunt you down," Jamie suggested. "Most of the ones I killed were nowhere near here. Maybe they're looking for something to get the shade here."

"If that theory is right, then we need to figure out what they're after. It would buy us some time against the shade, keep her in the Shadowlands while we figure out how to fight her."

"And what's wrong with you." Jamie added and gestured to me with the book. "No offense."

My other theory was that instead of coming here, the shade was luring me to her. Why else would the voice tell me to go to the lake? It sounded female. It could be her trying to skip a step by getting me to find her.

"It's funny," Jamie said. I looked at him, but his eyes were roving around the room.

"What is?"

He smiled. "I guess, I expected it to look different in here. It's felt like a long time since I was in here."

"It's only been a few weeks, Jamie." I said the words, but knew it had been longer. It was more like a month, and I realized now that the photos he took of me, the spoon bangle, and the display he'd created on my bulletin board were all the same as the last time he'd been here. I tried avoiding him for so long but couldn't remove the traces of him from my most private space. The blankets we used to form his bed on the floor were still folded in the closet.

Jamie looked at me again, a smile spreading across his face. He pulled a spoon from the pocket on his hoodie and held it up. His challenging smirk didn't last long as I used my powers to fold the metal over his knuckles without doing more than blinking. He looked at it and back at me, impressed.

"Not everything is like old times, Mindfreak."

"You're going to need more spoons if you keep testing me like that, Tightass."

Jamie smiled. "I'm a little disappointed that nickname stuck." He said and tossed the spoon on the mattress beside him.

"If the shoe fits ..."

Just like that, having Jamie sitting in my bedroom while I worked on my history essay felt the way it had when he was sleeping over because the ferryman was on the loose. It was nice and having his years of wisdom helped when it came time to proofread my essay and make final adjustments. Even thought it was super early, I turned it in online.

"You like your job?" Jamie asked me. He was lying on my bed while I finished handing in my essay at the desk. I waited for the confirmation screen that my essay went through.

"Yeah," I told him and sat on the bed once the confirmation came. "Willow pays me well and it's easy enough. I'm not very good at the coffee part though."

Jamie snorted and propped himself up on his elbows. "Which is the whole point of working in a coffee shop, right?"

"There are books there too," I defended.

He lay back down and looked up at the ceiling.

"And that barista."

My stomach twisted in knots as my brain flooded with images of Angel. Angel making lattes. Angel twisting his hair into a bun atop his head. Angel lifting bags of coffee beans onto the wire shelves in the storeroom.

"What about him?" I asked.

Jamie folded his hands behind his head.

"Nothing," he said at first. There was a beat of silence before he added, "The guy looks like he stepped out of a renaissance painting. That's all."

Was that why I found him so attractive? Was it my love of period pieces on Netflix and McKellen's Shakespeare class? My face warmed and I tried to erase the image of Angel's forearms as he pushed his sleeves to his elbows. He's a normal boy, not a guardian, and would attend New York University in the fall like a normal boy and move on to a career after like a normal man. He was out of my reach even if I wanted him, which I didn't.

"You okay?" Jamie asked, sitting up.

"What? Yeah. I'm fine," I said and tried hiding my embarrassment by gathering my pajamas from my dresser. The old volleyball T-shirt and sweatpants seemed ... I swapped them for a clean T-shirt and pair of flannel pants from a drawer that actually matched. It was slightly better.

"You like him," Jamie said.

I whirled around to face him, cheeks flaming.

"No! God, no," I said, "First of all, he's older. Second, he barely has his feet under him. He's only here to save money for college. And third, I'm not his type."

"You know his type?" Jamie asked, suddenly more interested in the subject.

I let out a frustrated sigh.

"He likes blondes. He told me. We've talked about relationships and stuff. Let's change the subject," I said and left for the bathroom.

I finished getting ready for bed and when I went back to my room, Jamie wasn't there. I checked my phone and found a text from him, saying he wanted to do one last sweep of Burbrook before going to the estate for the night. I knew it was for the best. It was better this way. Still, I couldn't help but feel a little disappointed.

We had a circle meeting the next day at the estate to review what Jamie and I had discussed, all of us but Macy who was lying by the beach in Florida. No one asked me more about how I knew the figure after me was a shade. My time there had been horrifying enough and I didn't want to relive anymore of it than I needed to.

"The ferryman failed, so the Shadow Mistress sends the Shade of the Shadowlands," Puck said, summarizing everything Jamie and I just told him and Izzy. We both nodded.

"Pretty much," I answered.

"Who's to say that the shadow demons aren't here to get Tori's blood? We know that's what the Shadow Mistress wants," Izzy said.

"We think she wants the shade to do that for her. The shadow demons are a means to an end, scouts to figure out how to get the shade through the gate," Jamie said, handing over the notes he and I scribbled out the night before. Izzy started flipping through the pages.

"I don't know about you guys," Puck started, "but I'm noticing more and more shadow demons as the days go." The warning was obvious. We needed to work fast to figure out what they were looking for before they found it.

I nodded. Jamie let out a deep breath.

"We're all keeping in shape, right?" he asked, looking to each of us in turn for confirmation. I exchanged glances with Puck before we both nodded. I was running three miles most mornings now, the effort easy. I started including some strength exercises with Puck's help when we reached the railroad station. I'd started to see the results of our workouts in the mirror.

"I think Tori should start hunting," Jamie said.

The shock on Izzy's face when she looked up from the notes would've been funny if I hadn't been just as surprised.

"Really?" I asked.

He nodded.

"It's like you said. You're stronger than you look." His words and the slight smile on his face reminded me of our training sessions a month before. I had yelled a similar sentiment at him after escaping the Shadowlands. Jamie was relaxing his controlling tendencies.

Or maybe he was finally letting go … Letting go of me.

I couldn't find the right words to say, so I just nodded, and we began discussing how we would divide our patrols.

CHAPTER 13

My new patrol consisted of mornings training with Puck. We did our normal run, up to four miles now, and did strength training at the railroad station before showering and joining Izzy. Usually, we drove along every street in Burbrook, which didn't take that long. We were finding that the shadow demons were much more active at night, because for every one we killed Jamie killed three.

I picked up extra shifts over the break to try saving a little more money, so I went into Beans and Books at one o'clock. Willow was there about half the time and always left by four, explaining why I never saw her during my normal shifts after school.

"Can you cover tomorrow's shift by yourself?" I asked Angel, a little hesitantly, on Friday as we closed the store. I had swept the same spot multiple times, not realizing until I finally convinced myself to ask him.

Angel looked up from the rag he was using to clean the counter, his expression amused. "You actually have weekend plans?"

"You say that like it's the first time I've ever been busy on a Saturday night," I told him.

He snorted and asked, "Do these plans include studying?"

"No," I said, muttering, "not this time," under my breath.

"I can handle it," he said with a shrug and finished wiping down the counter. "What are your big plans?"

"A girls' night out in Holston to celebrate my birthday," I said, feeling a little rush of excitement. I haven't been out for fun in weeks. I hoped this time didn't turn into guardian work the way the last time did.

"Eighteen?" Angel asked.

"Yup."

"Big milestone," he said and clapped his hands. "Have a good time. Buy some cigarettes. Buy a lottery ticket."

"I don't plan on going that far," I said and went back to work. Izzy and Macy planned the night. I didn't exactly know what we were doing and now that I thought about it, it would be just like them to do something on the wild side.

⁂

I bolted from the kitchen when I heard the frantic honking from the driveway. Becky followed me, giving me her usual spiel to be safe, keep my phone charged, and make good choices.

"I will," I called back. "I have my portable charger and the credit card you gave me for emergencies."

I pulled the front door closed and turned toward Izzy and Macy's cheering. Both waved their hands out the windows of a car I'd only seen in the corner of the Quinn's garage. It was a black SUV, modest considering Izzy's tastes, but sensible considering the snow we'd had this week.

"Get in, birthday bitch!" Macy yelled the words loud enough that I was sure Becky and all the neighbors had heard. I hurried to the back door, my feet sliding from under me after taking two steps on the sidewalk. I fell on my butt, cushioned by the snow Becky had shoveled off the driveway that morning. Both girls laughed hysterically as I struggled to my feet and then got to the car like Bambi on ice.

"Did you pregame or are you just uncoordinated?" Izzy asked and started to back out of the driveway.

"Definitely uncoordinated," Macy answered for me and then glanced back. "But when it's your birthday, you can have both." She sang the last words, flashing a pink flask.

I snatched it and stowed it under my thigh.

"Macy," I chided as she laughed.

"Don't worry. No one is drinking except you. It's about time I take care of you on a night out for a change," Macy said.

I wasn't against a good party, but drinking in the back of a car seemed ...

"What is it?" I asked.

"Bourbon," she said. I took a whiff at the same time, the smell strong enough to make me shudder. "My mom drinks chardonnay exclusively. My dad liked bourbon and he left his stash behind when they split, and she's never even looked in the cabinet since. She'll never know."

I took a swig and grimaced. Not my thing. I shoved the flask deep in my purse. "Where are we going?"

"You'll see," Izzy said as we headed toward Burbrook High. Evergreens replaced the view of the abandoned parking lot and the Starbucks across the street, snow clinging to the branches and covering what was left of the autumn leaves on the ground.

"How was Florida?" I asked Macy.

She launched into a day-by-day itinerary of events. Macy's

aunt flew from France to Orlando to spend time with her and her mom under the sun. The entire trip consisted of days on the beach, snorkeling, and a lavish shopping trip which included a new wardrobe that wouldn't be weather-appropriate in Colorado until May. Macy swore it was a great trip, but her story slowly weaved its way into a comparison of their last one to visit her aunt in Paris. Her aunt had taken them to a part of the countryside that had a vineyard where Macy was allowed to try different wines and even escargot, which she swore was better than expected. By the end of Macy's long story time, I wondered if she actually enjoyed their trip at all or had spent the entire time wishing Florida was Paris.

"Have you been to Paris, Izzy?" Macy asked, finally finishing her story now that Holston was visible in the distance. The twinkling lights from the town made the snow up the mountain behind it glitter like a fifth-grade art project.

"The last time I was in Paris ..." Izzy let the words hang in the air as she thought for a moment. "I don't remember. I think I'm confused about what I did with different trips. The last time was either the time Jamie got drunk and started a screaming match with some guy in a bar or it was the time Kim Kardashian bought everyone in the restaurant champagne to celebrate the launch of one of her things."

Macy gasped so loud that Izzy didn't hear me ask about Jamie until she promised Macy that she didn't remember anything else about the Kim Kardashian event.

"Jamie speaks French?" I asked.

Izzy laughed.

"I didn't know he did until he and that guy were in a full-on screaming match," she said and slowed the car as we entered the edge of town. "He speaks a few languages. French. Spanish. German, I think?"

"What about you?" Macy asked.

Izzy shook her head and turned onto a street that had twinkling Christmas lights zigzagging above the road and along the streetlights.

"Fine art and languages are Jamie's thing," she explained.

We went halfway down the street before pulling into a spot. The roads and sidewalks in Holston had all been treated for the weather, so they were almost bone dry and easily walkable.

Walking was exactly what we did next.

We walked, arms linked at the elbows, for a block before Izzy surged forward on her own in that confident way that I envied. She went straight past the valet standing at a podium and through the doors of the fanciest restaurant I'd ever been in. This was nicer than that Italian place she took me to. Every member of the staff was better dressed than I was. My black pants and off-the-shoulder sweater paled in comparison to the cocktail dresses and suits in the room. Now I knew why Macy told me to wear heels, a requirement I disregarded.

"You look fine," Macy whispered to me as Izzy talked to the hostess.

"Just fine?"

"It's cute," she promised. "Simple is elegant."

The hostess led us into the restaurant before I could argue. The restaurant was one large room beneath a massive chandelier made of twigs and fairy lights. Each table had a similar centerpiece that illuminated the faces of the diners; the room otherwise low-light.

"Enjoy," the hostess said as we took our seats at a round table.

"Izzy, this is ..." I started, still taking it all in.

"Amazing?" she asked.

"A lot," I finished, breathless.

A waiter appeared at my shoulder to fill my glass with water from a bottle that he left on the table once he finished. Izzy, who clearly had been here often, ordered us an appetizer of oysters before the waiter left.

"Happy birthday," Izzy told me, both her and Macy giggling at me.

"Izzy, this is ..." I started again. I wanted to say it was too much, too much for me, but I felt myself relaxing a little when I realized no one was looking our way. The room was filled with mostly couples on dates, a few families, and a lone table of what looked like businessmen with their glasses raised in a toast. They were all laughing. Every single person was having a wonderful time and it was infectious. There were no demons here, no hooded ferryman, and for once none of them brought up any guardian business. I felt the smile spread on my face and Izzy and Macy laughed again when I looked back at them.

"I really needed this, guys," I said, feeling my eyes burn. I blinked back the tears. I was already underdressed. I wasn't about to have smudgy makeup, too.

"We're having dinner here. Then, we thought we'd take you to see that new movie you won't shut up about. And if you're still up for it, Izzy thinks she can get us into a bar at the ski lodge," Macy said with a squeal.

"No ski lodge," I told them as the waiter came back with the oysters. "That puts me too far past curfew even more Becky, but dinner and a movie sounds amazing. Thank you."

I'd never had oysters before, so I just mimicked what Izzy and Macy did. It was salty, with a hint of sour from the lemon juice Izzy squeezed over the top. It was good and after I got used to how to go about eating them, I had two more.

I ordered beef Wellington, which Izzy told me was a classic.

Also, a dish I'd never had. The meat practically melted in my mouth, and I ate the entire dish while I listened to Izzy tell Macy about the different countries she'd visited throughout her life. She had enough stories to carry the conversation through the entire dinner.

When I wasn't looking, they must've ordered dessert because the waiter brought out a decadent-looking piece of chocolate cake with a small sparkler on top. He wished me a happy birthday and then I smiled as Izzy and Macy insisted on taking photos of me. Once they finished and the sparkler was dimming, I excused myself to go to the bathroom while they waited for their own desserts to come.

The bathroom was around the corner and down a long hallway filled with abstract canvas paintings. I paused in the doorway when I opened the door to the women's room. The strong smell of cherries, smoke, and potpourri was overwhelming.

"Oh, sorry," a woman said and waved away a cloud of smoke before her. She stowed her vape pen back into her purse.

"It's okay," I lied. The smell was still choking me a little, but I went to a stall anyway.

"I should really quit," the woman told me as I peed. "That's why I originally switched to vaping. I figure it's better than the cigarettes."

"Yeah," I said, not really sure if I should answer or not. I finished up and joined her at the marble vanity. She was wearing a black dress with red heels the same color as the lipstick she was putting on.

"What are you celebrating?" she asked. I hesitated before the sink, water dripping onto my pants until I hurried to the paper towel dispenser. "Unless you're super rich, people only come here when they're celebrating something," she explained.

"My birthday," I said, drying my hands and tossing the paper towel into the bin. "You?"

She smiled like it was the best day of her life. "I feel like things are moving forward with my boyfriend. I think we're celebrating early. It's not like he's asked me—I don't even think he will tonight or even this week." She said the words into the mirror, focusing on her own reflection with flushed cheeks.

"Well, congrats anyway," I said awkwardly.

She put the cap on her lipstick and stuck it in her purse.

"Happy birthday," she said and walked ahead of me as though embarrassed by something she'd said. I watched as her heels clicked on the hardwood floors down the hallway and back into the restaurant. She took a left, slipping past a waiter and nearly upsetting the tray of food he was holding. She leaned over her table to talk to her boyfriend, pulling out her wallet and beginning to count out bills onto the table.

I nearly turned toward our table when she moved aside, and I caught sight of the man she was with. I thought I imagined it, but suddenly all these clues flooded by brain. The smell of cheery vape pen. The way the smell clung to the seats of his truck. The tube of red lipstick.

Mark rose from the table, hand-in-hand with the frantic woman. He caught my gaze as they moved away from the table, and he paused for a moment before letting the woman pull him toward an exit at the back. I followed them through the tables of happy couples and past the businessmen. The cold air made me shiver when the woman opened the door, but I forged on.

"Mark?" I asked, still hoping I hadn't seen what I thought. Maybe it was a mistake. Maybe it was a business deal.

It wasn't.

The woman called him her boyfriend. Not just a boyfriend, but they were a serious couple.

"Tori," Mark said, turning to face me. He let go of the woman's hand and she backed up a few paces so I couldn't see her behind him.

"What is this? She said you're her boyfriend. She's serious about you. What's going on?" I asked, the tears burning my eyes. I was unable to contain them, and it only made me angrier.

"Tori, I told your aunt that we would talk when I got home. I planned on telling her this whole time."

"So, you are cheating? How long?"

"Tori, you shouldn't have to be in the middle."

"Just tell me. Becky will tell me. Unlike you, we don't keep secrets and lies," I said. I heard two pairs of feet behind me. I didn't budge, glaring through the tears at my uncle.

"Tori," he started again.

"Terry was never your work buddy, was he?" I asked.

Mark let out a sigh and massaged his temples the same way he did when he was mad at me. It made me tremble with anger that I was the one crying and begging for answers. It should be him. He should be asking me to keep his secret or swearing never to do it again.

"No," he said. "Terry was never a man."

I looked at the woman's face, tears streaming down her cheeks.

"How long?" I asked, trying and failing to make my voice firm.

"Tori, you shouldn't have to hear all of this," Mark said, reaching out for me.

I stepped back, far enough that Izzy or Macy, whoever it was, had to move aside to avoid being stepped on.

"How long?" I asked again, this time sounding so serious that I almost didn't recognize my own voice. It made an impression. Mark looked anxiously at me, glanced back at Terry who nodded. He sucked in a deep breath and looked back at me, keeping his eyes low.

"I started seeing Terry four years ago," he said.

My stomach dropped. He said he hadn't been on a date with Becky since the Christmas party they went to. I was a freshman. Just like that, he chose Terry over my family. New tears flowed down my face.

"She said you're serious. She thinks you're going to propose," I said, pointing to Terry accusingly. Mark wasn't stunned like I thought he'd be. He looked resigned to the fact, almost relieved that I knew. "You are, aren't you?" I asked, my voice cracking. I knew it was Macy's hand on my back because I could feel her rings. If anyone understood, it was Macy.

Mark nodded. "I guess you'll find out anyway," he said under his breath. He shifted from one leg to the other, put his hands in his pockets, and then pulled them back out again.

"What?" I asked.

He took a deep breath and said, "Terry and I have a son together. He'll be one in January."

Izzy paid the bill while Macy and I waited in the car. I drank the whole flask of bourbon as we drove back, feeling especially wobbly as Izzy and Macy helped me though the front door. I went to the kitchen for a glass of water, stopping when I saw Becky sitting at the table with a bottle of wine. Her phone sat in the middle, the screen broken.

When she looked up at me with puffy eyes, I collapsed into

her lap like a toddler who'd lost her favorite toy. Macy cried with us as she filled glasses of water. Izzy emptied what was left of the bottle into the sink and then started to inspect the damage to Becky's phone.

"I'm so sorry," I said into Becky's shoulder.

"Me too," she said back. "Me too."

CHAPTER 14

ark didn't come back like he said he would. He sent Becky a text that he was going to stay in Holston for a little while to give us space.

Becky spent all of Sunday in her pajamas and when we got up Monday morning, she told me she called in sick to work and that she'd call the school for me if I didn't feel up to going. I could've gone. Our entire circle knew. It wasn't like I'd walk into Burbrook High as all my classmates whispered behind my back. Becky needed me though, so I stayed. We started a rewatch of *Gilmore Girls* yet again while she wore those same pajamas, and we ate leftover birthday cake for breakfast.

I stayed home Tuesday, the last day Becky said she'd let me wallow in self-pity with her. She called her friend Margot from the book club between episodes of *Gilmore Girls*. She'd been divorced a few years earlier and after the second call ordered Becky to shower and get dressed saying that it would make her feel a little better. It didn't seem to, but at least Becky had grease-free hair now.

Becky managed to get out of working in the office the rest

of the week but agreed to show a few houses. Margot came over Wednesday and I went to school.

It was cold, cold enough that my old volleyball sweats didn't look at all out of place among the sea of students. Even Macy who was normally very fashion-forward kept her jacket on over her favorite sweater all day.

By Thursday, Becky and Margot had set up dinner plans for every Friday for the next foreseeable future. I stayed home instead of going to the Moore Estate and watched Margot's four- and six-year-olds build a castle out of old DVDs on the living room floor while Margot and Becky drank wine and watched *The Bachelor*.

"I'm going to get rid of those," Becky said, motioning toward the TV stand with her wine glass. The kids looked up at her with concern.

"Don't worry, they go to their father's on the weekends," Margot joked, getting a groan from her six-year-old daughter. Becky smiled.

"I mean it. Those DVDs are Mark's, and he hasn't touched them since we got Netflix. It's not like they're a collection or anything. The only collection on that shelf is the dust all over the DVDs."

"Are you sure you want to?" Margot asked and sat her glass on the coffee table.

"Yeah." Becky shrugged.

"You should probably ask Mark," I said carefully.

Becky filled her glass again and started saying what I knew would be the F-word. She caught herself though, glancing at the kids playing on the floor.

"Mark shmark," she said at last and sat the bottle down.

"That's right," Margot said and lifted her glass. "Mark shmark."

They clinked glasses and drank.

Once the kids had settled down a little, Margot's four-year-old son curled up with a blanket in the armchair and moments from falling asleep, I headed upstairs. I had just looked at my reflection in the bathroom mirror when I heard the voice again.

The lake.

I was more frustrated by the message than startled. What about the lake? Was I supposed to go there or ...

We're coming to find you.

The voice sent a chill over my skin this time. It wasn't the same breathy voice as before, but a man's whisper. I looked toward the hallway in case it actually had been a man and he was waiting to attack.

Nothing.

I heard the floor creak in my bedroom. I ran back into the hall and into my bedroom, with my hand in front of me. There was a figure standing in the middle of the room when I let my power loose, raising the man in the air so his hair brushed the ceiling.

"It's me!"

I felt my heart slow and my muscles ease as I lowered my hand. Jamie landed on his feet, the squeak of the floor particularly loud. I knew Becky and Margot were too occupied with their TV show to check on me.

"How did you ..." I looked past him at the window, surprised that it was open.

"It was open, so I just assumed it was an invitation," he said. He let out a deep breath and I could see his concerned expression in the moonlight now. Something happened.

I closed the window and used my power to turn the light on. Jamie walked slowly around the room, peeking in my closest.

"What's wrong?" I asked.

He glanced at me before getting to one knee to look under the bed. He didn't speak until he was on his feet again.

"Do you remember right before the hellhounds came? The way everything got quiet in Burbrook?"

"Vaguely," I said.

"I didn't see a single demon tonight and neither did Izzy or Puck."

"Is that why you're here?" I asked with a laugh. "You did too good of a job ridding the town of demons and now you're bored?"

He shook his head. "I wanted to check on you."

His gaze didn't linger on me the way it usually did. He glanced out the window as I sunk onto the mattress.

"I'm fine. I haven't seen any demons either," I said. It was strange and now I remembered the conversation we'd had last time. When the demons suddenly stopped appearing, it meant something more powerful was on the way. The worry must have been on my face because he nodded when I looked at him.

"I'm going to stay," he said. It was a comforting response, not a firm declaration. When I nodded, he went to the closet to gather the blankets on the floor.

I collected my pajamas and went to the bathroom. I changed and slipped the amulet back under my shirt. All of this was so frustrating. Everyone would be watching over me again, Jamie, Puck, Izzy, even Macy. I could defend myself. They knew that.

I wasn't going to resign to their protection this time. I wanted to stand beside them in the fight.

Jamie lay on the floor with a leg poking out from under the purple blanket. I had to move in slow motion to keep the floor from creaking as I gathered my running clothes. I got ready in the bathroom and escaped to the street without any problem.

I already felt better as I settled into a pace, my muscles loose and relaxed after taking a few days off from running. I didn't run with music anymore for safety reasons, but I found myself wishing I had stuck my AirPods in today. I let my mind wander, replaying the most popular song on the radio right now and trying to remember all the lyrics as I ran.

I must've been running faster than I normally did, because I'd already run up and down Burbrook Mountain and was a block from the main road before the sun peeked over the horizon. Maybe I had just gotten an early start. Whatever it was, I was glad for the sunrise. Not only was it beautiful, but it brought with it a little relief from the bitter cold.

I ran across the main road when it was clear and started in the neighborhood on the other side. I ran the same streets I did most mornings with Mr. Puck, only I found myself picking up speed again and feeling a little on edge. I was sure I was just paranoid. I felt like I was breaking the rules being out here to begin with. Jamie would probably be mad. I bet he'd text me once he got up.

I realized that I'd left my phone on the charger in my bedroom. Damn. That was probably why I felt so off. I never went anywhere without my phone, especially not running.

I passed the entrance to the railroad station and all thoughts went out of my head when I heard a strange whoosh.

I didn't get a chance to scream before something wrapped its arms under mine and I was lifted into the air. Once the panic passed and I realized I was being attacked, I tried freeing myself before we flew too high.

I freed one arm, and the shadow demon lost its grip,

sending me falling sideways toward the gravel. I screamed, the air rushing from my lungs when I landed. My arm went numb, my entire body aching. Thankfully, nothing seemed broken, and I was able to hold up my hands when the demon swooped down again.

It shrieked when it hit the invisible barrier I put between us, rising in the air again before landing on its feet behind me. I stood up, feeling a little unsteady from the fall, and braced myself for the coming attack.

It moved much quicker than I anticipated. The demon smashed into me, dragging me backward. I felt claws rake across my shoulder as we stopped against the metal of a shipping container. The demon glanced to the left just as I saw a blur of green pass behind it.

The distraction was all I needed to raise my arm and use my powers to shove the demon away. Mr. Puck ran between us this time, starting to race in a tight circle around the demon the way he had in the maze. The shadow demon looked back at me and to my surprise, it spoke.

"The shade will do worse to you than I would," it said. His voice was a deep growl. The demon raised both hands to his throat as the air was sucked from the vortex.

"Stop!" The words came out more like a command than a plea.

Mr. Puck stopped running, looking back at me in confusion. Before the demon could recover, I used my powers to pin it against the shipping container. It let out an angry shriek.

"Tell me about her," I said. When it laughed, I tightened the force on him, strangling it. "I'll bring you to the brink of death and back again for as long as you refuse to answer me."

When I loosened the force again, it spoke.

"The shade is coming."

"When?"

"Soon."

"How soon?" I asked.

Puck appeared next to the demon with a demon blade in his right hand. He was looking from me to the demon like I'd lost my mind.

"When is she coming?" I asked again, choking the demon again in warning.

"She's already here," he said with a deep laugh.

I stepped closer to him, ignoring Puck's orders to stop.

"How? I know she can't just come through the gate on her own."

"She possesses a body," the demon said.

"Whose body?" I could feel the answer in my bones before the demon spoke.

"The dead girl. The blonde."

"Alison Rivers," I said in a whisper.

Puck turned to look at me in shock. My stomach was doing somersaults. I was right. I hadn't been hallucinating all this time. The dreams of Alison in my backyard, the girl in the maze … The shade had been here much longer than we thought, and I'd already faced her.

The demon laughed. "You can't stop her now."

"Do it," I told Puck.

He shoved the knife into the demon's chest, and it hit the metal side of the shipping container with a squeal, leaving behind a scratch once the demon vanished in a plume of dark mist. Puck looked back at me in terror.

"We have to figure out how to kill her," I said.

"Kill who? What just happened?" Puck asked, motioning to the spot where the demon had been with his knife.

"The shade. How did you not make the connection? Alison is the shade, or, the shade is possessing her dead body." I started to walk toward the entrance, but Mr. Puck was standing in my way. Damn his super speed.

"Tori, I didn't hear a thing either of you said. It was just a bunch of hissing ..." He let the words trail off, glancing at his watch.

My chest hurt. Had I spoken another language? How did I not know? It sounded like plain English to me.

"Let's go somewhere safe," Puck said. "Come on."

He led a quick jog back to his apartment. I followed him up two flights of stairs and to a navy door at the end of the landing. He unlocked the door and motioned for me to go in.

The apartment was just three rooms. The main room was a combination kitchen and living room. Mr. Puck had a TV propped on a coffee table on the other side of the room. The only other piece of furniture in the entire space was a dilapidated couch in a moss-green color. The door to the right of the kitchen went to a small bathroom and the door next to it was the only bedroom. I couldn't see very far into the room, but I had an idea that the only thing inside was his bed.

"It looks like you're not planning on living in Burbrook for more than a few months, but you've been here at least four years," I said.

When I looked back at him, he held up a finger for me to wait. He pulled his phone from his pocket and groaned before pressing it to his ear.

"Jamie," he answered. I let out a deep breath and sat on the couch, sinking deeper into the cushions that I was used to. "She's with me. She tripped on our run today and broke her arm. She'll be healed in a bit."

Puck glanced my way before turning toward the window, peeking out of the blinds. "If you go to the estate now, you'll be late to school." Mr. Puck motioned for me to follow him.

We didn't have to go far. I stopped at the island in the kitchen while he adjusted the phone to his ear. His jaw tightened as I could hear Jamie on the other end. Mr. Puck pulled a frying pan from a cabinet and went to the fridge, coming back with a carton of eggs.

"Don't come here. We don't need you. Go to school," Puck said. After a beat, he smiled. "That was a creative insult." Puck sprayed the pan with non-stick spray and then turned on the heat. "Tori will be healed in a moment. Nothing happened. Go to school, Jamie, or I'll call you in for skipping."

Puck hung up the call and began scrolling through his phone.

"Thanks for not telling him," I said. I wasn't ready to talk about whatever it was that enabled me to talk to that demon, and I definitely didn't want to tell Jamie that the shade was already here. I wanted to try figuring out a few things out first.

"I hope he takes my advice and goes to school. I looked at his record and he can't afford another skipping offense," Mr. Puck said.

"Would you really turn him in?" I asked.

Puck paused and I could see that he meant what he said. He pursed his lips for a moment and let out a breath, cracking an egg into the pan with a sizzle before answering. "I will if he calls me that name again."

Puck cracked four more eggs into the pan and then took two mismatched plates down from a cabinet. My stomach growled loud enough for him to hear. He smiled and slid a fork across the island to me. He pulled out his phone again and dialed a number while the eggs cooked.

"Mr. Thackery," Puck greeted, prodding the eggs on the stove. "I had something come up at home unexpectedly and I have to take care of it. I'm not going to be in."

He gave the frying pan a shake so the eggs wouldn't stick and then slowly walked back toward the couch as he talked, relaying where a substitute could find his emergency lesson plans and what assignment his classes needed to turn in or work on for the day. His fist clenched and unclenched as he listened silently before finally telling Thackery that he really needed to get back to his apartment and would update him when he could.

"What happened back there?" he asked, turning around to face me.

I turned the fork in my hand. "I don't know. I didn't know I wasn't speaking English. I just heard it talk and I answered."

Puck thought for a moment, going back to the eggs. He worked in silence, seasoning the eggs before splitting them between both plates. He pushed one toward me and I dug in right away.

"Has that happened before?" he asked. "You think it could be a …"

"A Tori thing?" I said, finishing his thought.

He shrugged. "Something is weird about you compared to the rest of us. You can go to the Shadowlands without your match and survive. Your blood is important somehow. It wouldn't be out of the realm of possibility."

"Yeah, but I don't think that's it. It would've happened before, I think." First, I was hearing voices. Then, I spoke some demon language. I thought back to when it all started happening. I'd been having the weird dreams since homecoming and I thought those were some unique things, but I know now that it was the shade's influence. Nothing else had changed about me during the dance. Not only was I not injured that night, but I got a warning from the ferryman.

That wasn't the only thing he gave me.

Mr. Puck ate silently, not noticing me until I had pulled the pendant from under my shirt and held it in my palm. "What's that?"

"Something that belonged to our circle," I said. "I want to tell you something, but you can't tell anyone else. At least, not yet."

Puck looked at me a little anxiously at me before setting his fork down. "Okay."

I took a deep breath and dove right in. I told him about my interactions with the ferryman and then about chasing him into the forest. I told him about the pendant and that when the ferryman went up in flames, I could see that it was Jamie and Izzy's father. I told him everything about that night except the vision the ferryman had shown me of Jamie and I matching and Jamie's death as a result.

"I didn't wear the pendant right away, but after I put it on, I started to hear voices," I said, watching a little nervously for his reaction.

"Voices," Puck said under his breath. "What do they say?"

"Well, usually it's the same. Normally it just says *the lake,* but I think I might have spoken to it. I didn't mean to, but I was sort of telling it off in my head and a new voice responded. It said, *we are coming to find you.*"

I waited for him to speak, but he didn't. He looked like he was still taking in all the information, eyebrows furrowed.

"Can I see the necklace?" he asked.

I lifted it over my head and handed it to him. He turned the pendant over in his left palm, studying each side.

"That pendant can't just be a simple necklace. The ferryman wouldn't have insisted on me having it if it didn't mean something more. I think that maybe it's giving me the ability to hear the demons," I said, watching as Puck ran his finger over the metal circle.

"I wonder what this anchor means," he said.

"Anchor?"

Mr. Puck looked up with a surprised expression. "Yeah.

There's the Roman numeral for six on one side and an anchor on the other."

"That wasn't there before," I told him, holding out my hand. He turned the pendant so I could see the anchor etched into the metal on one side, turning it to show the numerals. He sat the pendant in my palm, anchor-side up. When I pulled it closer to me, the anchor was gone. I ran my index finger over the smooth metal.

"No way," I said. I held the pendant by the chain, turning it slowly to see if the anchor would reappear.

"Let me take it again," Puck said, reaching for the chain. We kept our eyes on the pendant as he took the chain. Just like before, the anchor appeared on the pendant. I reached out to touch it, but it felt smooth, and I noticed now that when I touched the metal circle, the symbol vanished again.

"Great," I said and straightened up. "One more weird thing about me."

Mr. Puck handed the necklace back and I tucked the pendant safely under the collar of my shirt.

"I'll drop you off at home so you can get ready for school," Puck said and took his keys from the counter. I didn't argue and followed him back onto the landing. Now that my sweat had dried, the cold air hit me like knives as I waited for him to lock his apartment door.

I walked with him to the ground floor and down the road lined with covered parking spots. I recognized the silver BMW as one of the cars that has lined the garage at the Moore Estate. Sure enough, it hummed to life with the press of a button before we reached the doors.

I climbed into the passenger side, thankful for how quickly the seat warmer worked. Mr. Puck told me he wouldn't tell the others about our morning until we both decided it was impor-tant. He said he was going to check out the national park and see if there was anything weird about the lake since the voices kept trying to lure me there.

I did say a word during the short drive to my house, just listening as he explained his plans for the day. He told me that just like he wouldn't spill my secret about the pendant, it would be best if I didn't say anything about what happened this morning until he could check things out first. I agreed as I got out of the car, shutting the door behind me when I heard the window roll down behind me.

"Do you need a ride to school?" he asked, leaning over the passenger seat to look at me through the open window.

I paused on the front lawn to answer. "No, I'm good."

Puck nodded. "I'll let you know what I find. Can you come back to the apartment after school? We may need to talk more about ..."

I knew he meant the voices, the necklace, the fact that my strange guardian abilities seemed to grow every day.

"I work after school," I said. "I could probably call and get Angel to cover for me, but he did that last weekend." Not only had he so graciously seen to the store by himself, but I didn't want to call off today. I wanted to talk to him. I wasn't sure why, but I wanted to tell him about my birthday weekend. We'd been too busy the last few days to talk much, and Friday nights were normally slower for us.

"Okay. I'll let you know what I find out and we'll go from there," Puck said.

He rolled up the window and I went to the front door. He waited until I was inside to pull the BMW away from the curb. I hurried upstairs for my phone, finding several texts and two missed calls from Jamie. The last text was after he'd talked with Mr. Puck and it told me to let him know when I got back to my phone. I sent him a short text that I was getting ready, and I'd meet him at school later, probably at lunch.

The hot shower felt heavenly. I lingered until my skin was turning pink under the hot water and the bathroom was full of steam. I thought for a moment about skipping the entire day but decided against it when I remembered that we had a quiz in history.

I pulled on a pair of jeans and a sweater, let my hair hang around my shoulders in its natural state, and left for school.

CHAPTER 15

I zzy must have gotten called to something with the athletic trainer, because Macy and Jamie were the only ones at our lunch table when I got there.

"Are you okay?" Macy asked, cutting off Jamie's own concerns.

"I'm fine. We were doing sprints and I went a little too hard," I told them and sat down with my tray of nuggets, green beans, and orange slices. "It's a little embarrassing now."

"I was worried when I noticed you left your phone behind," Jamie said.

"I know. I'm sorry."

"So, I'm new to this," Macy started, taking a bite of a nugget. "Does it hurt when you heal? How long does it take?"

Macy had been so calm about becoming a guardian that I forgot most of the time that she'd only been a member of the circle for a little over a month. Jamie started explaining how it worked. Yes, it hurt sometimes. Healing time depended on how bad the injury was. First-aid practices could help speed it up, like the way he cut my healing time in half when I broke my ankle by setting the bone first.

"Do you think there's a way to trigger Macy's powers?" I asked.

Jamie stopped midway into his explanation to look at me. Macy smiled.

"Yes, please. Please tell me there's a way to do that," she said, looking to Jamie next. Jamie had been so hesitant to wake me when I first made the change, so I was surprised by his answer.

"It's possible to trigger them. That's how it worked for all of us, but knowing the right trigger is the hard part." Jamie ate the last of his lunch and stood up with the empty tray. Macy gave hers to him and he started for the trashcan at the front of the cafeteria.

"Any ideas?" she asked me.

I shrugged. "Maybe Izzy can help."

"I'm tired of being the baby guardian," Macy said with a groan. "I want to be able to help in a fight."

"As far as I can tell, all our powers appeared when we most needed them to. Maybe being around for a fight would be enough to trigger your power," I said.

Jamie would have hated my answer. It meant putting her in danger, but I know I hated being a sitting duck for the ferryman. If she could help, why not let her?

Macy nodded, twisting the end of her blonde ponytail around her index finger. I checked my phone under the table, hoping that Mr. Puck had sent me an update and I just hadn't felt it vibrate. No such luck.

"Mrs. Hawthorne will give you detention all week if she catches you with that," Jamie said, retaking his seat next to me.

I pushed the phone back into my pocket. "I was just checking if the work schedule was up for next week."

The idea of anything at work being digital was absurd. Willow Jackson didn't even have a digital register. Angel ordered an iPad and set up a Square account for Beans and Books a few weekends ago. Willow still didn't know how to work it.

"Are you working tonight? If not, you should come over and watch a movie or something. My mom mentioned that it's been forever since she's seen you," Macy said.

The bell rang and chairs squeaked against the tile floor as students hurried for the halls.

"I work four to eight tonight," I told her, taking a chicken nugget from my untouched tray and popping it in my mouth. I tossed my lunch as we moved across the cafeteria. I could see the annoyance on Jamie's face about my not eating lunch, but he didn't say a word as we joined the students in the hall.

"Would Becky let you stay over?" Macy asked.

I adjusted my backpack strap on my shoulder. "Probably. She has plans with Margot every Friday for the foreseeable future."

Macy's expression fell a little, but she recovered before Jamie could see. I wasn't ready to tell him yet. I was a little worried that it would cause a moment of weakness for me and I'd end up letting him get close to me again.

"It's a date," Macy said with a wink before going down the hall ahead of us, blonde ponytail bouncing as she went.

"Finals schedule came out today," Jamie said as we stopped at my locker.

Crap.

"I've been so distracted that I haven't been paying atten-tion to school stuff," I said and swapped my morning books for my afternoon books. The history textbook nearly slipped from my hands, Jamie stopping the fall with a single-handed catch. "Thanks," I said.

"You've been a bit tense all week," he said and tucked the book into my backpack. "Did something happen?"

He looked at me with the sincerest gaze, warm eyes that nearly melted me.

"Nothing," I said and turned back to my locker. I adjusted the stack of books on the shelf, so they were in descending order, the smallest textbook at the top and the largest on the bottom. Jamie stepped into the space between the door so I couldn't shut it.

"When's the last time Mark was home?" he asked.

"He has a contract in Holston," I said. It wasn't a lie, but Jamie could tell it wasn't the truth either.

"He's doing the remodel at the hunting store. He's been there every day when I drive past after school," Jamie said.

I didn't bother with the locker door. I turned and started down the hall for Mrs. Hawthorne's class. I heard Jamie shut the locker behind me and he was at my shoulder a moment later.

"I'm fine," I told him, trying to put on my most sincere smile.

He eased a little, the corners of his mouth twitching upward. "Would you tell me if you weren't?"

I wanted to. His words made my stomach twist with guilt. I missed talking with Jamie. I missed sharing my thoughts with him, but whenever I did, I felt my heart softening toward him. It was easier this way.

"Things aren't great at home," I said. I had to tell him some part of the truth. "But it will be okay."

He accepted my answer. We paused at the door to my classroom and for a second, I thought he'd leaned in for a hug.

"I'll see you later," Jamie said and turned for the stairs.

The rest of the school day was fine. It was a Friday, so other than my history test, the discussion in every class was about what to expect for our upcoming semester final. How I lost track of school enough to forget about our test schedule, I didn't know. What I did know was that I would have to start studying now if I wanted good enough scores to maintain my A-average.

Friday evenings weren't too busy at Beans and Books, so we served a handful of coffees and spent the rest of our time cleaning. Willow wanted us to do a deep clean of the shop over the weekend, so we decided to spread it out and get the bookshelves done while we didn't have any customers.

"I've never been much of a reader," Angel said as he lifted a stack of books from the floor. He followed me to the farthest edge of the shelf, and I began reorganizing the books.

"I find that a little hard to believe," I said. "We've talked about books before and I think you've read more than I have."

Angel shot me a sideways smirk when I turned for another book. A jolt shot through my core. It always did when he got that playful look on his face. He was just that handsome. It was like a kind of superpower. I swear, with that one look, he could bewitch entire countries.

"I've read a lot, but it's not really my activity of choice," he said.

I took a book from the top of the stack and moved farther down the shelf to place it with the rest of the mystery books. "So, what is your activity of choice then?"

"Traveling," he said. "I don't like to be tied to one place for long."

"I would get lonely moving that much," I said and shelved

another book. I was Burbrook born and raised and the idea of leaving for college seemed like a big step to me. "Don't you miss your family?"

"Don't have any," he answered easily.

When I turned to face him, he was placing the last books in the stack back on the shelf.

"Are they back in Mexico?" I asked, worried a little that I was overstepping by asking at all.

He smiled. "I'm not from Mexico," he said and went back to the counter. I followed him, duster in hand and face on fire.

"I'm sorry. I shouldn't assume."

"I do speak Spanish, but not that Spanish exactly," he said. "I'm from Spain. I left a long time ago. My family all died and there was nothing left for me. I told you I love to travel, so I left."

He said it all like it was simple, as if he wasn't talking about the death of his entire family. I couldn't imagine. I still felt my throat close, and chest tighten at the thought of my parent's deaths.

"I'm sorry. I know family is a difficult subject for you," Angel said.

I looked up at him, a little surprised to find him staring at me with concern. I wasn't the one all alone in the world. Well, at least not really. Maybe I was feeling lonely right now and that's why I missed Jamie and missed the way things used to be with Macy. Izzy spent her free time with Mr. Puck, not with me like we used to.

"My parents are dead too," I said.

He nodded. "Willow told me that you live with your aunt and uncle."

"Not for long," I snorted. I was a little surprised at how easily the words flowed from my lips.

Angel glanced at the clock above the counter. We would

close in about thirty minutes, but we hadn't had a customer in over an hour at least. He pulled his apron over his head and tossed it toward the rack to the right, the apron catching on a hook and swaying there.

"What's going on?" he asked and leaned his elbows on the counter.

Maybe it was the sincerity in his beautiful face, or the strength of his bare forearms. I told him how my birthday had gone, all about Mark and Becky, and I told him more about Jamie than I probably should've. I made sure to tell him that Jamie and I wanted different things and that a relationship wouldn't work no matter how much I wished it would.

"That's hard," he said. "Sometimes, we're better people apart than we are together."

I nodded. Becky and Mark were some of my favorite people, but they must bring the worst out in each other. They were terrible when they were together, stressed and even rude. Becky already seemed a little more balanced now that he wasn't around. I was sure Mark was living happily with his new girlfriend. I'd almost forgotten that they had a baby together.

"I haven't told anyone any of that, not even my best friend."

Angel smiled. "I promise I won't tell anyone."

I didn't think he would but having a secret between us felt intimate.

"Are you seeing anyone?" I asked. I felt my entire body warm up. I wanted to duck behind the counter. Why did I ask that? It wasn't like I was interested in him that way.

"No," Angel said. "I haven't been with a woman in a very long time."

I scoffed, only making the embarrassment worse.

Angel smiled. "I haven't been with a woman in *that* way in a long time."

My phone vibrated in my pocket, and I dismissed the call without pulling my phone more than an inch from my pocket. I joined him behind the counter to start cleaning the coffee makers, but my phone began vibrating again. I glanced at the screen and saw that it was from Mr. Puck, and he'd already tried calling once.

"Hey," I said into the phone, moving away from the counter and toward the front door for some privacy.

"You said you thought the voices were trying to lure you to the lake," he said.

"Yeah. I don't know why, but it seemed that way."

"Whatever you're doing, stop," he said, his voice firm. "Come to my apartment now. The voices weren't trying to lure you in. I think they were asking for your help."

"Oh. Okay. I can ..." I glanced back to the counter. Angel looked up and motioned for me to go. "I'll be there in a few."

I left the front door and rounded the side of the building for the employee parking. Thankfully, one turn of the key and the Beetle rumbled to life. I drove a little recklessly considering the light snow falling from the sky. Instead of asking Puck for his gate code, I used my powers to unlock the gate. Once it was open enough, I drove through and found my way to his building.

I forgot I was still wearing my apron until it caught in the door, tugging me back and causing me to slip. I fell sideways onto the concrete, hanging by the strings tied around my waist. Once righted, I tugged the apron off and tossed it into the passenger seat.

I didn't knock on the door. I was sure it was his apartment from this morning, so I walked right in. He was kneeling on the floor in front of the couch, massaging a towel against the top of an unconscious girl's head.

I pushed the door closed behind me, stunned. The girl was buried under three blankets, her pale face and blue lips the only part of her that was visible. Puck stood up with the towel in hand so her short blonde hair splayed over the couch.

"Do you have a coat?" he asked, looking over me.

I shook my head. I was so focused on getting here that I hadn't even registered how cold it was. My coat hung on the rack in the corner of Beans and Books.

"W-who is she?" I asked.

Puck shrugged. "I went to the lake like I told you. I walked around the entire thing and when I got back where I started, she was facedown on the bank."

"She's not anyone from Burbrook that I know," I said. She looked young enough that I would probably have known her if she was local.

Puck nodded in agreement. "I don't have a clue who she is either. She didn't have any information on her. She's wearing a sundress."

"She's been in that lake a long time then," I said, the hair on my arms standing up in fear now. Had he brought a corpse back to his apartment? Was this a crime?

He gave me a serious look as if I'd missed something obvious. "I teach science. I know what happens when you die and if she'd been dead for months, she'd look a lot worse."

"Are you saying she's alive?" I asked, leaning a little closer to look at her face.

"I think she came through the gate," he said.

"Why haven't you stabbed her yet?"

Puck looked back at me as though the answer was obvious. He reached under the blankets and pulled her bare arm out from under it to reveal the tattoo wrapped around her forearm.

"Tori, she's one of us," he said.

After a moment, I joined him. Her hair was a bit shorter than shoulder length and it wasn't entirely blonde. I could see now that she had some light pink and ice blue on the underside of her hair. She looked moments from death, like I could reach out and jostle her awake.

I held out a hand to touch her but stopped. What if she really was dead? What if she'd been asking me for help all this time and I failed her? I lowered my hand but used my powers to reach farther instead. I kept extending my power until I felt a resistance. It was like electricity. It took me a moment to realize it was her pulse. It would beat and beat, growing faster and faster until it stopped entirely. After a few seconds of silence, the rhythm would start all over again. I noticed the second time that just before it went silent, her chest rose a little and then fell.

She was a guardian, so she couldn't die unless she had a match. She was still wet from being submerged in the lake. My heart skipped as I realized what my powers were sensing.

She was drowning over and over again.

I focused on the resistance I felt, letting my powers isolate the feeling. I sucked in a deep breath and pulled my power back toward me.

Puck let out a yell of surprise as a fountain of water shot from the girl's mouth. It fell onto her face with a splash. Her eyes flew open, and a gasp filled the room. She struggled against the blankets, and I came to her aid, pushing the fabric from her body to reveal the floral sundress underneath. She sat up, coughing as water dripped from her chin and hair.

"We should get her some hot tea or crank up the heat," I said, turning toward Puck.

He shook his head. "Izzy is on her way. She can warm her up."

No sooner had he spoken than the door flew open. Izzy looked from Puck at the girl and then at me.

"Who is she?" she asked before the door even banged into the wall behind her.

"We don't know, but she's a guardian," I said.

The girl opened her mouth to speak, but only a rattling sound came out between the chattering of her teeth. She'd have to recover a while before she was able to tell us anything. Her eyes fell on Izzy, who was frozen in shock staring back at her as though she was a ghost. When she recovered, Izzy moved toward the kitchen and raised her phone to her head.

"I'll start some tea," Puck said, glancing at Izzy who was telling whoever was on the other line to hurry.

The door opened again as Macy came in. She was just as surprised as Izzy had been except instead of stopping to stare, she immediately jumped in to help. She took the discarded towel from the floor and began drying the girl's hair the way Puck had been before.

"Do you have more blankets?" I asked him.

Before he could turn from the kettle on the stove, Izzy walked out of the bedroom with a blue comforter piled so high in her arms that it was a wonder she could see where she was going. I pulled the damp blankets from the girl's legs and began draping the thick material over her. Izzy took Macy's spot and began using her powers to dry the girl's hair, running fingers through her locks.

"Can you say your name?" Macy asked.

The girl opened her mouth to speak, but only a hoarse whisper came out. She tried again, but it was too quiet to understand. She raised her quivering hand when Puck rejoined us with a steaming cup of tea. The girl winced when she raised it to her lips immediately, drinking the tea and probably scalding her throat in the process. She blew on the top of the mug before drinking again, taking several small sips.

She opened her mouth to speak, getting a moaning sound out before she could finish the words. The door opened behind me, and her eyes widened.

"Emily?" Jamie asked.

The girl shoved the mug away from her, missing the coffee table. Puck's hand was there in a flash to catch the tea before it spilled even a drop. Jamie brushed past me, sinking onto the couch and holding the girl's face between his hands. The girl nodded vigorously, tears slipping down her cheeks.

"I thought she looked like … It can't be. She went into the gate alone," Izzy said.

Jamie pressed his lips to the girl's forehead. He'd told me about her when I was dropped in the Shadowlands and came back out without needing a match. This was the same girl he'd taken to the meadow, the one he never matched with and was devastated about. *Emily*.

She was Jamie's Emily.

This was the girl he'd fallen in love with.

The girl he was still in love with.

CHAPTER 16

I felt like my chest was caving in.

We waited until Emily had recovered enough to speak and wasn't ghostly white in the face, Jamie never once leaving her side. Once she felt well enough, we all drove to the Moore Estate where Izzy loaned Emily a pair of sweat-pants and a hoodie. Her blonde hair hung in loose waves around her face now that it was dry. The icy blue piece of hair only made her blue eyes more electric.

"We thought you died," Izzy said, handing Emily what was probably her third cup of tea. She liked chamomile. Jamie made a stop while we all drove to the estate so he could pick some up especially for her. The blush on her cheeks when she saw him making the first cup in the kitchen told me it had been his idea, not hers. One of those memories of a lost loved-one that you cling to for comfort, like how I remembered the hint of spice that lingered on his skin when we'd held each other in the corn maze ...

"I did too," she said, her voice light.

"What happened?" Jamie asked, rubbing the back of her hand with his thumb.

She gave his hand a squeeze. "Well, that demon pulled me into the Shadowlands. From there, I just sort of started a new life. I had to. I tried leaving, but the ferryman wouldn't let me pass. I was stuck."

"Tori went there," Macy said, prompting all eyes to find my face. "She was able to come out though."

I shrugged. "The ferryman needs payment for demons to pass though, but he didn't need anything from me. It was like I got a pass for some reason."

A curious expression came over Emily's face as she studied mine. I was sure she was trying to figure out what made me different just as we had been since I woke.

"There's something special about Tori," Jamie told her. "And we aren't exactly sure what that is yet. The Shadow Mistress wants her blood. Whatever makes her different, it's important to the Shadowlands."

Emily looked at Jamie and then back at me. "How strange." She said the words slowly, almost in a whisper. Silence fell for a beat.

"So, what did you do in the Shadowlands?" Izzy asked.

Emily adjusted both hands on the mug of tea and held it just underneath her chin.

"The Shadowlands is like purgatory. It's not an afterlife the way I thought it was. There's a gate on the other side of it and if you are ... I guess, if you are worthy of it, you can pass through the gate."

"What's on the other side?" Puck asked.

Emily paused, looking down at her mug as though she'd made a mistake. Whatever it was, she had not been worthy enough for what was behind the gate.

"It was beautiful," she said and looked up at us. "It was a

dirt road with sunflower fields on both sides. I could see a city in the distance. I kind of remember now... There were words etched into the gate and a place to put your hand. It said something about being worthy." She thought for a moment. *"Only those free from their pasts can venture into their futures."*

The words were haunting. It reminded me of the gate at the end of the dock and how I was able to go through it without the ferryman. Emily looked a little ashamed as she stared down at the tea.

"So, you were stuck in the Shadowlands because you hadn't let go of being human?" Macy asked. Jamie shot her a look of frustration, like she'd insulted Emily.

"Maybe," Emily said in a sigh.

"What did you do all this time?" I asked.

She shrugged, starting to fidget with the mug. I saw her eyes glisten before she lowered them to the tea, rubbing her thumb over the Q printed on the porcelain.

"You don't have to say anything else about what it was like," Jamie said, wrapping an arm around her shoulder. She let her head rest at the crook of his neck, and she sucked in a deep breath. They stayed like that for a long moment, long enough that it felt too private to be a witness to.

I went to the bar behind the couch they sat on. When I popped the cork off a bottle of wine using my powers, a hand appeared on my neck before I could pour a glass. Mr. Puck's firm expression melted into sympathy, and I thought I would cry on the spot.

"Drinking when you're upset is not a habit you want to start," he whispered to me.

I let him have the bottle. I took a calming breath. Instead of thinking about Jamie and Emily cuddling, I thought about how she was here at all. She'd been tossed out of the Shadowlands. She was just as surprised as we were to see her. She hadn't left on purpose.

"You found her when we went back to the bank?" I asked Puck.

"I walked around the lake. When I got back to the place I'd started, she was washed up on the bank." He paused to glance back at the space. Izzy was crouched at the fireplace. She held a hand over the logs and a fire crackled to life.

Nothing more romantic than cuddling by the fire. Great.

"How long have you been wearing that necklace?" Puck asked.

I looked back at him, his concerned expression a little unnerving. "Since the ferryman gave it to me at homecoming. Why?"

He let out a sigh, catching Izzy's gaze now. She looked from him to me, a little confused.

"You're wearing it now?" Puck asked me.

I thought about lying. Something told me this was going to become a problem. I didn't a have a chance to answer him before he walked around the couch to face Jamie and Emily.

"Emily, how did you get here exactly?" he asked.

She sat up. Jamie looked a little annoyed at Puck's question, but he looked at Emily for the answer now.

"I don't really know," she said. "I was arrested. These two demons came at me from nowhere and they dragged me away. They took me to the castle, and I was in a big room when she came in."

"She?" Jamie asked.

"The Shadow Mistress," I said.

Emily nodded.

"Then I was in your apartment," she said.

"Why would the Shadow Mistress send you here?" Macy asked.

"I don't know. She didn't say. She just told me I got lucky."

I rubbed the bridge of my nose. Was this just another distraction the way the shadow demons seemed to be? Was the idea to distract me with Emily and Jamie rekindling an old flame so that I didn't see any of the moves the shade made against us until it was too late?

"What did she look like?" Macy asked.

Emily's expression changed drastically. She looked away from Macy and her horrified gaze caught mine. She shook her head.

"You don't have to answer that," Jamie said and sent us all looks of warning.

"You didn't hear any voices, did you?" Mr. Puck asked. His words sent a jolt through my chest.

Here we go.

"Voices?" Emily asked.

"Where did that come from?" Izzy asked, taking a few steps from the fireplace.

Please, no.

Puck sucked in a deep breath and gave me a look of apology. "Tori's been hearing voices," he said and looked at the others.

"What kind of voices?" Jamie asked. He was on his feet now, turning to look at me.

"It's nothing," I cried out.

"She said a voice has been telling her to go to the lake. I thought maybe that voice was calling Emily as well or maybe it was Emily. Clearly, it wasn't her."

"Why didn't you tell us?" Izzy asked and sat her hands on her hips.

"Why are you hearing voices?" Jamie asked, looking from me to Puck.

"She has an amulet that's enabling her to hear the voice. It also allowed her to speak to a shadow demon that attacked her this morning," Puck said.

"Jesus," Jamie said under his breath. "I knew something happened."

"It's not anything bad. It has actually been helpful," I said, tugging the necklace from under my shirt. "I was able to find out that the shade is already here."

Macy gasped. Jamie looked horrified now, the same expression he'd worn when he picked me up at school after I'd survived being in the Shadowlands.

"The shadow demon told you that?" Izzy asked.

I nodded. "He said the shade is here and she's possessing Alison River's body. I thought I was going crazy. I was seeing her in my dreams standing outside my house. I was sure I saw her running around the maze, and I was right. The shade has been here for weeks."

"Tori, this is so dangerous. You should've said something!" Izzy yelled.

"Take it off," Emily said. Her words were quiet, but they stood out to me as if she'd yelled them over Izzy and Jamie's concerns.

"What?" I asked her. "Why?"

"It's connecting you to the Shadowlands somehow. You can suddenly speak with demons. You are hearing voices luring you to the gate. The shade already seems to know where you are. That amulet is probably like a beacon." Emily looked scared, the same way she'd look when she talked about meeting the Shadow Mistress.

"Tori, what if that's like a GPS?" Macy asked a little hesitantly. "Maybe Emily's right. Take it off for a little while. Just stop wearing it to see what happens."

"No, destroy it," Emily said. Her words were firm, like if I didn't do it myself, she might snatch it from me.

"No," I said and tightened my fist around the amulet. If they knew what I knew about the ferryman, who he had been, then it would be different. Even now, I couldn't bring myself to break it to Jamie and Izzy. "It belongs to our circle, so it's not a dangerous item. It's important somehow."

"How did you even get that thing?" Jamie asked.

"When the ferryman died or whatever he did, this was left behind," I said, the lie sliding off my lips easily. Lying wasn't something I did very often, but I knew how to do it. Keep your lie as close to the truth as possible.

Puck caught my gaze, giving me a curt nod. Good to know he wouldn't expose *that* secret.

"See?" Emily asked, looking at Jamie and Izzy. "It was from the ferryman. He works for the Shadow Mistress. He does her bidding, so who's to say he didn't leave it to make finding her easier?"

I could see in the way they looked at each other that they were exchanging silent agreements. My heart sank into my stomach.

"The ferryman was able to find me without any kind of magical device. This isn't a Shadowland amulet; this is a sixth circle amulet. It belongs to us."

"Sometimes, things aren't always what they seem," Emily told me. Her eyes were soft. Something about her was comforting and I was almost swayed by her concern.

"Toss it here," Izzy told me.

"No," I told her, pulling the collar of my shirt out. Before I could drop the necklace beneath the fabric, it was snatched from my neck. My hand went to the nape of my neck where the metal had scratched the skin.

Jamie straightened up from the back of the couch with the necklace in hand. "I'm sorry," he said quietly to me.

I lowered my hand from my neck as he passed the necklace

to Izzy. I wanted to protest, but I knew it wouldn't change anything. I watched as she went to the fireplace. She held the amulet over the flames by the chain before letting it fall onto the top log. It shimmered in the firelight when she turned.

"It's a safety thing," she told me.

"I get it," I told them, unable to keep the venom from my tone.

This time, when I turned to the bar for the bottle of wine, Mr. Puck didn't stop me.

After a stretch of silence and half a glass of wine, the conversation went back to Emily. She asked questions about the town, how things were different than the last time she was here. Jamie told her about different places in town. I noticed my glass was empty when he started telling her about a burger place that hadn't existed in Burbrook in a long time. Apparently, it was one of their favorite places.

I thought about going back to the bar for a refill but knew I wouldn't be able to stand their flirting much longer and the more wine I drank the less I might be able to control how I reacted to them.

"Where's Macy?" I asked. She wasn't sitting in the armchair across from Jamie and Emily like I remembered. Izzy looked around the room and shrugged, leaning against the fireplace again.

"I must not have noticed her get up," she said. "She's probably in the bathroom or something."

"Much better," Macy said, practically bouncing into the room.

"Where were you?" I asked her.

She shrugged, looking suspiciously excited about something. She grabbed her purse off the seat of the armchair and draped it over her shoulder.

"We are leaving," she told me with a wink.

"Now?" Izzy asked.

Macy looked at the group as if just now noticing them in the room.

"Well, we are unless there's something else to talk about," she said with a shrug. "Are we done here?"

Puck smirked a little in amusement. Izzy glanced at Jamie who didn't look away from Emily when he said, "I can't think of anything else."

"Good. Then, let's go," Macy told me and held out my purse by the strap. "We have a sleepover to start."

I stood in shock with my purse in my hands, following her before she could get too far ahead. She picked up her pace once we reached the front door, meaning I was nearly jogging after her as we went to our cars.

"Macy, what's going on?" I asked her.

She opened her car door and looked back at me just long enough to say, "I'll tell you at my house" before climbing into the seat.

The Charger's engine hummed to life, and I hurried to get into the Beetle while she did a three-point turn and started driving toward the main road. I followed.

Macy's house was a little farther down the mountain, close enough to the bottom that you could see the entire town of Burbrook from a bird's-eye view. Like the Moore Estate, her house was at the end of a long driveway, but it wasn't a gated property, and the house wasn't nearly as big as the Quinn's. The three-car garage was empty when the door rolled upward, and Macy pulled inside. I stopped behind the Charger and turned the Beetle off while she climbed out.

"Come through the garage," she told me. I joined her inside and she pushed a button, so the door slid shut behind us.

"Macy, you know something," I said as we walked into the house.

The garage was right off the kitchen, white cabinets and light-gray countertops a stark contrast to the dark wood and matte finishings at the Moore Estate. Macy turned away from the kitchen island with a giddy smile on her face. She held up a hand and the sixth circle necklace hung from her finger.

"What ... How?" I gasped. I took the necklace from her as she laughed and turned the amulet over in my palm to confirm that it really was the same necklace that I'd watched Izzy place in the flames.

"I thought destroying it was a little harsh. I agreed with you that it belonged to the circle and maybe it wasn't really bad. So, I stood up and went to stop Izzy. No one acted like it was weird and that's when I noticed that no one could see me," Macy said. She let out a girlish squeal.

"You were invisible? That's your power?" I asked her.

She nodded.

"Yes. None of you could see me, so I fished the necklace out of the fireplace and went to the kitchen to get a grip on myself. I was pretty excited about finally having my powers. Finally!"

She squealed again as I hesitated with the necklace in both hands. Maybe I shouldn't wear it for a little while. Maybe their concern was at least a little valid. I tucked it into my pocket.

"Thank you," I told her.

"I got you," she said and opened the fridge. She turned back around with two cans of Coke, handing one off to me before cracking hers open. It let out a loud hiss.

"I can't believe that after all this time, just when I reject Jamie, she suddenly appears," I said, snapping the tab on the can hard enough that it came off in my fingers. I tossed it on the counter.

"I don't like her," Macy said.

"She's nice enough," I said. I wish she wasn't.

"Not as nice as you," Macy told me.

"Thanks."

"Did you notice that one of her boobs is bigger than the other?"

I paused with the Coke can at my lips. "Don't most women have one boob that's bigger than the other?"

Macy shrugged. "Yes, but hers was so noticeable and her forehead is kinda big too. Your boobs might not be as big as hers, but at least they're symmetrical. I think they're nice."

"You're just saying that to make me feel better," I said with a laugh.

"Is it working?"

I relaxed a little. Better was not even close to what I felt. Annoyed was pretty accurate.

"At least there's another member of our circle," I said.

"Does it count though if you are regurgitated from the Shadowlands?"

"I guess, we will find out," I said. She held her coke can out in a toast.

"To us," Macy said. "You are my ride or die. Friends forever."

I pressed my can to hers and said. "Always."

CHAPTER 17

When I got home from Macy's house, I could tell Becky was crying. I heard her muffling her sobs when I shut the front door and I saw her turn toward the sink in the kitchen, the water turning on. I stopped in the doorway and watched as she started to wash a plate, something she'd never do. Even the larger dishes like pots and pans, she'd just cram into the dishwasher. She said it grossed her out to touch plates with cold bits of food clinging to them.

"I'll be in my room doing homework," I told her.

"Oh," she said. "I didn't hear you come in. That's fine. I thought maybe we could go out later."

"Sure," I said and left her to her pretending.

I shut my bedroom door behind me and went to my desk. Underneath an old volleyball sweatshirt was a stack of books I'd taken from the secret library behind the hutch at the Moore Estate. I draped the sweatshirt over the back of the chair and sat down to look at the books.

I'd read two of the four and was mostly through a third. I'd have to return to the hutch soon for more. No one had reported anything interesting from their research, but part of me thought everyone but Jamie and I had forgotten about our agreement to search for answers.

I took the book I'd been reading and sat it on top of my laptop, my student ID number stuck to the corner of the device making me pause. We had two weeks left before winter break. One week to prepare for semester tests and then test week, which would put us on a different schedule at school and might just kill any chance I had at maintaining a perfect GPA.

I wondered when I'd hear back about my application to CU Boulder. As little hope as I had in any kind of future involving college, my heart skipped in my chest at the thought of getting a response. It was a good kind of anxiety, the type that kept you on the edge of your seat and made you smile all at once.

My phone rang and after taking a moment to control my urge to groan into the receiver when I saw his name, I answered.

"Hi, Jamie."

"Hi. It's Emily actually," the sweet voice said.

I sat back in my chair, pulling my knees to my chest. "Hey. Is everything okay?"

"Yes. Great as a matter of fact," she said.

"Oh. Well, did you need something?" I wasn't sure why she was calling me. If nothing was wrong and things were going great, what did she need me for?

"I already talked to Izzy, and I called Macy. They both thought it would be fun to all get together some time, just the girls. Macy said you worked at the best coffee shop in town. Did you know that Beans and Books used to be the old Burbrook Public Library?"

I was hoping I didn't have to see her for a few days so I could process her being here. I must've been quiet for a while, because she asked if I could still hear her. "Yeah. I heard you. That would be fun, but I don't know about Beans and Books. I spend a lot of time there as it is."

"That's fine," Emily said. "Izzy mentioned a place in town called Starbucks. Can you meet us there at two today?"

I leaned my chin on my knees. For the first time, I wished Beans and Books was open on Sundays, so I had work as an excuse. "Sure. Starbucks will work."

"That's perfect. I'll see you then," Emily said and hung up.

I studied for semester tests until I forced myself to get ready for the coffee date. When I went downstairs, Becky was sitting in the living room with her laptop propped on her knees and *Friends* playing on the TV. She looked up at me with a smile as if she hadn't been crying when I got home this morning.

"Tori, what do you think about going on a ski trip with Margot and her kids?"

"Cool," I said with a shrug before fully realizing what she'd said. I froze with my coat in my hand. We hadn't gone on a vacation in years. "Wait a minute. Like, go on a vacation?"

"Yeah. Margot takes her kids to this cute ski resort a few hours away every January for New Years and she asked if we would like to go this year," she said, motioning from herself to me. Of course, Mark would not be going.

Becky's smile dimmed a little and she looked over me, noticing my backpack on my shoulder. "Where are you going?"

"Studying at Starbucks," I told her. "Do you think I'll get an email or a letter about CU Boulder?" I wasn't sure why the question burst out of me. I hadn't been thinking about college since Emily called.

Becky lifted the remote and paused Netflix. "Probably both. You might get an email first though just because it's quicker. All those universities like to send fancy acceptance letters. My cousin Cathy got a card that played the school song when you opened it."

I pulled my coat on and slipped my backpack over my shoulder again. Becky didn't speak as I stood there, twisting my car key between my fingers.

"I'll be back before dinner," I told her and opened the door, shutting it before she could say a word.

I was on my third attempt at trying to get the Beetle to start when I heard someone honk behind me. I turned in the seat to see Izzy's Jeep blocking the driveway. I got out of the Beetle and went to the backseat, letting out a moan when the warm air from the heater hit me.

"I should've just asked if you wanted a ride," Izzy said. I could hear the insult to my car in her voice. Emily turned in the passenger seat to smile at me. Her blonde curls were a little more refined now, light blue-and-pink strands of hair spiraled throughout the blonde.

"Jamie told me you play volleyball," Emily said as we pulled from the curb.

"I used to," I said. I adjusted the vents around me, so the heat was on full blast. It wasn't a long drive, but my fingers were like ice from holding the cold steering wheel of the Beetle. "I had to quit after I became a guardian."

"I'm sorry. He said you were good."

As far as I knew, the last time I played was also the first time Jamie had ever seen me in action. I wasn't the best on the team, but I was good enough to play a little of whatever our team needed for each game.

"Do you ever miss it?" Izzy asked me.

"Not really," I said. After I started running as a replacement for the training I got from volleyball practice, I found myself enjoying that more than hitting drills and serving practice.

We got through the stoplight before it turned yellow and went down the road. Izzy turned into the Starbucks parking lot. I spotted Macy's red Charger a few spots over from us as we all climbed out of the Jeep.

"When's the last time you came here?" Izzy asked me as we walked to the door.

"Homecoming? Maybe?" I said as I tried remembering who I was with. I used to come with Macy every day after school. Whenever that was, it had been long enough that I didn't recognize most of the staff behind the counter.

Macy waved us over to the largest round table in the place. She already had a cup of coffee for herself, and she pushed another so that it sat in front of the seat next to her.

"I got you the usual," she told me.

I slipped into the seat while Emily stood a few feet away, looking at the menu.

"You didn't have to buy my coffee," I told her and took the lid off, the steam hot on my cheeks. I took a small sip, noticing something a little off about the coffee. It was a little strong, but not in a coffee way. It was a little like someone had done something to the beans before pouring hot water over them.

"Don't tell me that you're a coffee snob now after working with Willow," Macy said with a smirk.

I blew on the top of the cup to cool it off. "I'm not the one who orders that fancy thing," I said and pointed to her cup. Macy's coffee was always more cream and sugar than coffee. She stuck her tongue out at me.

"Being here is weird," Macy said. "I mean, we used to come all the time and then we stopped. Being here with you again made me think about school and how things were before guardian things took over. You know, we only have six months left until we're graduated?"

She was right. I'd lost track of time and now that I was trying to set my focus on other things than the shade and the shadow demons, I was realizing that it is December and everyone at school was talking about prom and what they were going to major in at college in the fall.

As if reading my mind, Macy brought up the very subject that had plagued me all day. "I think I might just major in business or something. Have you heard back from CU Boulder?"

"What are we talking about?" Emily asked as she slipped into the seat next to me with a cup of coffee in her hand. I could smell the pumpkin spice latte.

"College," Macy said as Izzy sat next to her.

"Oh! I had a great time in college. Don't major in anything medical though. It sucks all the fun out of parties," she said.

Macy laughed. "That's what I was thinking. I want to major in something fun, but practical. I was thinking business."

"Tori will study law, of course," Izzy said.

Emily turned a little in her seat to look at me.

"I didn't go to a lot of college," she said.

Izzy scoffed. "You finished four degrees."

"Yeah, but that's not a lot considering how long I've been immortal. You and Jamie have dozens of degrees." Emily took the lid off her cup and licked the bottom where the caramel drizzle stuck to the plastic. She looked at me again and asked, "Why law?"

Ugh. I didn't want to talk about it.

"I don't know. I like a lot of things. I guess it's more about what I hate about the justice system though, like it's unfair to people of color and some crimes are punished harsher than others that are way worse. I think family court is really interesting. I guess, I'll see. Who knows," I said, turning my cup in a circle as I talked.

"You'll see?" Macy asked with a laugh. "You've wanted to be a lawyer since I met you in middle school. You're going to crush college the way you crush high school."

"Maybe you can represent Sean Peterson in court some day?" Izzy said.

Macy groaned. "More like be the one to put him away from the shitty way he treats women."

I felt the smile pull at my lips for real this time. I did like the sound of that.

"So, what kind of degrees do you have, Emily?" Macy asked.

Emily sat up a little straighter in her seat, her face lighting up. "Photography, art, graphic design, and art again with an emphasis on digital arts. My favorite thing is photography though."

"You were one of the earliest photographers, weren't you?" Izzy prompted.

Emily blushed and nodded. "I used to paint and sketch, mostly. My life before I woke was before the invention of the camera. Women weren't allowed to do much at the time like work outside the home, but I have always been a bit different. I would paint portraits for the other families in the country like mine. I saved the money away, never spent any of it. My family wouldn't need it and my parents had enough to ensure I married wealthy. The money and painting were mine."

"What happened?" Macy asked. "I mean, how did you wake?"

Emily sipped on her coffee. When she lowered it to the table, she kept both hands cupped around it and leaned forward on her elbows. She kept her voice low enough so only we could hear as she told her story.

"I was seventeen at the time. My family was one of the three richest families in the county and all three of us lived in the countryside in New York State. There was my family, the Masons. There were the Saxons, who kept to themselves most of the time. They were rich immigrants from Scotland and didn't really fit in with the other families. Then, there was the Covington family, which is the family that mine was close to. My father wanted to invest in their family business, and they had a handsome son who was nice enough named Elliot. He wasn't exactly the business mogul his father was, but he was nice and thought my painting was a cute venture and didn't want to take it from me the way I thought any other future husband would. So, we started seeing each other, which had my father over the moon."

"How handsome are we talking?" Macy asked with a coy grin.

Emily smirked, a slight blush creeping into her cheeks. "Handsome enough to keep my attention, despite his short-comings."

"So, handsome and nice enough to charm anyone into his business, but not smart enough to run it?" I asked.

Emily nodded. "He cruised through life on his family's money, that's what happened in the end. I wasn't around to see it all in action, but I heard he did well for himself."

"So, where did you end up?" Macy asked.

Emily leaned over the table again to continue.

"Elliot Covington and I were seeing each other. It was apparent from the beginning that we would end up married. There wasn't anyone else of our status around. He was nice enough. I've already explained that a bit, but I really did like him as a person. He wasn't the smartest, but he thought my rebellious side was cute and didn't act like he wanted to change that about me. We were courting, but I hated the chaperoned dates and family dinners that ended up being all about business. We started seeing each other in secret. I was visiting his house while his family were away. He had pretended to be sick to get out of his father's business talk, so everyone was gone."

"Sounds like a romance story," Macy said with a lilting tone.

Emily wasn't smiling now.

"We weren't as alone as we thought. One of the servants came to check on Elliot. I snuck out and started home on foot. We were only a few miles away and since it was December, the river that separated our properties was frozen over. I decided to make the walk a lot shorter by crossing the river instead of going down to the bridge miles away. The river was deeper in some places than others and I didn't think about how that would make a difference in how frozen it would be. I must've been at a deeper portion where the ice wasn't as strong, because I fell through, and the current drew me down the river."

I shuddered at the thought. Emily let the silence hang in the air for a moment. The barista at the counter called out a name and a man came forward to collect his order.

"I drowned twice. The first time was when I had my death experience that changed me to a guardian," Emily said, watching as the man left the store. "The second time, I came out of unconsciousness to find myself under the ice. My clothes were soaked, and the fabrics back then were thick, the kind that soaked up water and got heavy, so I couldn't even try breaking the ice. I focused on getting out of my coat and I must have, because when I woke up the third time I was only in my dress."

"How did you get out?" I asked. As a guardian, she could've been stuck there for days dying repeatedly.

"Paul Saxon," she answered.

"The Scottish family," Izzy said in confirmation.

"I thought I was going to suffocate again, but he smashed the ice and pulled me out," Emily said. She took a sip of the coffee and held it below her chin as she spoke. "He was happy to see me, but not in a *I'm so glad we found you* kind of way. He told me right then what happened to me, about being a guardian, and it triggered my power when I tried to run away from him."

The confusion must've shown on our faces because she explained more in detail next. "He told me I was a guardian, but not a member of his circle. He ripped apart the sleeve of my dress to prove it to me. I was shocked by the tattoo, but more shocked that he enjoyed the fact that I tried to cover myself. He got that look on his face and when he lunged at me, I ran. I used my power to freeze the river again and crossed it. But he had powers like you," Emily said and looked at me. Her expression was serious, a hint of fear in her eyes.

"That's horrible," Macy said in a whisper.

Emily nodded. "I told you I have always been strong-willed. I told him I was going to tell everyone what he did. He told me that I had two choices. I wasn't a member of his circle, but I was a member of someone's circle. He said I needed to leave to find my circle, or he would bury me alive and I could spend the next hundred years suffocating over and over again."

"Asshole," Izzy said under her breath. It was clear she'd heard the story before, but no matter how well you knew the tale it didn't make the crime any easier to hear.

"So, you left?" Macy asked.

"Not right away. He was nice enough after that, even acting the part of a good gentleman," Emily said. "He took me to his family's house. He got me cleaned up and into some warm clothes. His sister packed a whole wardrobe for me and helped me figure out how to get started on my own. They wanted me to just disappear, but I couldn't do that to my family. I had to at least see them before I left forever. I was going to tell them that I was leaving to take my life into my own hands, but I found out before I could even get near the house that the entire countryside thought I was dead. Elliot was worried about me after I'd left, and he went looking. When he didn't find me at home, my family started searching and they found my coat stuck under the ice. I couldn't explain how I escaped that, so I left. I had a bunch of adventures after that, but eventually I found Burbrook and the Quinns."

I knew she meant Jamie by the way her cheeks flushed. I didn't feel the same pang of jealousy though after everything she'd just said. How could you hate someone who had been through so much and lost so much along the way?

"I'm sorry," I said.

Emily gave me a small smile. "It was a long time ago," she said with a shrug. "I'm just happy to be here and not stuck in the Shadowlands anymore."

"You make our circle stronger by being here," Izzy said. "It's one more person to help. Maybe we need your Shadowlands experiences. Maybe you can help us figure out what makes Tori so different."

"Yeah. Maybe," I said. It was my turn to shrug.

"We'll figure it out," Emily said, so positive about the fact that all I could do was sit and drink my coffee as they started talking about how Emily would work in our rotation of duties.

CHAPTER 18

On my way to school the next morning, I passed a news crew. The dark-haired woman stood before the Burbrook city sign, speaking into a microphone while a man filmed her. The sight already had me on edge, but I knew something serious had happened when I got to campus and saw all the students milling about the front lawn.

There were more teachers outside than usual, not the normal crew of coaches who did morning duty every day. They were gathered in groups of three, talking about something pulled up on their phones rather than watching the student body. Not that it mattered that they paid attention. The students were doing the same thing.

I parked in the first spot I saw and hurried to the lawn to find Macy. She was pale-faced when I found her among her usual crowd of girls. No one gave me any side-eye as I approached like they had since I quit volleyball. I noticed that one of the girls was in tears, Sean Peterson looking more dumbfounded than he usually did as he stood next to her with a limp arm over her shoulder.

"What's going on?" I asked.

Macy let out a deep breath and passed her phone to me. I felt my muscles relax and I let my backpack slip off my shoulder and land with a soft crunch in the snowy grass. Alison's photo was at the top of the article, the same one plastered all over town.

Burbrook Teen Victim of Wolf Attack

"They found her?" I said, my voice so soft that the breathy tone sent chills up my spine. I looked at Macy who didn't move, staring over the parking lot in a daze.

I felt queasy. The images of Alison from that night flashed through my mind. That wolf had shredded her. She was covered in blood. The way her neck had been ripped open ...

I nearly gagged at the memory, only brought back to reality as I heard Alison's friends whispering around us. They didn't understand how it was possible. They didn't know how she could've been in that forest all this time after all those searches.

"The report said she must've been preserved by the cold. Her body was ..." The girl didn't finish her thought, but it reminded me of the way I'd last seen Alison. The shade was possessing her. She looked perfectly fine. Well, a bloody mess, but alive. Anyone who'd been mauled and left in a forest since homecoming would look much worse than that.

I forced myself to look down at Macy's phone again to read the article.

The Rivers family have been searching non-stop for their daughter since she went missing the night of the Burbrook High School homecoming dance. Alison was a good student, member of the student council, and had just started discussions about joining the University of Colorado volleyball team in the fall where she planned to study sports medicine. Alison was last seen by her friends at the dance, friends who never saw her leave until they realized she was gone.

Local police have been searching the town and the surrounding area since her disappearance, saying nothing of this scale has ever happened in the small town of Burbrook. A month before the dance, alerts went out in the town about a large wolf in the area. A wildlife research team has been stationed at the national park since the beast's pawprints were found, putting the animal at record size not just for the Colorado wolf population, but for any known wolf species.

The team of specialists have found more tracks, but no other signs of the wolf until Alison Rivers's disappearance, which they say happened in the same area of the national park where the wolf is believed to be. Local community members had their worries about holding the homecoming dance at the national park this year with a wolf on the prowl, but the Burbrook High School administration team, local police, and the wildlife team felt confident in their plan to keep students safe.

Alison River's body was found in the forest near the national park building where the dance was held. Police said that the area had been searched multiple times and it's believed that her body may have been dragged there since their last search. The teen was identified by photos the police had on hand, her homecoming dress and jewelry matching the photos and descriptions given by her friends and family. No details from her autopsy have been released, but police are sure her cause of death was related to an animal attack and noted that they were surprised to find her body preserved given the time that has elapsed since the date of her disappearance. The combination of cold weather and animal behaviors this time of year have been offered by experts as an explanation. A spokesperson for the Burbrook Police said that if it hadn't been for the cold weather, her body might not have been so easily identified.

I felt my stomach turn again and I walked with heavy feet toward the trash can near the front door in case I did get sick. The bell must have rung for the start of school because the crowd on the lawn was thinning and the teachers had gone.

"Let's go! First hour," Mr. Thackery yelled from the door, propping it open with his foot and whistling at the remaining groups of students.

I took a few deep breaths, the cold air like knives in my lungs, and passed him for the warm air of the entryway. I made my way to chemistry in a stupor, not coming out of it until Macy sat down at our table next to me and pulled her phone from my fingers.

"We've lost three classmates in one semester," Macy said.

I looked up and caught the gaze of Jamie Quinn as he walked into the classroom. He paused in the doorway for a moment, his expression worried. His jaw hardened and he turned on his heel and went back into the hall. I was out of my seat and following him despite Macy's protesting.

"Tori," Mr. Puck said as I brushed past him. He caught my bicep and held it firm. I looked toward the front door, watching as Jamie slipped outside. When I looked back at Mr. Puck, his expression said it all. He wouldn't stop me. He understood. But he couldn't keep me from whatever happened as a result.

He let go of me and I ran after Jamie.

He was parked in the back row like I was, his silver Audi humming to life and windows already fogging from the heater. I climbed into the passenger seat.

"Have you found out anything about the shade?" he asked immediately.

I was a little stunned. It was like he'd wanted me to follow. "Nothing that we don't already know. The shade had to possess a body to leave the Shadowlands, but I'm not sure how she did it and now that that body has been found ..."

Jamie nodded. The car was silent for a long time. The warmth from the heater and our bodies had completely fogged the windows now and made it stuffy. I turned the dial, so it wasn't blowing hot air directly into my face.

"Do you know anything more?" I asked.

"Emily thinks that the shade was using that amulet you had somehow. She thinks that when we destroyed it something severed the ties to the shade, and it might have vanished. That's why Alison's body was found. The shade might have been sent back to the Shadowlands." Jamie didn't look up from the steering wheel.

"You don't believe that though, do you?"

He let out a deep breath. "I don't know."

"Well, I know that the voices I heard were different. The amulet allowed me to talk to that shadow demon, but it wasn't what you think it was. It was just an ability provided by the amulet. I think it's another thing that only works for me, because of whatever is so different about me. It's the same thing that has the Shadow Mistress after my blood. I don't think that amulet was dangerous, and I don't think that just because Emily's been in the Shadowlands this whole time makes her an expert on all things related to it."

Jamie looked at me now, his eyes a little shocked at what I'd said.

"She knew that the Shadowlands was just a transition to another gate."

"I saw that gate myself when I was there," I told him, remembering the gate from afar before I'd been captured alongside the witch. "I think that I'm connected to the Shadowlands on a deeper level than even the other guardians are. I know that we have a higher power there than other supernatural beings, but it felt different for me. Why else would the Shadow Mistress want my blood so badly?"

"I don't know, Tori," Jamie said in frustration. "We have other things to worry about than that right now. The shade may be back in the Shadowlands, or she could be in a whole new body. For all we know, she used Alison as a transition to a better physical form and is here as the assassin that she is."

"I understand why it's important to track her, but shouldn't we be focusing on what makes me different? If we can figure that out, we can fight the Shadow Mistress head-on. We don't have to wait around for the next demon to come after us."

"We don't have anywhere to start," Jamie said, raising his voice. He looked back at the steering wheel, gripping his hands on the top and then relaxing with a sigh. "We've searched the library. Puck doesn't have any ideas. I've been looking through the hutch since we started doing research on the shade and there's nothing there. I've talked about everything we know about you with Emily, and she hasn't seen anything like it in the Shadowlands or has any idea where we could even go for answers."

I opened my mouth to tell him how the voices were different. I know that amulet allowed me to speak with that shadow demon. It seemed to work differently for me based on how the anchor on the amulet would vanish at my touch. I paused for a moment before spilling my secrets. Jamie wanted answers as badly as I did, but he was also a protector, and I didn't want to risk being put on lockdown again.

Still, this was Jamie.

"I think that amulet is the key. I don't think that the voice I was hearing was the shade or even anything from the Shadow-lands," I said.

Jamie looked curiously at me, weighing what I said. If someone else was speaking to me, maybe it was because they knew the answers. Maybe the mention of the lake wasn't to try and lure me to the gate but to meet me there.

I jumped when a figure darkened the window behind Jamie, knocking on the glass twice.

"Out," Mr. Thackery demanded and stepped back from the car.

I sat with two wooden chairs separating me from Jamie. The main office of Burbrook High was quiet aside from the occasional ring of the phone and the beep of the printer. I hadn't looked up from my boots since Mr. Thackery led us into the office and told us to sit. I'd heard him on the phone, calling Becky first and then calling whichever number Jamie had listed as his parents'.

Izzy came into the office after ten minutes of sitting.

"What did you do?" she asked Jamie as soon as she came in, only looking up when Mr. Thackery came out of his office to greet her. "Our parents are out of the country for work and their flight is delayed due to weather."

"That's what your mother said on the phone," Thackery said and stepped to one side of his office. Izzy shot Jamie an annoyed look before heading into the office.

"Tori?" Becky asked as she walked in. "What's wrong?"

Of course, she would think something was wrong and not that I'd gotten in trouble.

"Mrs. Greenwood," Mr. Thackery greeted.

"Johnson," Becky replied, so quickly that I saw her glance my way and blush. I felt my own cheeks heat from embarrassment. *Johnson*. So, that's how things were going.

My stomach twisted. This was the last thing I needed. This was the last thing Becky needed right now. She should be focused on what to do about Mark, how to deal with the fact that her husband had an affair. Not only an affair, but he also had a whole life with a woman he'd been with for years. He had a child. My heart sank with guilt.

"Unless you and Ms. Quinn would prefer to keep matters separate ..." Thackery started.

"What's wrong?" Becky asked again, looking from the principal to me.

"Ask Jamie," Izzy said, clearly enunciating each word and casting a questioning gaze at Jamie. Becky was looking at him now too and when she looked at me, I couldn't help but lower my eyes to the floor.

"Let's move into my office," Mr. Thackery said.

I stood up and followed Becky into the small room. Jamie let out a groan and came in last, Mr. Thackery shutting the door behind him and telling both of us to sit.

There were two wooden chairs sat before the large principal's desk. They were hard, clearly not placed there for welcoming conversations. Izzy crossed her arms and leaned against the wall while Becky stood awkwardly next to her, looking just as uncomfortable as I felt.

"Thank you for taking time from your day to come here, Ms. Quinn. Mrs. Green—" Thackery caught himself before the whole name could leave his lips. He cleared his throat before correcting himself. "Mrs. Johnson."

"I don't understand. You said on the phone that there was a problem and I needed to come," Becky said, trying to look at me again before I focused my gaze on the mug full of pens on the corner of Thackery's desk.

Mr. Thackery sat down behind the desk and moved a sheet of paper toward himself that he began to read from. "Victoria Johnson and Jamie Quinn were caught at the back of the student parking lot sitting in an Audi, which had a parking pass that identified it as Jamie's vehicle. They were found there twenty minutes after the start of first period this morning. The windows were steamed up when I got to it."

"Oh boy," I heard Becky said under her breath.

I could've died. I wanted to sink through that hard chair and into the carpet.

"We weren't doing anything," Jamie said. "It was fogged up from the heater and we were just talking."

"You admit that you were skipping class?" Thackery asked.

"Yeah," Jamie said.

"Victoria?" Thackery asked.

Ugh. No one ever used my full name. It made my heart skip in my chest as I looked up at him, only managing a tight-lipped nod.

"When we catch students skipping, especially when they are in groups like this, we always search their belongings. It's school policy and it's for student safety," Mr. Thackery told Izzy and Becky.

Jamie groaned next to me but bent over for his backpack

anyway. I followed his lead, placing my backpack on the desk and hoping that Jamie didn't have any guardian weapons in his.

"Jamie, stand up and pull out your pockets," Thackery told him.

He watched as Jamie stood, pulling a wallet out of his back pocket and letting the lining hang out. He did the same with the two at his hips, the key to the Audi going onto the desk next to the wallet. Thankfully, that was as far as the search went. I was sure that if Thackery insisted on patting him down, he would've found a demon blade at Jamie's waist.

Mr. Thackery made me stand next, not that I had any pockets to turn out. The pockets on my jeans were so small that he was happy with me just running my fingertips along the inside. I took my phone and car key out of my coat pockets and placed them on the desk.

We both stood silently while Principal Thackery unloaded our backpacks and peered in each zippered pocket until it was clear we didn't possess any weapons or drugs. The bell for the start of second period.

"Nothing happened. We were just talking," Jamie said again.

Mr. Thackery looked at Jamie as though daring him to speak again. "About?"

Jamie opened his mouth to speak but closed it a moment later. Thackery scoffed and held the empty backpacks over to us. I took mine and busied myself by slowing stuffing my things back into it.

"Jamie, you a good student and a nice kid, but you've made quite a few poor decisions just this one semester, right?" Thackery asked.

I finished zipping my backpack and looked at Jamie beside me. He shrugged.

"Right," Jamie said.

"That's just one semester. In the last few months, you've had just about all the second chances you can get. I'm sure that you know that. What is the offense you've been caught doing the most this year?"

"Skipping."

Mr. Thackery let the room go quiet for a moment as though letting Jamie's admission sink in. Jamie looked a little too comfortable sitting back in his chair. It wasn't like anything serious would come of this. He didn't have parents to answer to. Izzy would be annoyed at him, but she wouldn't care beyond the scene that his actions created and the attention it brought. Just like last time, Jamie would take his suspension and use it to do research or hunt demons.

"You've worked your way up the discipline matrix, but I'm not the kind of administrator that thinks discipline is one-size-fits-all and it clearly isn't in your case," Thackery said.

Jamie's serious expression cracked. It was subtle, a little twitch at the corner of his mouth that told me he wouldn't have the upper hand. I looked past him at Izzy. Her mouth parted and she pressed her index finger to the bridge of her nose.

"I mean no offense to your parents," Mr. Thackery said to Izzy and Jamie. Neither of them spoke, so he continued. "Being out of school on suspension doesn't seem to have an effect, so you can spend the rest of the week in in-school suspension. You'll come here for the rest of the week, and you can do your schoolwork at the table in the lobby."

Jamie's jaw tightened. He nodded.

"Victoria," Mr. Thackery started. His tone was much softer, and his expression melted from anger to disappointment. He sat his elbows on the desk and leaned forward. "You've never been in trouble before, but I did notice that Mr. Puck expressed some concerns a while back about your behavior. You are set to be salutatorian at graduation but cutting class and the senioritis your teachers have noticed does not show dedication to academics or your future for that matter."

"I know," I said, my voice so small it was barely recognizable as my own.

Mr. Thackery spoke to Becky as he gave my sentence. I would serve detention for the rest of the week. He let me pick between before- or after-school detention. I chose to serve my time before school, so I didn't have to adjust my work schedule.

"Mr. Thackery," Becky started as we all gathered our things and moved into the main office again. "Tori has a dentist appointment this afternoon, so I will just take her home for now if that's okay."

It took me a moment to realize that Becky was lying on my behalf. Mr. Thackery didn't argue, letting the secretary know so she could note it on my attendance record for the day.

The drive home was silent. When we pulled into the garage, I got out and went into the house immediately. I took the stairs two at a time and didn't stop until I was in my bedroom. I dropped my backpack in the middle of the floor, the hardwood creaking as I walked to my bed and laid down with my boots skimming the floor.

I stared at the ceiling for a long time until Becky appeared above me. She sat on the edge of the bed and with a sigh, laid down beside me. I almost sat up; I was so surprised. When I looked sideways at her, her gaze was focused on the beams above us.

"Things have been so hard lately," she said.

I didn't know what to say. An apology seemed overdue, but also inconsequential considering all the rules I had willingly broken the last few months. "Since when are you a Johnson?"

The words came out of nowhere. I was a little worried that they'd gone deeper than I meant them to, that they might make Becky cry. Instead, she turned her head on the mattress to face me, a small smile on her face. She took my hand and gave it a squeeze before standing up and leaving the room.

CHAPTER 19

I understood why Jamie didn't mind being suspended now. I spent the rest of the day reading the books I'd taken from the Moore Estate, finishing both and then going to Google to see what I could find. It resulted in nothing. I wasn't any closer to answers about the shade as I'd been when I started, except that I was sure the amulet had nothing to do with her.

Becky knew my work schedule, so she didn't question me when I left the house for my shift. Angel was surprised to see me though.

"I wasn't at school today," I told him before he could ask.

"Why?"

"It's a long story." I took my apron from the hook by the counter and pulled it over my head.

"Does it involve that boy you like?"

I slowed my pace toward the counter, catching his gaze. His expression went from taunting to apologetic and he added, "Just a lucky guess," a moment later.

"He's with someone else," I said and started checking how

much coffee we had brewed to keep from showing my flaming cheeks.

"Ouch." Angel opened the dishwasher, and a plume of hot steam came out the top. He waited a moment before unloading the top rack of mugs onto the shelf above the counter.

Something about his response made me relax. It didn't just make me feel more comfortable, it made me want to tell him more. We hadn't talked in-depth about Jamie, but it was like he could infer everything I wasn't saying, and I liked him for that. I liked that he didn't draw things out or press for information.

Even now, as I looked over at him, he'd moved on from the conversation to his work. He spooned beans into one of the small grinders and plugged it into the wall. He stepped closer to the counter and wrapped a hand around the grinder and let the other sit on the lid. The muscles in his forearms flexed as he pressed on the top, so the grinder hummed to life.

Why, no matter how cold it was in the store or even if we were walking to our cars after closing for the night, did he always have his sleeves pushed up to his elbows? Why was the skin there so unblemished? Did the guy not have a single freckle on his entire body? Why did I notice this about him every time I came to work?

I went back to checking each roast, glad to find the light roast carafe with no more than a cup left. I gathered the beans I needed and began grinding away. When I was finished and turned back to prep the coffee maker, I found a mug of coffee sitting on the counter. A pour-over, no cream or sugar. Black, the way I liked it.

Angel was in the backroom now. I could hear the heavy sound of bags of beans being moved onto the wire shelves. I hit brew on the coffee maker and shifted to the right just enough that I could see him working. It reminded me of how Jamie looked behind the hutch, moving books around the small room. I'd been trying to avoid the daydream of Jamie setting me on that desk instead of the books ...

With those forearms, I'm sure lifting me onto the metal table in the stockroom would be just as easy for Angel. The image sent a jolt of shock through me and then my body warmed at the new thoughts. I replayed the daydream behind the hutch except instead of Jamie, it was Angel, and we were in the Beans and Books storeroom.

I realized a beat too late that he was staring at me now. He straightened up from the lower shelf with a smirk on his face.

"Thanks for the coffee," I blurted. I should've turned away and pretended like that's all I'd stood there for, but I didn't. Why? Why couldn't I just walk away and keep the one place in Burbrook free from my guardian drama?

The bell at the front door rang. I turned to greet the customers before any more awkwardness could pass between us.

Getting to school early for detention was annoying, but with Jamie locked away all day without any way to send a text, it made things feel almost normal again. Izzy was too busy keeping up her charade of fake college classes to check in with Macy or me during the school day. Things around Burbrook were oddly quiet, which everyone in our circle took as a good sign.

The only time I'd seen Jamie all week was when we held a circle meeting at the estate to discuss what we'd seen around town. Nothing. Nothing had happened since Alison's body was found and everyone assumed that meant the shade was back in the Shadowlands and we were safe. I didn't voice my opinion and Jamie hadn't said a word the whole meeting, but when our eyes met for just seconds across the room, I knew that he had the same thought.

When the forest grew quiet, it wasn't because there weren't any animals among the trees. It was because they were making space for something bigger, something more threatening.

It had gotten colder each day and snow became the norm on the way to school each day. I was a little thankful for the weather and the extra time off guardian duty to study. I had not done a good job keeping up at school and it made me feel guilty.

"You're not off for a run now, are you?" Becky asked me Sunday morning.

I hadn't been running before school last week after I slipped on a patch of ice and bashed my head. Sure, I healed fast, but I wasn't keen to take another fall like that soon. Today though, I felt like I needed to exert some energy. I'd been studying all morning and things were going well, but I had missed more questions on my calculus practice test than I had hoped. My GPA had dipped, and I had my eyes on that CU Boulder Valedictorian Scholarship, not that I knew if I was even going to college at all. It was a lot. I needed to get out.

"I'm only going like a mile and I'm going to stick to the salted roads," I said as I tucked my AirPods into my ears.

"I was hoping you would paint with me," Becky said. She was dressed in her painting clothes, a pair of old shorts and a volleyball T-shirt she'd stolen from me when I tried tossing out all my gear after I quit. The sight was becoming common around here. I could almost expect to find her wearing the same outfit with a paintbrush in hand as she worked to redo some corner of the house.

"I'll help when I get back," I told her as I went to the door.

"Take your phone," she called out.

After my last run-in with that demon at the railroad station, my phone was practically glued to my hand. I held it up to show her I had it before I went out the front door and into the cold.

I shivered. I had pulled on an extra layer, but the goose-bumps still rose on my arms underneath the long-sleeve T-shirt and the hoodie. I knew that after a warm-up and a few blocks my body would warm up though. I kept moving as I did my stretches and was glad when I started jogging down the street.

I listened to a YouTube video I'd queued up of a college professor discussing *MacBeth*, the primary subject of Mrs. McKellen's English test. I had already watched the BBC's version of the play once since we'd read it in class. The thought of plays reminded me of the students I saw discussing the Odyssey when I visited CU Boulder.

The shade was a ghost of her former self and needed to possess a body to be in the mortal world. How did she know to possess Alison's? Could she possess someone who was alive, or did it have to be a dead person?

I watched the woman who ducked into a shop down the main road, wondering if the shade was hiding as some ordinary person in Burbrook now.

Instead of taking the normal route, I decided to run the sidewalks downtown. I had turned down the main road instead of crossing it to go to the railroad station like I usually did. The sidewalks outside the shops were salted often and I felt comfortable running there. At least, I did until I'd turned down an alleyway to run the backside of the strip mall.

I got that same strange feeling along my neck as I had the morning that demon chased me. I didn't look back right away, just quickened my pace. The parking lot behind the shops had been cleared of snow, but not salted the same way the sidewalks were. Just as I considered slowing now, my right foot slipped on a patch of ice, and I fell face-first into the pavement.

My left knee hit the ground first, tipping me onto my right side where I tried bracing the fall with my elbow. The leggings tugged down at my right hip, the skin there grating against the concrete. I let out a yelp of pain, hearing a snarl behind me that confirmed my fears.

I didn't look back. I ignored the pain in my hip and scrambled to my feet, running full force toward the end of the parking lot. It was mostly empty, only a few employees parked there. The early birds. I didn't have time to make a call to anyone in my circle, not that they'd have enough time to find me before whatever demon was chasing me ran me down. I did the only thing I could think of to try scaring the demon away. I screamed.

I yelled for help, the effort leaving me breathless and a little dizzy. I heard a hum behind me, gaining speed until it sounded right next to me. A black SUV sped past me, wheels squealing as it made a sharp turn and came to a stop at the exit. The passenger door flew open and I didn't hesitate. I barely slowed my pace as I climbed inside. The door shut behind me by force as the car shot forward, tires squealing. That's when I finally looked at the driver and realized who'd come to my rescue.

"What are you doing here?" I asked.

Angel sent a confused look my way before speeding through the yellow light and heading toward the outskirts of town. "Are you really questioning me after you ran screaming through a parking lot?"

I felt my cheeks heat. "Thanks for that." I glanced behind us, the line of shops obscuring the view of the parking lot now.

There wasn't a single person in sight. Had I imagined it? Maybe no one was chasing me after all, and I was just paranoid.

"You're hurt," Angel said. He slowed the car and turned onto a side road that led up Burbrook Mountain.

"How do you know?" I asked. The adrenaline was fading now, and I could feel the cuts on my hip. I raised my shirt to look at them. They were fading to smaller scrapes now, pink skin slowly knitting back together.

"That's when I pulled around the corner," Angel said. "You fell."

If he'd gotten to the lot at that point, then he would've seen my attacker. That meant two things; one, there had never been anyone chasing me or two, he was acting really relaxed for someone who'd just seen a demon.

"You know who was chasing you?" he asked.

I let out a deep breath, my heart still coming down to normal pace from my sprint. "No."

Angel pulled the car to the side of the road where the turn was to start up the mountain.

"There's a first aid kit in the glove compartment," he said.

"I'm fine," I told him and really looked at him for the first time since I got in the car.

He wore a long-sleeve shirt, sleeves pushed to his elbows like always. His hair was pulled into his normal topknot, but there were pieces of leaves trapped underneath a few locks of hair as though he'd been in the forest. A look at his boots told me he probably had been.

"What were you up to this morning?" I asked.

He shrugged. "I restocked at the store."

"We aren't open Sundays."

"Which is why it was the perfect day to stock the store."

"Willow didn't say anything about us stocking the store this weekend."

Angel scoffed and shifted in his seat to look at me so one knee was resting near the center console. "You're lucky I was stocking the store and was on my way out when I heard you scream. A thank you would be nice."

The smirk on his face told me he was more amused by my questions than he was angry that I had so many. I lowered my eyes to my phone, so I didn't have to look at him anymore. The unanswered message from Izzy was there in my notifications, taunting me. She invited me over to swim in the pool. She said she could use her powers to keep it warm for an hour. I hadn't opened the message, because I wasn't sure how to say no. I didn't want to go over there if it was her and Puck together and Jamie and Emily. I imagined them all in skimpy swimsuits, both couples stealing kisses and flirting.

I needed to visit the Moore Estate though. I was out of books for my research and without books to read, all I had to fill my time was studying for semester tests and that was only worsening my mood. Running didn't work to relief any stress and now that I was staring at the message on my phone, I only felt worse.

I groaned. "Can you take me to a friend's hous?."

"Doesn't sound like you want to go to a friend's house," Angel said and faced forward. "But, sure."

"I want to see my friend, but I don't want to run into someone else while I'm there."

"Him?"

My first thought was to change the subject, but I'd already told Angel all about Jamie. I nodded in response. We sat in silence for a long moment before he put the SUV in drive and pulled away from the shoulder.

"Where to?"

"Up the mountain."

We drove in silence. I gave him directions as we went and

he followed my lead, not asking any more questions. I was glad about that. It made me feel a little bad for asking him so many though.

"Remind me," Angel said as he turned onto the driveway to the estate. I felt my insides twist when I saw that the gate was closed. When did they fix it?

"Let me call Izzy," I said and pulled my phone out.

"Remind me," Angel started again as he stopped in front of the gate. "You like this guy, right?"

I didn't answer. I looked up from my phone when I heard his window slide down. He was parked next to the call button.

"I don't want to see *her*," I blurted.

Angel's fingers froze halfway to the red button. He looked back at me, confused. "You don't want to see your friend?"

"No, the other girl. His ex-girlfriend showed up and I don't want to see her."

"You don't like her?" Angel asked.

Couldn't he just drop me off at the gate?

"She's nice. I mean, I don't *not* like her. She's a good person."

Angel smirked in a knowing way. "You don't want to see *them*."

The way he said the words made my heart skip. Them. Jamie and Emily.

Angel reached over and clicked the button before I could react. I sat back in my seat, holding my breath. The speaker crackled and I relaxed a little when I heard Mr. Puck's voice.

"Quinn's residence," he said.

"It's Angel. I'm dropping off Tori."

I could hear all the questions in the silence. *Who is Angel? Why is Tori with him?*

"We'll meet you out front," Puck said.

The speaker crackled and a loud clang rang out as the gate

swung inward. Angel rolled up his window and put the car in drive. He drove slowly towards the white house.

"What do the Quinns do?" he asked, looking at the house in awe as he came to a stop behind Mr. Puck's car in the driveway.

The garage door rolled open and Angel's amazement only grew as the line of sports cars were visible. While he stared at the display, I watched as the door to the house opened and Jamie came out, dressed in a pair of swim trunks. He pulled on a T-shirt on as he walked, Emily coming out behind him and then Izzy. Mr. Puck came out last, the only one not yet dressed for the pool. He looked strange in his sweats next to the others. Izzy wore a pair of shorts and her bikini top, not acting as though the cold bothered her at all. Emily came out with a kind of sarong around her hips and a blanket pulled around her shoulders.

"Thanks for the ride," I said and hopped out of the SUV. I walked just a few feet when I heard Angel's door shut. I stopped walking and he joined me, offering the others a kind wave.

Jamie slowed his pace but kept walking to meet us. He looked annoyed to see Angel but smiled anyway.

"You work at Beans and Books, right?" Jamie asked.

"Yes. I'm Angel," he said and held out a hand. For a moment, I didn't think Jamie was going to shake it, but he did. I caught Izzy's sly smirk for a moment, and I knew I'd be bombarded with questions about Angel afterward.

"You're new to Burbrook," Mr. Puck said. It wasn't a question. We knew most everyone in the small town or at least knew of them.

Angel nodded. "I'm just here for a few months. I go to NYU in the fall."

"Good school. What are you going to study?" Puck asked.

Angel smiled. "I'm still deciding. You work at the high school, right?"

"Yeah. I teach chemistry."

"And I can't really stick around for very long. I was hoping you could drive me back home," I said to Izzy, hoping my expression was enough of a plea that I didn't have to say more.

"Tori, I can wait around and then drop you off," Angel said. The corners of his mouth tugged upward in an almost devious way. "I could say hi to Becky."

In that moment I knew what he was doing. He was playing wingman, trying to get a rise out of Jamie. It worked. Jamie's expression faltered for a moment before his smile returned.

"That's okay. I'll just go with Izzy. We could use some girl time," I told him, surging forward and grabbing Izzy's hand.

"See you tomorrow," Angel called out as Izzy and headed for the garage.

I practically dragged her into the house, ignoring her laughter.

"He's sexier than you described him," she said once we were inside. The door shut a moment later as Puck, Emily, and Jamie joined us. I could feel my cheeks burning and I turned away from the others to try hiding the fact.

"He's just a work friend," I said and led the way to the kitchen. I could see the steam coming from the pool. I had probably interrupted them just before they all dove in.

"You sure you don't want to join us for a swim?" Emily asked. She tossed the blanket onto the counter to reveal a crop top in the same pink color as the sarong, the straps of her swimsuit peeking out the top.

"No, I was on a run and remembered that I needed to get new books from the hutch," I said.

"On a run with Angel?" Izzy said with a teasing tone. I sent a glare her way.

"Have you found anything?" Jamie asked, leaning against the hutch.

I shook my head. "Have you?"

"I wish," he said.

Izzy groaned. "This day wasn't supposed to be about guardian things. It was supposed to be a relaxing day in our make-shift hot tub."

"Exactly," Emily said, slapping Jamie's chest playfully. He smiled a little at her and captured the offending hand, pressing it to his lips.

"Izzy, show Tori what you found. We'll catch up later," Jamie said without looking away from Emily. I was glad to leave the room.

"What did you find?" I asked as she led me back to the hall.

"I'll meet you by the pool," Puck told her.

Izzy moved quickly, practically running down the hall and into the library.

"It's one of Mom's diaries," she said and went to the couch where a box sat. "We have been so focused on Dad's work with the circle guide and the books in the hutch that I didn't think about checking anywhere else until Will and I found them."

She took the lid off the box to reveal a stack of notebooks. She lifted the first one out and began flipping through the pages.

"Mom and Dad used to take the train to different places. They were usually making trips to find other circles and compare notes. That's why Dad's circle guide had so much in it. He made notes about different circles and where they were in the country. Mom wrote more about who those people were though, and she had this photo ..."

Izzy flipped a few more pages before she found the one she was looking for. She turned the notebook so I could see it. The entire page was filled with her mom's cursive, but the bottom corner had a small photo taped to it. I recognized her mom in the picture, long dark hair and a smile. Next to her was a girl that looked to be seven or eight. She had black hair that was cut short around her face. She had blunt bangs that hung just over her brows, which were knitted together in a serious expression.

"Look at her neck," Izzy said.

I looked closer at the girl. A chain hung around her neck. It went low over her dress and nearly disappeared between the zipper of her coat, which was where I spotted the same pendant that was concealed under my shirt. I stared at the girl for a long time before I read the diary entry.

Today was one of the more interesting circle visits we've done in a long time. We found this circle in New York. We weren't planning on going there, and we didn't really want to take the train that far, but we did and I'm glad. This circle was one of the largest ones we've found. So many different powers! The most interesting member was a seven-year-old girl named Suri. She has powers of telekinesis that were amazing. She has stronger powers than most adults and I found out why very quickly. She was the leader of this circle. She may have been in the body of a seven-year-old, but Suri has been a guardian since the early 1800s. She said she couldn't remember the exact date anymore.

I stopped reading when I realized the rest of the entry was about a demon they hunted while in New York. Was it possible that there was a pendant for every circle? If Suri had one and we had the same power, then there had to be a connection there as well. Maybe there were more guardians in other circles who were exactly like me.

"Maybe the answers are outside of Burbrook," Izzy said.

I didn't get a chance to reply. Izzy got a phone call and moved across the room to take it. It only took a few words for me to realize it was Puck from the pool. As the pink tinge rose to her cheeks, I knew it was my cue to leave.

I sent Izzy a quick text that I was going to pick new books and then needed a ride back home before Becky wondered where I was. I was a little surprised that she hadn't called already, but with her newfound redecorating obsession it wasn't *that* surprising that she'd lost track of time.

I glanced out the kitchen window to see Mr. Puck swimming from the shallow end of the steamy pool to the deep end. Seeing his exposed back reminded me of the night I'd caught him and Izzy in the hallway. I quickly turned my attention to the hutch across the kitchen. I'd have to return the books I had at home another time. With semester tests this week and Christmas Break starting after that, I would probably have whatever I picked today finished in days and need to come back anyway.

I grabbed the side of the hutch and pulled it back, my heart leaping into my throat when Emily gasped. She was lying across the tiny desk, her upper body pressed against one of the bookshelves. Her eyes went wide, focused on me as her face turned red. Jamie stood between her thighs, lips pressed against her neck. One hand was under the fabric of her crop top and the other had hiked up the sarong at her hip.

He looked back at me, his expression falling before he stepped back from the desk.

"Tori," he started, apologetic.

He didn't need to apologize. I had rejected him. I'd rejected him several times. I should be the one apologizing, but I couldn't help the anger that was spreading hot in my chest. I wanted to scream at him for kissing her, for even picking up their relationship where it left off as though time and space couldn't separate them. I wanted to yell at him, because seeing him between her legs and her spread across that desk ruined the only dream that I'd been replaying in my brain of Jamie and me together. I could never imagine us together again without seeing Emily's face and Jamie's lips on her throat.

The tears came hot before I could stop them, one, two, and a third rolling down my cheeks and over my trembling lip.

"Tori," Jamie said again and took a step toward me.

I turned and ran. I went out the door and ran through the garage toward the end of the driveway. I used my powers to push the gate open, hoping that it would break again like the last time I'd passed it. I didn't care that Izzy would wonder where I went or that Emily had seen me cry at the sight of them. I turned at the end of the driveway and ran back down the mountain.

CHAPTER 20

I would've avoided everyone if I could've. Instead, I avoided Jamie, which was easier than I thought it would be. It seemed like he was trying to avoid me too. He was out of in-school suspension, which meant that he was back in classes. I didn't pass him in the halls at all, which meant he was taking a new route to class.

I was sure that Izzy found out why I'd left, but she didn't bring it up. I had to tell Macy though and she was a great friend and listened to me as I cried about it all over again. It was Becky's turn to comfort me, which involved late-night coffee and lots of redecorating. Becky wanted the master bedroom to look completely different than before, reminding me of the way Macy's mom had repainted their entire house when she divorced Macy's dad.

"Are you leaving Mark?" I asked her, eager to change the subject from my recent drama.

"He left me, don't you think?" she replied in a grumble.

I couldn't argue with that. She finished rolling the gray paint over the brown wall where the bed used to be. Her plan was to get rid of the old bed frame, a heavy chestnut thing, and replace the headboard with paint instead. She wanted to paint a large arch where the bed would go with several smaller ones within it, all different pastel colors. It was the kind of girly thing Mark hated having around the house, which explained why so many things were around the place now.

"I already filed the paperwork," Becky said and stepped back from the wall. "He signed over the weekend."

"So, what's next?" I asked. Would they split custody of me or something? Did it even matter since I turned eighteen?

Becky let out a deep breath. "First, we go on our girl's ski trip with Margot. Then," she turned to me with her roller in hand and pressed it to my stomach, "we do whatever we want."

I stood in shock, staring down at the gray line left along the old volleyball shirt. When I looked up at her, she was smiling mischievously.

"Keep that up and I won't paint with you anymore," I told her, flicking my brush her way so a spray of gray dotted the front of her shirt.

She smiled and went back to work on a new wall.

Willow was nice and let me have most of the week off so I could prepare for all my tests. It also made avoiding people easier. I don't know why Angel decided to show off to Jamie, but it hadn't made things any easier.

It was a short school week with each day having dedicated testing periods. Monday, I had my English and history tests. They were the subjects I was worried about the least, which was a good thing since I was so distracted by trying to avoid

Jamie. Tuesday was Shakespeare and drama. I had to recite a memorized monologue for my drama class, which I'd been dreading. I'd managed to not do a lot of speaking in front of the class all semester, but Mrs. McKellen denied my request to give the monologue to her in private. By the time it was my turn to go, I was shaking so bad that I was sure I'd lowered my grade based on performance alone. McKellen assured me after class that I'd done fine though.

Wednesday, our last day, was the worst day of the week.

Mr. Puck was serious about test days, and he went to the extreme on semester test days. He made everyone put their bags in the hallway before entering the class with just a pencil. He mixed up the usual seating chart at random, so I ended up sitting at a table with Sean Peterson and Jamie sat at the one across the center aisle from us with Connor Taylor.

I did my best to ignore Jamie, which was a little easier once I had the test on my desk. I was focused on the periodic table and the graphs. There were several long paragraphs detailing different labs with questions that followed. After answering the final one and looking up, I noticed that Mr. Puck was watching me expectantly. He gave me a kind smile and motioned for me to come to his desk.

I rose from my chair with my test and handed it over when I reached him. He sat the test inside a green file folder and then reached around me. Jamie handed his test over next, glancing at me anxiously before I looked away.

"You can go to the library to study for the last of your tests," Mr. Puck told us.

I hurried from the room, looping my arm around the strap of my backpack, and making it halfway down the hall before I heard the feet running after me.

"Tori, wait," Jamie said.

Before I could round the corner for the library, he grabbed

the other side of my backpack. I turned to face him, my arm looped in one strap and Jamie's wrapped around the other, so the backpack was held between us.

"I've dedicated the week to trying to salvage my GPA," I told him. It was a poor excuse for my absence, I know. Still, even if it was a little immature, I couldn't stand the idea of bringing up the incident at the estate.

Jamie kept a tight grip on my bag. "Why don't you like her?"

"What?"

"Emily told me that you've been giving her the cold shoulder any time the two of you are around each other. She said she's tried being friendly and tried getting to know you, but you aren't having it."

"Wait, what?" I let go of my backpack and Jamie took the weight of it in one hand. "I don't ... Emily is nice. I don't have anything against her. I don't understand what you're saying."

Jamie shook his head in disbelief. "She told me you don't like her, and she was in tears about it."

"*She* was in tears?" I asked, unable to keep the venom from my tone.

Jamie scoffed. "Yes. She was. She can't figure out why you won't be nicer to her. Tori, we are all part of the same circle. We can't let something petty divide us."

"I'm not being petty," I shot back.

"Sure about that?" Jamie looked straight at me, waiting for my reply.

My eyes burned with angry tears. "I just want to be left alone. I have my calculus test after lunch and I'm stressing out about it. There's nothing going on between Emily and me and I don't understand why she thinks there is."

"Well, you should actually talk to her instead of dodging her texts."

"Texts? I haven't gotten any texts from her."

That was the truth. I hadn't gotten a text from Emily since she set up our coffee date. She never reached out to me in any way, not even when we had circle meetings. She was always glued to Jamie's side. She contributed to the group, but past that we never had time together.

"She said you are," Jamie said. He let go of my backpack, so it settled between his feet.

"Well, I'm not," I said and reached for the backpack. "She hasn't sent me any texts and maybe you should ask her about why she's saying she did."

Jamie shifted his foot so that it was over the strap of the bag, keeping me from lifting it more than a foot off the floor. I glared back at him, smelling the leather of his biker jacket.

"I don't know what to believe about you anymore," Jamie said, his voice low.

"I'm not the one lying," I said, tugging on my backpack again to no avail.

Jamie let out an annoyed sigh. "I don't understand you, Victoria." My full name sounded like silk on his tongue, too beautiful for the message he was sending. "One week your hands are soft in my hair and next they're tight around my neck."

I remembered the feel of his hair all too well. I wanted to think about that moment in the maze. I had nearly kissed him then. I was ready to forget about everything the ferryman had shown me until the reality of it came crashing down again.

"Leave me alone," I said, hating that my voice cracked when I said the words.

Jamie stepped back, taking his foot off the strap so I could lift my backpack to my shoulder again and walk toward the library.

Jamie never appeared in the library with the rest of our

class as they finished testing. I worried about him getting in trouble again for skipping, but quickly realized as the day went that teachers and even Principal Thackery weren't overly concerned with student behavior with it being the last day before break.

I had a hard time focusing on my calculus test, double-checking my work before deciding to hand in the test. I sat at the back of the library during the last period of the day, glad that there wasn't any work to be done. The library was empty and even the librarian was ready for the day to be over, not caring that all the books she put on the turn-in cart were facing different directions.

When the bell rang for the end of the day, the halls filled with the sound of students hurrying toward the parking lot. The speakers came on and Mr. Thackery wished us all a Merry Christmas before playing "Jingle Bells."

When I checked my phone, I noticed a text from Jamie in the circle group chat. He suggested that we have a meeting to discuss what everyone's plans were for the break. I typed out my message that I had work and tucked my phone in my pocket. It buzzed twice as I made my way to the Beetle, feet crunching over the fresh snow that had fallen while we were in school.

I had mixed feelings about going to work. I was eager for the distraction, but I both wanted to see Angel and not see him. I always felt better after I talked to him, but I didn't want to revisit all the emotions again.

I turned the radio up higher than normal as I made my way to Beans and Books. I parked next to Angel's SUV and forced myself to get out of the car before I could second-guess myself. I walked through the storeroom and passed the coffee makers for the aprons on the wall. The room filled with the clanging of porcelain mugs and pouring coffee as I tied the apron around my waist. I turned around as I adjusted the name tag clipped to the apron front. When I looked up, a mug of hot coffee sat on the corner of the countertop. The strong smell of a pour-over. Black.

Angel finished pouring freshly ground coffee into one of the machines before he turned to face me, brushing coffee dust off his forearms. He looked up at me with his usual smile.

"How was the last day?"

My lip gave a single wobble before the sob burst forth. The tears poured down my face, which heated with embarrassment. It was pathetic. I was so stupid to dump all my high school drama on him, but I couldn't help it. My chest was tight, and I didn't feel like a single breath filled my lungs.

"Not coffee," Angel said when I reached for the cup. He pushed it out of the way and quickly moved to the sink. He pulled down a glass from one of the shelves and filled it at the tap. "Water."

I took the glass from him and let him lead me to the storeroom. He went to the back and lifted two large burlap bags of beans from the wire rack, stacking them against the wall to create a seat. I collapsed on them, the sound reminding me of a beanbag chair I used to have in my bedroom when I was a kid.

"I shouldn't be ... I-I'm sorry. You shouldn't have to ..." I couldn't get the words past my lips. I squeezed my eyes tight for a moment and tried taking a full breath, but it caught in my chest, and I felt like I was starting over again.

"Drink," Angel said. His voice was soft, but his eyes were an order. "Cold water helps."

I did as I was told. I took a small sip first, then a couple gulps. Just like he said, I could feel my breathing return to normal.

"You shouldn't have to listen to all my—" I stopped when Angel shushed me.

"You're fine, Tori. I get it. You talk if you want to," he said. He was sincere, his firm expression soothing. I sucked in a deep breath and let it out slowly with a nod.

"Finish that," he said with a nod toward the glass. I took another sip, shivering from the cold water. He took my coat from the hook near the door and draped the thick fabric over my knees. Two more sips later and the glass was empty. I held it out to him.

"Can I have coffee now?" I asked him.

He smiled. "Sure."

I tried rubbing the moisture from my face as he went for the mug, but my hair was sticking to my face now. I pushed it behind my ears, but the front pieces fell back into my face and tried sticking again where the tears had dried on my cheeks.

"Here," Angel said as he returned. "Let me." He sat the coffee on the shelf next to me and pulled the elastic from his topknot. Dark hair fell around his shoulders in too-perfect waves. They were like effortless beach waves, the kind that took a hairdresser's touch or some professional styling product.

Angel slipped the elastic around his wrist and moved to my side, gently nudging my shoulder so I turned on the burlap sack so he could stand behind me. He was gentle with my curls, sweeping half the hair away from my face and pulling it into a ponytail at the back of my head.

"You sit there a while. Enjoy your coffee and take a little time for yourself," Angel said when he moved in front of me.

I shook my head. "I can't take another day off." More like I didn't want to. Sitting and thinking about everything was exactly what I had been hoping to avoid.

Angel shook his head. "You aren't taking the day off. I can take care of our shift. No one comes in this close to closing anyway."

My heart skipped in my chest from the generosity. I had forgotten that we were closing early today, the start of holiday hours. I wanted to thank him, but I couldn't utter a word. Instead, I slowly drank my coffee as he worked.

No one came into the store, but Angel kept himself busy by cleaning up. A part of me was glad for the silence until it was interrupted by the buzzing of my phone in the pocket of my coat. I pulled it out to look at the texts. There were several in the circle group chat, all of them discussing possible meeting times to discuss what our break would look like. Macy wanted to meet in the morning, but Jamie insisted it be tonight because he and Emily had plans.

My stomach turned as I read the words. The text that had buzzed on my lap was from Jamie, confirming a meeting time for later tonight. Three dots appeared next to his name as a new message was typed. It came in seconds later.

Tori?

I stared down at my name for a long time, my heart beating heavy. I could hear his voice. The way he'd said my full name today was so different than when he just used my nickname. It carried more meaning than just what he was saying. It was like he was begging me to understand why I needed to be friends with Emily. He wanted us to be friends.

Do it for him.

"Hey," Angel's voice came softly. He crossed the storeroom and knelt in front of me. He cupped my face with both of his hands, using his thumbs to wipe away the tears. His touch was so soft, softer than I imagined. His eyes were brown, warm, and cozy. I couldn't help it. I reached out to feel if his hair was as soft as the rest of him.

The dark locks were smooth. I let my hands sink into his thick hair, pulling him toward me by the back of his neck. His hands stayed on my face, but his forearms brushed my neck and collarbone, the touch like silk sheets fresh from the dryer. I wanted those arms to encompass me. How was it possible for his skin to feel so good against mine? It was otherworldly.

I pulled his lips to mine.

He kept them tight at first, a gentle kiss that deepened. His lips parted so mine could fit with his. I moved one hand down his neck and to his chest, tightening my grip at the collar of his shirt to keep him there. He kissed me like I'd never been kissed before. The deeper the kiss got, the stranger it felt. It wasn't his lips. It was almost like he had braces, but instead of bumpy, they were tapered. Pointed.

I pulled him toward me and rolled, both of us slipping from the burlap sack to the concrete floor. I pushed him into the stone under us with one hand and pulled my demon dagger from the waist of my pants, the point just under his chin. As he tipped his head back to avoid being jabbed, I could see the fangs more clearly.

"Explain," I told him.

"I'm not going to hurt you," he said.

I snorted. "Only because I'm going to get you first."

"No," he corrected, keeping calm as though we were having the most routine conversation. "I'm not here to hurt anyone."

"Vampires have to kill humans to survive," I said.

"I'm here because I need help," he said.

"What kind of help?" I asked.

He wasn't like any demon I'd ever encountered. Jamie had said before that witches and vampires were some of the most dangerous supernatural beings because they were as human as we were. They weren't as controlled by their beastly nature.

"Yours," he said. "Tori, I need your help."

Neither of us moved. It came down to one question. Did I trust him? I had no reason not to. He *had* saved me from a demon before.

I climbed off him, keeping my dagger raised at his chest. He propped himself up on his arms before slowly getting to his feet once it was clear I wasn't making any more moves.

"Why do you need my help?" I asked.

"You have telekinesis," he said.

How did he know? I hadn't used my powers when I was running in the parking lot.

"You've been watching me," I said.

"It's not what you think," he said.

"They call vampires night stalkers for a reason," I told him, tightening my grip on the dagger.

Angel held his hands up as though to show me he was unarmed. I knew better. Vampires are walking weapons.

"I was told I needed to find a guardian with telekinesis," he said.

"Who told you?"

"The witch."

My mind went to the blonde witch I'd met in the Shadow-lands. Something had been strange about her. Something about her was familiar.

"The blonde witch?" I asked.

Angel's expression changed. Confused. "No. She's a Black woman."

"Why do you need my help?" I asked. My arm had relaxed a little, so I switched the blade to my other hand.

Angel was quiet for a moment. It looked like he was trying

to decide if he should tell me. He let out a deep breath, his shoulders relaxing.

"There's a cure for vampirism," he said at last. "All I need are a few things and the witch can do the spell."

My stomach twisted. He was here for my blood.

"No," I said.

Angel looked offended. "You don't even know what I need."

"You need my blood," I told him, watching as the truth came across his face. "I know the mistress needs my blood. I won't give it to you."

"Mistress? You mean the mistress to the Shadowlands?" Angel asked.

What were the chances that he really did need my blood for his cure? It was all too convenient though. The ferryman vanishes and everything goes mostly back to normal until the shade and her shadow demons appear, then Angel comes to town ...

"How do I know that you aren't working for her?" I asked.

Angel scoffed. "You won't believe me even if I tried to prove that and I don't know that I can."

We stood for a long time. I wasn't sure what to do. I wanted to trust him, but I knew that part of that was his nature. Vampires appeared kind, attractive. He made me feel so comfortable because of what he is, but was any of that real?

I glanced toward the counter when I heard the bell ring from the front door. When I looked back, Angel was gone. He wasn't anywhere in the storeroom and a quick glance out the back door told he me wasn't in his car or in the parking lot. I went into the store, feigning a smile at the man with a little boy who'd come in. Angel wasn't in the store at all.

But I had a feeling he wasn't gone for good.

CHAPTER 21

"Tori! Tori, get up! Come down here!"

Becky's scream sent me bolting from bed, bare feet pounding on the stairs. I whipped around the banister and only slowed my pace when I saw the smile on her face and the reason for it clutched between her hands.

She held a letter, gold and black printed on the outside with the outline of a buffalo next to the address.

"Come here. Open it," she said and held the envelope out to me.

I hesitated for a moment before moving into the kitchen. I took the envelope and looked down at the address for the University of Colorado Boulder. Becky fidgeted with the bottom button of her pajama shirt; the compulsive gesture what made me rip open the envelop with a quick movement that tore the corner of the letter inside.

"What does it say?" Becky asked. "What am I saying? I know you'll get in."

I ignored her as and read the letter. The first line told me I'd been accepted, making my stomach twist tight instead of providing the relief I'd hoped for. Further down the letter were instructions about when to enroll for housing, for classes, and a small reminder to check the financial portal and keep my admissions information up to date through senior year in case I qualified for any of their scholarships.

Becky's laptop was open on the table. I turned it my way and opened a tab to log into my account. Just a few clicks and I was staring at the dashboard for all my financial information. There was a welcome message for all incoming freshmen that gave an estimation for tuition, fees, and housing. Under that were messages that only applied to me. The one at the top was a scholarship for valedictorian status.

You indicated possible valedictorian status at your high school. Submit your final transcript after high school graduation to confirm that you were number one in your class, and you will receive the Valedictorian Scholarship to be applied to four consecutive years at CU Boulder.

The message tallied a rough estimate of tuition that would be left over after the scholarship was applied. It was still a lot, but much more manageable to pay with a job and maybe a small loan. It would depend on several factors, of course, but money wasn't the giant barrier I worried it would be.

"I am so excited for you," Becky said and gave me a hug from behind, pulling me out of my thoughts.

"Yeah. It's amazing," I said, though not sounding nearly as enthused as I probably should.

"It's normal to be a little nervous," Becky said and went to the coffee maker when it beeped. She poured two mugs, beginning to mix a scoop of sugar and a pour of milk into hers.

I took my mug from the counter and blew on the top, watching the coffee ripple. "Nervous is becoming the new normal for me." I grumbled the words more to myself, but I knew she'd heard them based on the sympathetic way she looked back at me.

"What else has you nervous?" Becky asked.

I couldn't keep it in any longer, not from Becky anyway.

"I kissed the boy at work. I didn't mean to, but I was stressed about semester tests and everything with my friends is all messed up right now and I kissed the boy at work."

"Do you like him?" Becky asked, slipping into a chair at the table. She shut her laptop and slid it to one side.

I sat down across from her, sinking heavily into the chair. "No. Not like that. He's super hot, yes, but I don't want to be with him. I just did it. I don't know why."

Becky didn't *oh* and *ah* at me the way Macy would have, which I appreciated. Becky was always a good listener, never emotional or judgmental about anything I told her. That was probably why it all spilled out of me now.

"I have a feeling this has more to do with Jamie than the boy at work," she said.

I melted onto the table, letting my chin rest on my folded arms. "He's with someone else now."

"I thought you two were on the brink of dating. Wait— were you dating?"

"I don't know. Not really. I told him we shouldn't."

"Why?"

"It's complicated and I don't want to talk about it." I sat up in my seat and lifted the coffee to my lips again, not caring that it was still scalding as I let it pass my lips.

Becky didn't say anything for a long time. We drank our coffee until her phone buzzed on the table.

"I almost forgot," she said and stood up. "I am going

mattress shopping. I'll probably be out most of the day. I may look at some other décor and furniture pieces."

I wanted to ask her just how far her newfound obsession with remodeling the house would go, but I decided it might be more hurtful than helpful. Therapy could be just as expensive as all her projects anyway.

"I think I'll ..." I was going to say that I was going to study at the library, but I forgot that school was over, and Christmas Break started today. It seemed too early to be Christmas time.

"If you leave the house, can you stop by the store for things to make dinner? I'll send you a text." Becky was already in the entryway before I could reply.

I wasn't planning on going anywhere and after reliving the whole Angel thing again with her, I wanted to stay in my pajamas and watch Netflix on the couch the rest of the day. I decided that I'd start with a hot shower and see if I felt like doing anything afterward.

I took a long shower, complete with a face mask and body scrub even. I did feel a little better afterward. As I dried my curls, I thought about what I would wear. My first thought was the volleyball sweats in my closet, but I went the extra mile instead.

What started with just a shower and putting a little more effort into my appearance ended with me in one of my favorite sweaters, a full face of makeup, and sorting through what little jewelry I had tucked away under the bathroom sink. I had been searching for the gold bracelet the witch gave me in the Shadowlands before remembering that Alison stole it off me at the homecoming game.

Alison's funeral was a few days ago. Her family had her cremated, so Macy said. She left school after her semester tests to attend the service and said that her family were going to plan another memorial to spread her ashes when the weather warmed up in the spring.

Would the guilt ever go away? Why did I feel so guilty anyway? I didn't kill Alison. I tried to stop it. It wasn't anyone's fault. She'd just been in the wrong place at the wrong time.

Getting dressed up made me feel more confident, less embarrassed about what had happened with Angel and how I'd walked in on Jamie and Emily. The last part still haunted my dreams. But I looked pretty, and I didn't want to waste that on a day stuck inside the house. I wanted to show off. I wanted something to feel good about.

I was accepted to CU Boulder this morning. I had a real shot at a scholarship that would pay for most of my expenses. I felt good about how my semester tests went. It was Christmas Break, which meant no school and Becky's homemade enchiladas, which were a Christmas Eve tradition at our house. I even had a real reason to get away on our upcoming ski trip before school started back up.

I found myself typing the text message before I could second-guess myself.

Want to go for a drive?

Izzy's reply came just moments after.

Yes. I'll pick you up in five.

Izzy and I picked up coffee at Starbucks and drove around Burbrook, talking until our cups were empty. It turned out that she was a little annoyed with Jamie and Emily too. She said they were always sitting on the couch together or standing next to each other or sitting on the same side of the booth when they went on a double date to the diner.

"You know, you and Puck are also glued at the hip like that. I never see you anymore," I told her as she turned into a parking spot downtown.

"Not like this though," she said and turned off the car.

We both got out and moved onto the sidewalk. All the downtown shops were decorated for Christmas now. There were green trees with baubles painted on store windows. Twinkling lights outlined displays of featured items. It was festive enough to chase away a little bit of the blue feeling I'd gotten so used to this week.

"They are always together, in a way they weren't the last time," Izzy said.

I groaned. "Well, the way he used to talk about Emily ... It was a bit obsessive."

"He loved her, but he wasn't obsessed with her," Izzy said as we made our way into the first shop. It was a small boutique that mostly sold custom T-shirts.

"Is he obsessed now?" I asked, pretending to be interested in a T-shirt with the cursive words *Sleigh All Day* on the front.

"No ..."

The way she said the words, like she was thinking aloud, made me look back at her. Izzy stood on the welcome mat, repeatedly scraping her snow boots over the mat.

"What?" I asked. Her expression made me nervous. Was something else going on with Jamie? Had he found something out or gone rogue on some mission the way he had when he'd been hunting all night for demons?

Izzy let out a sigh. "Jamie's been different since they got back together. Not in a bad way. He's just different and I feel like he's far away from me. He doesn't worry about things the way I do and it's not like him. I'm not supposed to be the overly concerned one. That's always been his thing."

What was she concerned about? I let the T-shirt fall from my hands and I moved a little closer to her so the employee behind the register couldn't hear.

"What are you concerned about?" I asked.

"Something he told me," Izzy said. She sucked on her bottom lip for a moment. "When we all met last, we hadn't seen any signs of demons, or the shade, and we thought after Alison was found that the shade had gone back to the Shadow-lands. I thought that too, but Jamie made a good point. He said that the demons vanished after the ferryman showed up in Burbrook and since it's been so quiet ... I don't think the shade ever left."

My heart picked up pace. "I think she's here in a different body."

"Whose?"

"I don't know. I need to find out more about how shades work," I said. That would require returning to the estate to get more books.

Izzy nodded and moved to one of the racks, looking through the Christmas-themed sweaters. I moved to a table with jewelry laid out. Maybe I could find a gold bracelet to replace the one Alison took. It was the only bit of gold jewelry I had, and I did like the way it looked with some of my tops over my usual silver jewelry.

"Emily mentioned you never look at her when we are all together," Izzy said as she made her way around the rack to me.

"What?" I asked, looking up at her. Her expression was

accusatory. I let out a sigh. "Why does everyone think I have something against her?"

"Because we all know you like Jamie."

I felt the heat rush to my cheeks. I looked back down at the table, lifting a pair of dangly earrings that were longer than I liked.

"I like Emily. She's nice. I don't have a problem with her, but it is weird being around her. Like you said, she's always with Jamie and ..." I didn't really have a good excuse for feeling strange about them other than the fact that I liked him. I knew we were a match. I knew that if I kissed him, we'd fall deeply in love and be together forever. I also knew that if we matched, he would die.

"You should make a point to be nice to her," Izzy said.

I sat the earrings down. "I am nice to her."

"I mean that you should make a point to be *really* nice to her, so she knows that. All she sees is that you feel weird around her and she's taking it the wrong way. She wants to be friends. She is a member of our circle."

"Jamie already gave me that lecture," I said and moved toward the door.

We both gave polite waves to the cashier when she told us to come back again. The cool air whooshed over us, making me shove my hands deep into my coat pockets for warmth.

"Was he an ass about it?" Izzy asked. I didn't reply. She groaned and said, "He's always an ass."

I laughed, glad to see that she was smiling too.

We walked through two more shops before going back to her Jeep, turning the seat warmers on high as we considered going back to Starbucks for a second cup of coffee.

"Oh. We're having a Christmas party," Izzy said. "The whole school will be there. They're all dying to see the mysterious Quinn family house." She laughed.

"How are you getting away with that with Puck and all?" I asked. No way would Puck allow it.

Izzy backed out of the parking spot and pulled to a stop at the light. "It was Macy's idea, but her mom will be home. She asked if we could use the estate. Will and I are going to the ski resort in Holston next weekend, so we will be gone the Saturday of the party. You're welcome."

"After what happened in the fall, isn't a party up the mountain a bad idea, especially when you consider the weather?" I asked. I didn't want to imagine how that party would've been worse with snow and ice in the mix.

"Because it's the rich neighborhood, the county does a good job salting the mountain roads anyway, but since Will and I matched ..." She let the words hang in the air, a coy smile spreading on her face.

"Your powers are strong enough to melt the ice and snow for the whole mountain pass? Seriously?"

Izzy laughed. "That and into Burbrook. It didn't take a lot when I tried it out. It's not supposed to snow at all starting Thursday, so Macy and I are going to do a little at a time. The roads will be bone dry for the party. Plus, the gate is working again, and we have to open it for everyone who comes and goes, so you can keep anyone who is too tipsy from driving."

It did sound like a pretty safe night, but the idea of a party made me just as nervous as it did before I went to my first one at Connor's house. I knew Jamie wouldn't approve, so that meant that Macy was making it all a surprise. He wasn't connected with the gossip at srchool to find out about it. The way Izzy talked, he was too busy making out with Emily to notice anyway.

I had been prepared to reject the idea before the thought of Jamie and Emily came to my mind. He deserved to be pissed off about something and the idea of unwinding from the stress of it all with a drink sounded very enticing.

"So, Saturday," I said as we made our way back to Starbucks for round two.

"Saturday," Izzy echoed.

We sat inside the store for a while, long enough that she finished her pumpkin spice latte, and I got halfway through my cup. Before we pulled from the parking lot, I remembered that I promised Becky that I'd pick up ingredients for dinner.

"Can you stop at the grocery store? I have to pick up something for Becky," I said.

Izzy turned onto the road. "Sure."

The local grocery store, Rainbow Grocers, sat on a corner on the way out of town. As usual, the parking lot was filled despite only a couple cars being there. They were all either pulling RVs or towing trailers with snowmobiles. They took up most of the parking spots, so Izzy stopped the Jeep in a space between the parking lot and two gas pumps.

"I'll just be a few," I told her as I got out.

She pulled out her phone and opened Instagram. "Sounds good."

I hurried toward the door, nearly slipping on the concrete when a dog barked at me from the backseat of a truck. The heat was on full blast in the store, warm and inviting despite the harsh florescent lighting. I pulled out my phone and checked the text Becky sent me hours ago. Most of what she needed was canned food to toss in the chili, but she also needed a pound of ground beef. It could only mean one thing we'd be eating chili for a while.

I picked up a plastic basket next to the register and found my way to the canned food section. The bell from the front door rang distantly as I filled my basket with canned beans and what

Becky considered her secret ingredient, a jar of salsa. There was no better way to describe Becky's cooking than the way she made chili. Not just because every dish she made consisted of using already-made ingredients and heating them up, but because chili was one of the few dishes she made. Mark did most of the cooking at our house and he always cooked from scratch.

That, I was going to miss about him living at the house.

The temperature in the store dropped as I moved away from the giant heater at the front and toward the freezer section at the back. I planned to get the beef from the butcher at the counter, but a handwritten sign was taped on the door to the back that said he'd gone on break. The lights behind the counter were turned off as if he planned on being gone for a while.

I checked my watch. It was four, close to the time people would be in to pick up groceries after work for dinner. Something must have come up for him to leave the counter empty like that so close to the rush.

I turned from the counter to the other side of the aisle where the packaged meats were sitting in their little Styrofoam containers. I reached for the ground beef just as something heavy smashed into the side of my head.

My vision went black. For seconds, all I could hear was the hum of the freezers and the sound of my frantic breathing. Someone clapped a hand over my mouth and pulled me backward. I heard the swinging door of the butcher counter open as my vision came back in a blur of florescent lights.

I turned my head to the left to try uncovering my mouth and froze when I saw the mess. The body of a man with a bloodied apron laid spread-eagle on the tile. Blood was still running from the cut on the side of his neck, eyes wide and mouth opening and closing as though asking for help.

I was so struck with fear that I didn't move until I felt the cold air prick my skin as we moved from the store to the alley behind it. I twisted hard, setting us enough off-balance that I slid from my attacker's grip. I swung my fist at him, missing as he took a step away. He looked like any other human man, except his eyes were a vibrant red and when he sent a sinister smile my way, I saw that his teeth were tapered to sharp points.

Before he could lunge at me, I thrust a hand toward him and he flew backward, going several feet before smashing into the dumpster. I turned to run just in time to see the cinder block.

CHAPTER 22

My head throbbed terribly. Everything was dark for a long time as I endured the horrible pain. I didn't hear the voices until the pain had faded a little. Their voices were deep. I could see their dark shapes moving near a tree as my vision slowly came back.

After another minute, I could see them clearly in the forest and the pain in my skull was no worse than a headache. I propped myself up a little to see if I recognized any of the surroundings. We were among the trees, a small pool of blood staining the snow where my head had been.

I heard the soft shush of metal on metal and turned just in time to be hauled to my feet by the same demon I'd tossed into the dumpster. He held a dagger under my chin, forcing me to raise my head to keep from being impaled.

"Who are you?" I asked.

I could see a glimmer of fear shoot through his red eyes. He glanced to the man next to him, a dark-haired man with blood caked on his chest that was likely from carrying me all this way as I slowly healed from his deathblow.

"How can you speak?" the man holding me asked.

"You know how," I said.

Despite the terror in his eyes, he held the front of my coat tight in one hand and kept the dagger poised in the other. I was glad for the amulet. It made me feel powerful, like I had something extra over the two demons who stared back at me, like I was much more than I really was. They feared me. I needed to make sure they continued to fear me.

"Unless you want to go back to the Shadowlands, you should take your hands off me," I told the man through my teeth. He didn't budge. I reached out and grabbed the collar of his shirt, pulling him an inch toward me so I got a whiff of the rotting smell on his teeth and the dagger brushed the bottom of my skin. "I'm sure you'll be tossed in the shallows if I'm the one to send you back."

The demon snarled and let go of me. He lowered his dagger and took a step to the side. The second man began to laugh, and I didn't understand why until I saw the black mist a yard ahead of us. It started as a haze, like looking into a dark fog, then became more and more dense until it was a thick cloud. A figure walked out of it, striding quickly toward me.

She was no taller than I was but wore the armor of a warrior. Dark fabric flowed behind her like a cape. She had a bodice made of silver that rose high to protect her neck. A helmet covered her entire head, complete with the angled face of a woman on her metal mask. Metal spokes rose inches above her head, and I didn't notice that they were antlers until she was a few feet away.

I took several steps backward, but she grabbed onto the front of my coat to keep me from moving any farther back. I could see her piercing eyes just past the mask, roving over my face and then over my body. I gasped when she tugged me to her metal chest, her hand going inside my coat and feeling along my stomach and the front of my pants until she came away with my cellphone in her hand. She held it up and the man who held me before came forward and took it from her hand.

"You're the shade," I said.

She didn't move, but I could hear a soft harumph from behind her mask. She shoved me toward the man, and he grabbed me from behind, the dagger rested against my throat. I stayed perfectly still, fighting to keep my breath even as the fear rose in my chest. I couldn't die. I knew that, but I knew I'd feel the slice of that blade across my throat.

The shade reached into her pocket and withdrew a vial, the same kind of vial the ferryman kept for this very moment. I couldn't help the panic that had me panting, trying to think of any way to slip from the demon's grasp as she stopped in front of me again with the vial. She raised it and I caught sight of the only shimmer of gold among the silver adorning her body. She wore a gold bracelet around her wrist, the same one Alison stole from me.

I raised my hand, harnessing my power and focusing on her face. I let out a yell and her silver helmet popped from her head. She turned her back on me, doubling over with her hands over her head. The helmet flew toward me. The demon let go, giving me just enough time to catch the helmet, turn, and run as fast as I could away from them.

I weaved around the trees, flying at a speed that would've impressed Puck. I could hear the demons tearing after me. A brief glance at the trees behind me was all it took. My foot caught on a tree root, and I fell, sliding along the snow. An elm stopped my momentum.

When I looked up, it was into the red eyes of the dagger-wielding demon as he raced toward me. Just as I scrambled to my feet in the slick snow, a dark shape swooped from the trees and carried the demon back into the treetops. I looked up and could see the tip of a black wing, a loud sound between an animalistic shriek and a human yell rang out as the attacker disappeared.

I gripped the helmet and started running again, not thinking about where I was going until now. My speed slowed as I got to a thinner section of trees where the snow was deeper. I could see something in the distance, some kind of structure. I focused my gaze on in and forced my legs to move as fast as they could through the snow.

I could make out more of the structure as I got closer, realizing now that it was the community building in the national park. I was in a stretch of forest I had run through months ago when I'd chased the ferryman. The recognition sent a wave of relief over me that vanished as soon as a pair of arms reached out from behind a tree and pushed me into the trunk of large oak.

My scream was cut off when a hand clapped over my mouth. I stopped struggling when I looked up into Angel's face. He shushed me but didn't lower his hand even after I'd quieted. I could hear what he had heard now, a pair of feet swishing through the snow behind us. He stayed still as a statue as the demon approached, not moving until I could hear the feet just behind the tree. When Angel moved, it was so quick that I hadn't realized he was gone until I heard the demon hiss.

I heard the creak of a tree and I moved away from my hiding spot just in time to see Angel's lips go to the demon's neck. There was a stomach-turning squishing and then ripping sound as Angel tore a hunk of the demon's throat away, black goo spraying over his face and onto the white snow.

The demon slumped to the snow, where it broke apart like black ash. Angel turned to face me, his expression apologetic beneath the gore. He spat a mouthful of dark liquid onto the snow and wiped his mouth with his forearm, smearing the black gunk over his skin. Before I could say a word, I heard the crunching of tires from the parking lot a few yards away. I glanced at the community building as Izzy's Jeep pulled to a stop behind Macy's red Charger. When I looked back at Angel, he was already gone.

"Tori! Tori, what happened?" Jamie asked.

I looked to the left and saw him running through the trees toward me, Emily trailing just behind.

"The shade," I said, noticing now that my hands were shaking. I felt like my entire body had turned to Jell-O and I was only standing by sheer will.

Jamie stopped a couple of feet away, looking from me to the dark goop over the snow and the pile of ash. Emily moved around him to reach me. She put her hands on my shoulders and looked me up and down.

"Are you okay?" she asked.

I took a deep breath, feeling for a second like I might throw up. "Yeah."

"What happened?" Jamie asked, coming out of his thoughts, and slowly moving toward me.

"The shade. It's her. It's the witch," I said, the words falling from my mouth quickly.

Jamie's brows furrowed. "What witch?"

"The witch from the Shadowlands. She's the one who got me out of the castle, the one who saved me."

"How do you know that it's her?" Emily asked, dropping her hands and moving back from me in shock.

I took two steps toward the oak tree and leaned against it. "I saw her bracelet. She gave me a bracelet to pay the ferryman for passage back through the gate. He let me keep it. It's what's allowing her to be here. That bracelet is how she can stay here."

They both stared back at me in awe for a long moment. Jamie broke first with a deep sigh. He nodded.

"Okay," he said. "We know who we're looking for. What does she look like?"

I shook my head. Why couldn't I remember her? I thought about how I woke up on the dock first, retracing my steps until I was reeling her boat in from the lake and then to the moment when she stepped onto the dock. I know she was built like me, short and slender.

"She had long blonde hair, like to her hips long. She's ... She's around my size ..." I didn't have anything else to go on. She was an ordinary woman. I was so frustrated that I came face-to-face with the shade, and I still didn't know what she looked like. I could feel my eyes burn.

Jamie let out a sigh, his expression so sympathetic that it hurt. His arms rose to from his side but stopped halfway. I wondered if he would have hugged me if Emily wasn't with us. I wondered if I would let him.

"Let's get you warmed up. It's freezing," Emily said and wrapped her arm around my shoulders.

I let her lead me toward the community building, Jamie trailing after us. Macy got out of her car first, crossing the parking lot and nearly slipping twice on the way. Izzy opened the door to her Jeep and stepped out while Mr. Puck leaned over the center console to try looking around her.

"Are you okay?" she asked, breathless. She wrapped her arms around me.

"Nothing that a little immortality can't heal," I said. She wasn't tolerating the dark joke though, reaching out and giving my shoulder a gentle shove. It nearly sent me falling into the snow, regaining my footing with help from Emily.

"How does hot cocoa sound?" Emily asked.

"I'm meeting Becky for dinner. I need to go home," I said. I remembered the reason for the trip to the grocery store now. I guess pizza would have to do.

Macy groaned. "I want to do anything but go home right now, but I have to. My mom has started to notice that I'm never home and she thinks that I'm turning into my brother."

"Next time," Izzy said. "I think everyone could use a break after this. I about had a heart attack when I realized you were gone."

Puck snorted from the passenger seat. "I've never heard that many curses strung together. She's inventive."

Izzy's cheeks flushed.

"We can take you home," Emily said.

I hadn't noticed Jamie's Audi parked near the entrance of the parking lot until now. I wanted Izzy to come to my rescue and offer to take me home. She had before our plans were derailed. Instead, she said I should sleep with my knife under my pillow tonight before she climbed into the driver's seat of the Jeep.

"Shit," Macy said under her breath, pulling her phone from her pocket and pressing it to her ear. "Hey, Mom. I'm on my way home."

I waited until Macy's door shut and I heard the hum of the Jeep engine to look at Emily and Jamie. "I guess it's decided."

Emily smiled and linked her arm in mine, leading me toward the Audi as Jamie pressed a button to start the engine.

"There's a blanket in the backseat," Jamie said when we reached the car.

I opened the door and stared at the fluffy pink blanket. Emily's. I couldn't help but think about them cuddled in the backseat, car parked in one of the campsites in the national park. I was too cold to refuse the warm blanket, even with those thoughts racing through my mind. I felt my muscles relax as I sank into the warm seat and draped the blanket over my body.

Emily tugged her beanie from her head, using the mirror in the visor to flatten her hair.

I watched Jamie's face in the rearview mirror as he buckled his seatbelt. He let out a long sigh, massaging is temple for a moment. With a deep inhale, he put both hands on the wheel and looked up. Our eyes met in the mirror. I looked down at my lap until he finished reversing and we moved forward.

He drove slowly. The wheels of the car crunched over the ice until we were on the salted pavement of the highway again, heading toward Burbrook. Emily set her hand on top of Jamie's which was draped over the gear shift. She had barely touched him when he moved his hand from hers. He turned on the radio and then set his hand on the steering wheel, looking a little awkward with both hands positioned there. Tense.

The radio host finished reading an ad for a tattoo parlor in Denver and then "Helter Skelter" by the Beatles filled the silence in the car. I saw Emily's annoyed expression in the rearview mirror before she pulled her knees to her chest and leaned on the door, watching as the snow-covered trees whizzed by.

No one spoke until we pulled up to the curb outside my house. My body didn't want to leave the warmth of the fuzzy blanket, but I didn't want to sit in the car any longer. The air was stifling with frustrated energy between Emily and Jamie.

"Hey," Jamie called out after I'd shut the back door. His window rolled down and he shifted in the front seat, obscuring my view of a confused Emily.

"Um ... What's up?" I asked, wrapping my arms around my torso in an attempt to keep warm.

Jamie hesitated. He leaned out the window, one forearm

propped on the car door. Snowflakes landed in his hair as he sat there. "Do you still leave your window open?"

The question made my stomach twist. I wasn't sure what to tell him. He must've taken my silence for a no because he nodded his head after a moment in defeat.

"We'll talk another time," he said.

I nodded, pulling my arms tighter around me as if I might fall apart. "Yeah. Um, another time."

He nodded. He stayed hanging out the Audi window for a long moment, sincere eyes looking back at me as though he wanted to say something important. Finally, he sat back in his seat and rolled the window up. I waved at them as the Audi pulled away from the curb.

My breath swirled in front of my face. I'd almost forgotten how cold I was. Talking with Jamie was always like that. I felt my stomach sink as I thought about how I had yet again pushed him away. The truth was that my window was closed, but I hadn't locked it. Not once.

CHAPTER 23

The first day back at work Angel never showed. I worked the whole store alone and by the end of my shift, I felt guilty for the times he had worked by himself. It was lonely. I had been prepared to lie and say he'd gone home sick when Willow made her rare afternoon appearance, but the first thing she said stopped me.

"Angel has the flu," she said. "And he put in his two weeks' notice when he called me this morning. He said he might be in by the end of the week but wasn't sure."

So, that's how I knew to bring something to work for the rest of the week.

Day two, I spent my shift going over practice SAT questions. Becky thought it was crazy that I still planned on taking the SAT in the spring after my acceptance letter from CU came, but a few extra points could turn into thousands in scholarship funds. Besides, it was the homework Mrs. McKellen advised us to do for the academic team. We had done a few practice meets and several by Zoom this semester, but the spring was when we would do our competing.

Willow had offered to work the Christmas Eve shift, but my dread for the lonely shifts had turned into a kind of meditation. I knew that the store would be mostly empty all day. We were closing at four thirty anyway, so it wasn't like I'd be working that hard or very late. I told her to enjoy Christmas and as a thanks, I found a red giftbag on the counter when I came into work that morning.

Before opening the shop, I pulled out the white tissue paper and found a candle inside that smelled like berries and a red scarf with a matching hat that I knew Willow had knitted herself. I put the gift on the hook under my coat and started getting ready for my shift.

I tied my apron around my waist and began brewing coffee first. Once the smell had filled the store and the sound of coffee dripping into carafes filled the silence, I unlocked the front door and switched the sign, so it read "open."

I poured myself a cup of the dark roast and sat behind the counter with my SAT book opened to a set of practice questions. I wrote the answers lightly in the book so I could go through and erase the pencil after I'd checked them. I nearly fell off the stool when someone cleared their throat a few feet in front of me.

"Shit," I breathed, my shock turning to annoyance when I saw Emily there. She had a pink beanie on her head with a little yarn pom-pom on the top, her blue, pink, and blonde hair in perfect curls underneath. She had a shoebox between her hands with a smaller box balanced on top.

"I figured now would be a good time to talk," she said and sat the box down on the counter. She reached over and dragged a barstool over so she could sit in front of me.

"I'm kind of in the middle of my shift," I started.

She smiled bashfully. "I know, but it's Christmas Eve and since it warmed up a little, it's also not the nicest outside with all the slushy roads and what-not. Also, you are not the easiest person to catch alone."

I groaned internally. "You know that nothing is secret in our circle."

"Well, almost nothing," she said. She looked back at me with such a questioning look that it made me nervous. She knew.

"I don't keep any secrets that might affect our circle," I told her.

"I know that you and Jamie had a thing a while back and I think that's probably why it's so weird between us," Emily said, moving the small box from the larger one and setting it in front of me. "Which is why I wanted to talk just us. I wanted you to have a gift and I want to try making things a little less awkward."

"Emily, I don't know if that's possible."

"Do you still have feelings for him? Is that why?" she asked, her tone honest. There wasn't a single threat in the way she said it, just curiosity and it made my stomach knot even more with guilt. Was I just being petty? I had no reason not to like her, but I wished I had a good reason.

"No," I said, trying to sound as firm as I could.

"Then, let's move forward and be friends," Emily said with a smile. "Open it."

She pushed the box closer to me. I pulled the top off to reveal a handmade bracelet. It was an intricate braid, with a golden disk in the center that was stamped with the roman numerals for six. On the other side was my name. Victoria, not Tori. No one ever called me Victoria.

"Thank you. It's beautiful," I said and lifted the bracelet from the box.

She shrugged. "I made one for everyone. Yours took the longest, because your name is the longest."

Which meant she'd used everyone else's nicknames like Will and Izzy.

"Jamie is kind of long to stamp on this disc," I said. My name was stamped in tiny letters, so the entire thing fit. I made sure to tie the bracelet on with the six-side facing up.

"I guess so. I hadn't thought about it. I put Jay on his. That's what I've always called him."

They had nicknames. Great.

"So, what's in the other box?" I asked, doing my best to keep the pettiness from creeping into the conversation. She moved it so it sat between us and took off the lid. The inside was littered with photos and a couple stacks of letters that were kept together with rubber bands.

"I wanted to share it with you," Emily said. "I thought we could get to know each other better and I thought I might as well be the one to start."

I picked up the picture on top and couldn't help but smile. It was a photo of Izzy, but her hair was cut short to her shoulders and hung in curls. She had more makeup on than I'd ever seen her wear, almost making her look like a different person. It was a girly version of her, complete with a miniskirt and pink top. She stared at herself in the mirror as she swiped on some lipstick. Emily must have taken it from the doorway before Izzy realized it.

"That one was before a party. Believe it or not, Izzy went through a period where she dressed pretty preppy before the black took over her wardrobe."

"I find that hard to believe," I said with a laugh and put the photo back in the box. Emily had removed a stack of Polaroid's and was laying them over the countertop. She wasn't in a single one, always behind the camera. Many of them were of Jamie, candid moments of him behind his piano, with a guitar propped on his knee, or outside.

Emily must have loved taking photos of nature, because there were many of them. They were professional in quality. I stared at a photo of a fall leaf with a raindrop clinging to it for a long time, studying every line in the surface before noticing all the oranges, browns, and yellows that were unfocused in the background.

"You're really good," I told her and handed back the stack.

She finished laying out the next on the counter before taking it from me. "Thank you. I love natural elements. I love the world exactly the way it should be, with the trees and snow untouched by winter boots."

I looked up at her as she studied a photo of a field. She didn't look like the kind of person who liked things naturally. Everything from her tri-colored hair to her trendy outfits seemed more urban.

"Have you always dyed your hair?" I asked, interrupting her thoughts.

She shook her head. "The Shadowlands made me a different person." She said the words slowly, like there was a darker meaning there that only she understood. My brain was suddenly full of images of the dock, the castle, the strange demons I saw as I tried escaping.

"You're lucky you got out. I was able to just leave somehow, but you ..." I watched as her somber expression melted, a small smile returning as she lifted her eyes from the photos to me.

"Can I ask you a question I've been wondering for a while?" she asked.

"If it's how I'm able to do that and about all the other weird things, I have no clue."

"No," she said with a giggle. "After that first circle meeting when we burned that pendant you had, I went to the fireplace to try and find it. After I gave it a little more thought, I felt bad for making you toss it. That pendent could be more important than we think. I still don't think it's a good idea for you to wear it, but ... Anyway, I couldn't find it and I thought that maybe you ..."

I wanted to lie, but the way she looked at me now told me she already knew. Who else would have it? She'd probably already asked the others. Macy would never admit that she used her powers to help me. She hadn't yet told them she'd even discovered her powers of invisibility.

The best way to tell a lie is to keep it as close to the truth as possible.

"I pulled it from the fire. I haven't worn it since though," I told her.

She wasn't mad. She nodded as though she understood.

"I just wondered," she told me. "Where do you keep it now? You probably should lock it somewhere safe."

"I do," I said and left it at that. It was becoming more common, this whole keeping secrets thing. There was no way it could be good for our circle.

I was thankful that she didn't ask any more questions about the necklace. Instead, we looked through all the photos from the box, Emily occasionally giving me an explanation of where the photo was taken or what she remembered about that day.

"You've always been an artist," I said and handed back the last photo from the stack. She placed the whole stack of Polaroids in the box and pulled out a new one. "Why switch to photography over painting like you did before?"

Emily started laying out the photos. These were all of people; I recognized most of them as Izzy or Jamie. A lot of Jamie.

"I love how candid photos can be. I love capturing a beautiful moment, not just the way it looks, but the emotion attached to it," she said.

I scanned the photos, my gaze stopping on several photos of Jamie sitting on a blanket. He was in a meadow, lavender bent with the wind behind him. This was the meadow he'd talked about. Izzy hinted that he hadn't been the same since the meadow and I figured it had to do with the girl he'd fallen in love with then.

"Can I ask you a question I've been wondering a while, since I answered yours?" I asked.

Emily smiled at me and shrugged.

"What happened in the meadow?"

Emily's smile dimmed and she lowered her eyes to the photos I had been staring at before. She picked up the one I liked the best. Jamie was sitting the blanket. A picnic basket was in front of him and a place setting for two already laid out. He was unpacking the basket when he must have glanced back to look at her, a sly smile tugging at one corner of his lips.

"I died," Emily said softly. "Well, I thought so. That's when I was swept into the Shadowlands."

"How?" I asked. The gate was in the middle of the lake. How had she ended up there when the meadow was a mile away?

"Jamie always said he liked to take things slow; he was a man of his time. I think he was just nervous," Emily started, holding the photo between her hands. "We went to the meadow that day because it was supposed to be the next level in our relationship. We hadn't even kissed yet and Jamie said he was ready for everything a match entailed. We went for lunch. We kissed and nothing happened. We didn't match. Jamie was devastated. I said that it didn't change that we were in love, but he felt … Jamie said it wasn't enough when someone else out there …"

"Jamie broke it off?" I asked.

Emily nodded.

"We had an argument about it. He wanted to go back to the car. I didn't. We fought the whole way back to the park. A few days after that, we were back in the park chasing a bunch of demons. Izzy, Jamie, and I chased them to the meadow where we could fight without the trees in the way. One of them caught me and that was it. It must have escaped back to the Shadowlands with my body, because when I healed and woke up that's where I was."

After a long moment of silence, Emily took a deep breath.

"I'm sorry," I said.

Emily began collecting the photos into a stack and then put them away, closing the lid on the box. She swiped a stray tear from the corner of her eye and then looked back at me with a forced smile.

"Merry Christmas, Tori," she said and stood up from the stool. She gathered the box in her arms and hurried to the front door, my call of "Merry Christmas" getting lost in the tinkle of the bell over the door.

CHAPTER 24

The whole house smelled of ham and fresh rolls. I went to the kitchen to find Becky bent over with the oven door open. Two pots were steaming on top of the oven. A sheet pan full of enough rolls for a family of four sat on a trivet on the counter. Becky straightened up and turned, her face lighting up when she saw me.

"Go upstairs and get changed," she exclaimed. She motioned to her outfit with the spatula in her right hand. She was wearing a pair of flannel pajama pants with Santa hats on them and a long-sleeve shirt with the word *Naughty* written across the front. "I got you a matching set."

"Be right back," I said and went for the stairs.

Just like she said, the same pajama set was laid out on the bed only my shirt had the word *Nice* on the front. Next to the outfit was a red envelope. I could tell from the handwriting that it was from Mark.

I ripped it open, and a check fell out. The letter was short.

Congrats on getting into CU! Here's a present you can put toward this next stage of life.
Love, Mark

I had to get on my knees to reach the check under the bed. When I saw the amount, I almost shoved it back under there. A thousand dollars stared back at me. I was sure this was coming, at least in part, from a place of guilt. Mark had always harped about how important it was that I save for college and how he and Becky wouldn't be able to help me pay for my education. Did he actually have money to help me pay for it and it was just going to Terry this whole time? Or was it that he didn't really have the money, but this was a bribe to keep me from being mad at him anymore?

I groaned and sat the letter and the check on my nightstand. Whatever the motivation, I needed tuition money.

I changed into my new pajamas and went back downstairs. Becky had pulled the ham from the oven and was transferring it from the pan to a platter. She moved it to the table before she noticed me standing in the doorway.

"How was work?"

I shrugged. "The usual shift."

"Was that boy there?" she asked.

"No," I said and sat at the table in my normal seat. "He called in sick for the whole week and he put in his two weeks."

"Maybe it's a good thing?" Becky asked, moving a bowl of green beans to the table next. I could smell the bacon and brown sugar.

"Maybe." I didn't wait for her to sit down, spooning a helping of green beans onto my plate.

"So, I thought we would start a new Christmas tradition,"

Becky said, staring expectantly back at me while I loaded my plate with mashed potatoes and ham.

"Like what?" I asked.

Becky smiled. It was the happiest I'd seen her since Mark left. She went back to the counter and began digging in the shopping bags that sat on the far side of the counter. She pulled out a brown box and then turned to face me, holding the box so I could see that it was a full set of gingerbread house cookie cutters.

"When is the last time you baked anything?" I asked with a giggle.

Becky shrugged. "I thought it would be fun. It's not like we have to eat them, so if I burn the batch, it's fine."

She wasn't wrong about that. She began unpacking the plastic bags until the counter was full of gingerbread ingredients and toppings.

"Shouldn't we at least eat dinner first?" I asked.

"Okay. You're right," Becky said and finished unpacking the final bag. She was halfway to the table when she stopped and went to the oven. "Let me preheat it for the cookies anyway."

She finally joined me as I cut into the slice of ham on my plate. We talked about plans for our New Year's ski trip with Margot and her kids. I'd never been skiing before and Becky hadn't since she was a kid, so we came to a mutual agreement to stick to the easy slopes and if those were too hard, we'd just bail and drink hot chocolate at the lodge.

I started making a list of all the things we'd need to buy on her laptop as she started prepping the cookie sheets for gingerbread. As she rolled out the dough, I double-checked the batter to make sure she'd followed the ingredient list exactly, and I price-checked the items on my shopping list.

"Margot told me a little about the New Year's Eve party the

lodge throws and it sounds pretty amazing," Becky said as she shut the oven door.

As she set a timer on her phone, my thoughts went to the party at the Moore Estate planned for Saturday. The idea of a party made me a little nervous for two reasons. The last party I went to ended up with my death and rebirth as a guardian. What bothered me the most was what Emily and Jamie would be like after a few drinks. Maybe Jamie would be too annoyed by the surprise party to canoodle with his girlfriend.

I doubted it, but it was the only hope I had left that didn't have me calling Macy to cancel our plans immediately.

"So, um," I started.

Becky sat down across from me and looked up from her laptop as she pulled it toward her.

"Something wrong?" she asked.

"Oh, no," I said, quickly feeling the warmth spread over my face. If I didn't just say it now, I'd be caught for sure. "Izzy wants to have a girls' sleepover on Saturday to celebrate Christmas. She wants to do a gift exchange with Macy and me and she has this whole movie thing planned at their house ..."

"Sounds fun," Becky said with a shrug. "What are you getting them?"

My hand went to my wrist, and I found the bracelet Emily had given me.

"Bracelets," I told her.

Becky smiled, already busy looking over my list. "That sounds like a nice gift. Man, who would've thought ski pants would be this expensive?"

"Yeah. Pay nearly a hundred bucks to look like the Michelin Man," I said, glad for the subject change. Becky burst into laughter, which eased some of the tension that had gathered in my shoulders.

Becky continued scrolling through my list, relaxing a little more as she found all my notes about what we could rent at the lodge to save some money.

"I should run this list by Margot. She goes skiing all the time," Becky said. A moment later, I heard the whooshing sound of an email being sent. Becky sat back in her chair and closed the laptop.

"Is now a good time to do the pick-a-gift tradition?" I asked. Every Christmas Eve, we each would pick one gift to open and leave the rest to be opened on Christmas morning.

Becky stood up and hurried for the living room, coming back with a small box wrapped in red paper. "Open this one," she told me and sat the box on the table.

"Okay, but let me go get your gift," I said. I stopped halfway to the tree in the living room. While I was at work, she had put all the presents under the tree. I'd only gotten one gift for her, the single rectangular box wrapped in plaid among the sea of red boxes. Some of them were huge, making me feel a little guilty that I hadn't used more of my savings on her.

I picked up the box and took it back to the table where Becky sat. She didn't wait for me to sit before she tore away the paper and pulled the lid off the box to reveal a green sweater and pair of earrings.

"Thank you," she said with a gasp, holding the sweater to her chest. "This is so soft. Where did you get it?"

"One of the boutiques downtown. I went when I was on my break," I told her, turning the box on the table between my hands. It felt heavy. I hoped whatever inside wasn't expensive, but whatever it was felt suspiciously like an iPhone or some other electronic device.

"Your turn," Becky said, scooting her gift to one side so she could rest her elbows on the table expectantly.

I hesitated for a moment before carefully pulling the paper open by the edge of the wrapping paper. I could practically hear her internally screaming for me to just rip the paper off. One more pull and I was able to pull the wrapping paper away in one red sheet to reveal the box underneath. It was a Polaroid camera, one of those new kinds that could connect to your phone if you wanted it to.

"Thank you," I said and opened the box. It had already been opened and I could tell from the weight of the device that she'd already loaded it with film.

"Let's take a picture in our pajamas," Becky said and stood up. "Let's go to the tree."

I followed her to the living room. She adjusted the lighting so that it didn't overshadow the beautiful twinkling lights of the tree. We took several photos, a couple of cute ones I planned to post to Instagram and a few I planned to put on my bulletin board and never let anyone but us see.

When her phone timer went off, we moved back to the kitchen to pull the gingerbread pieces out. We let them cool while we decided on our designs and talked about what movie to watch while we decorated. Once the gingerbread was cool enough, we moved the icing and toppings to the living room coffee table, queued up *White Christmas* on Netflix, and started to build our houses.

I planned mine so that it looked as suburban as it could, with icing shutters and a perfectly manicured gumdrop side-walk. Becky wanted hers to look as magical as possible, like Santa himself might live there. By the end of the movie, my house was finished and as ordinary-looking as I could make it. Hers had grown to include a petting zoo of animal crackers and a pool she made by crushing blue rock candy.

By the time we cleaned the kitchen, we were both tired enough that we went to bed. I set the Polaroid camera on my desk and laid out the photos we'd taken, picking the goofiest one of us to pin to my bulletin board. I stepped back and looked at all the photos together, remembering who had taken them.

I focused on getting ready for bed, but it took my brain a while to slow down as I lay under the sheets and stared at the moonlight casting shapes over the floorboards.

I was the first one up Christmas morning and I'd still slept in nearly an hour. I started a pot of coffee and decided to make waffles. I spooned the last of the batter onto the waffle maker when Becky joined me. I picked up my camera from the counter and snapped a picture of her as she yawned.

She gasped when she realized what I'd done. "Rude."

I smiled back at her, waiting as the photo was printed. "It's your fault. You're the one who gave me a camera and told me to document everything."

I handed her the photo and she shook it as the photo of her slowly appeared. "I meant to document college, not my muffin top."

She sat the photo on the table next to the camera and grabbed the plate I'd made for her while I pulled the last waffle off the griddle. I decorated both our plates with whipped cream and red and green sprinkles just to be festive. We ate more than we should've in front of the Christmas Day Parade on TV. Once we finished, Becky didn't let me bother with cleaning up.

"Let's open presents first," she said, already pulling a long box from under the tree.

"I didn't get you anything else," I said.

She shrugged. "For me, the fun isn't in getting gifts. You know that. Now, open it."

She only grew more excited as I opened the presents, but a part of me grew heavier as I caught on to the theme. The first box was a set of dainty lights that came with clips. Becky told me they were so I could clip Polaroid pictures to them to create a kind of beautiful collage of the next four years of my life. The largest box was a new bedspread. One gift held not just one, but two different sweatshirts with the CU logo emblazoned on the front. I got another box of spirit wear that included jewelry and a puffy CU coat that Becky told me was for the cold football games.

The smallest present was the one that sent me over the edge. It was a red envelope, like the one Mark had given me, except this one wasn't a check. It was a bank statement, and the account name said it was my college fund. I felt the sting of the tears and then the warmth of the ones I couldn't hold back on my cheeks.

"Becky, you didn't have to do that," I told her.

She got to her knees to hug me. "I didn't mean to make you cry."

"Well, you could've told me before," I said. In a way, it felt like permission to take everything I'd wanted. I wanted to go to CU Boulder. I wanted to study law and become a lawyer and appear in court. I'd still need some loans, but the amount already in the account would get me through a year of school once I added in my savings from working at Beans and Books. The only thing keeping me from going was our circle.

"What's that one?" I asked, trying to change the subject and put an end to my tears.

Becky gasped and picked up the small box. "That one is for me."

She looked so proud of herself as she held the little box.

"You wrapped your own present?"

"Sure. Why not?"

"You already know what's in it," I said with a laugh.

Becky smiled and pulled off the red paper to reveal a shiny wooden box. It opened on a hinge, and I read the upside-down cursive engraved on the top.

Love Yourself

She lifted out a silver necklace with a diamond pendant. She let out a long sigh as she held it to her chest, the diamond shimmering under the light from the tree too beautifully to be anything but a real diamond.

"That's gorgeous," I told her.

She held it out so I could look at the pendant. "I found a woman on Etsy who turns engagement and wedding rings into new jewelry."

I lowered my hand from the necklace and Becky began clasping it around her neck, using one of the silver baubles on the tree as a mirror. I thought about all the Christmases the two of us had sat around the same tree with Mark. He always got her the same gift, jewelry.

"Becky," I started. I was a little afraid to ask, but I could see in her dimming expression that she already knew the question. "Are you ..."

There were so many things I wanted to ask. Was she okay? What would happen next? What would things be like after all was said and done? Would she be okay if I went away to college? My chest hurt at the thought of her all alone in this creaky house.

"We are getting a divorce," she said quietly. "I already filed the paperwork. He signed. It looks like it's going to be ... smooth."

I already knew that, but hearing the words still felt like a punch in the gut. I had never known anything different. It had always been me with Mark and Becky. My aunt and uncle. Our family in this old house that groaned when you walked down the stairs. I knew I was too old for custody to play a part in this. Still, I couldn't imagine the two Thanksgivings or Christmases or deciding to visit on the weekends when I came home from college. If I even went to college.

"Mark is a good man," Becky said, the words coming out one at a time as through it was hard for her to get each past her lips.

"He cheated on you. He has a whole other family with her," I said, feeling my eyes burn again. Christmas was supposed to be a time of celebration and gratitude, but so far it felt like I was saying goodbye to everything.

Becky scooted closer to me. "He did something he shouldn't have, something unforgiveable. He made a bad choice. He should've ended things a long time ago."

"Yes! He could've told her no. He could've told her he was married."

Becky shook her head. "I meant me." Her eyes filled with tears, but her words were so firm that I knew she'd come to terms with their meaning well before now. "He should've ended things with me a long time ago."

"Why?" I asked, swiping at the stray tear on my cheek.

Becky shrugged. "It's hard to let go of something you've put so much time and work into. I knew our relationship was over years ago, but I tried pretending like all the fighting was normal until I noticed how it was affecting you."

"This isn't your fault," I said.

She snorted. "I know that. The bastard cheated on me

instead of just telling me he loved someone else. I'm not defending him, but I am saying that as shitty as it is, a part of me understands."

I looked down at the wrapping paper strewn around us, folding a piece of it in half.

"Life really is short, Tori," Becky said. She laid a hand over mine, so I was forced to stop fiddling with the paper and look up at her. "It's too short to deny yourself of the things you want and the people you love."

My chest ached as I thought about Jamie. The only difference between what she said was that we were immortal. Jamie and Emily could be together forever, for decades or thousands of years and I would watch until things were safe. Would they ever be safe though? Would there always be a threat or a demon after us? Maybe the ferryman hadn't shown me that vision so I could prevent Jamie and me matching and undoing our immortality. Maybe there was another way to protect him.

CHAPTER 25

I almost drove over to the Moore Estate as soon as I knew what to do, but I knew there would be no getting Jamie away from Emily. Sometimes, being in a large crowd brought with it a strange kind of privacy. People would be too enamored with the Moore Estate at the party to pay much attention to anything except having a good time. It wasn't the quiet, romantic way I wanted to tell Jamie about our fate, but it would be easier to get lost among the crowd.

"This is just like a romantic comedy," Macy said from my bed after I told her all the details. "This is your running through the airport moment."

I wanted to scoff, but she was right. This was a big moment. This was the moment that could change everything. If it went the way I hoped, Jamie and I could be mortal by morning and our powers would be stronger.

"My hands are shaking so much," I said as I raised the eyeliner to my lid.

Macy pulled the liner from me and led me to my bed. With

a gentle push, I sat on the mattress, and she pulled my desk chair over so she could sit in front of me.

"I'll do it, but please let me do it my way," she begged. "This is the moment you confess your love for him, and I would love to make your lips look kissable and highlight your cheekbones."

Macy pouted, lower lip on full display until I agreed. I had been through my closet twice already and still didn't know what to wear to the party that was warm but wouldn't swallow me whole like most of my winter sweaters.

"Macy, I don't know how to do this," I groaned as she began unloading powders and lipsticks from her purse.

"Don't play dumb," Macy said with a beauty blender in one hand. "You two had so much chemistry it was, like, unreal. I can still sense it whenever you're in a room together. You are going to be fine."

"Okay, but what am I going to wear?" I asked as she began patting my face with the makeup sponge.

"You are going to wear that leather jacket you had on at the last party, a long-sleeve shirt, and we are going to take Izzy's heeled combat boots. I doubt she took them with her."

Izzy didn't need a pair of heels with her on her ski lodge trip with Mr. Puck, but she was the kind of girl to have that kind of killer outfit ready to go if the moment presented itself.

I let out a deep breath and tried relaxing while Macy finished doing my makeup. She told me to leave my hair natural, so I ran my usual products through my curls and stared back at myself in the mirror. Macy was right. The outfit, though simple and casual, looked like that kind of effortlessly sexy thing models had going for them.

I sorted through my small collection of jewelry and decided on a pair of dainty gold studs when I noticed the pendant the ferryman had given me. I hadn't worn it since Emily convinced everyone I should take it off. Maybe it was out of spite, but I put it on and let the pendant rest over my shirt. I smiled back at my reflection. The necklace changed the entire look, made it edgier. I looked badass.

Macy's jaw dropped when I went back to my bedroom.

"You look hot," she said.

"I know," I said with a giggle. She joined in the laughter and grabbed my wrist on the way to the hall.

"We're going to the sleepover. I'll see you tomorrow," I called toward the kitchen.

"Have fun and be safe," Becky called back just as I pulled the front door shut.

I climbed into Macy's car, and she turned the radio on high as we backed into the street. I felt warm despite the cold air in the car, too excited for the night to let it cool my spirit.

"Who knows about this party?" I asked.

Macy turned onto the road that led up Burbrook Mountain. "The whole school."

"No, I meant in our circle."

"Everyone except Puck and Jamie," Macy said, driving a little faster now thanks to Izzy's work melting the road earlier today. It was bone dry, not even a dusting of snow on the pavement.

We all had the code for the garage, so we let ourselves in once we parked in the driveway. My heart raced as we hurried upstairs and into Izzy's room. Macy ducked into the closet and came back out with the heeled combat boots. I took them from her and started to put them on while she checked her phone.

"It's almost nine," Macy said, a blue glow falling over her face as she opened an app on her phone.

"What time are people coming?" I asked.

She locked her phone and stuck it in her pocket.

"Any time now," she said. "I'll get Emily to help me in the kitchen. You go find Jamie."

My stomach twisted so tight I felt a little sick. "Macy, wait."

I took one step after her and nearly fell from the weight of the shoes. They were heavy the way my snow boots were, far from the delicate feel of any other pair of heels. By the time I recovered and made it into the hall, Macy was gone. I could hear her calling for Emily. It was her usual battle cry, the classic whoop that was always followed by a wild night she'd talk about for weeks after.

"Tori?" Jamie asked.

I turned around. He was standing in the doorway of his bedroom, a demon dagger in his right hand. He replaced it in the sheath concealed at his waistband.

"Hi," I said.

"What's going on?"

"Well, um, I thought we should talk."

He looked confused for a moment before his expression melted and a kind of sadness replaced it. I could feel my resolve fading fast.

Jamie shook his head and the words he spoke came out in almost a whisper. "I can't keep doing this, Tori."

"That's what I wanted to talk about," I told him. "I don't want to keep doing this."

"I've been waiting for you to prove it," he said, angry.

The anger burned in my chest. Months ago, I wanted the same thing.

"Then why are you with her?" I asked, surprised at the venom in my tone.

Jamie looked conflicted. He looked at the floor before looking back at me. "I don't know."

Before either of us could do anything, cheers erupted

downstairs. Jamie brushed past me and stopped at the top of the stairs, leaning over the railing. He looked back at me with shock in his eyes.

"What ... I didn't ..." I struggled to find the words, but he didn't hang around for me to find them. He hurried down the stairs, calling out for Macy.

The bottom floor was already full of people, helping Macy connect her phone to the Moore Estate's sound system and passing around plastic cups. A group of boys I recognized from the football team came through the front door and kept me from grabbing the back of Jamie's shirt.

He lifted his phone to his ear, and I took the chance. I raised my hand and used my powers. The phone flew from his hand and into mine. I quickly hung up the call to Izzy before she could pick up, tucking the phone into my back pocket.

Jamie whirled around to face me.

"She's on a date," I told him.

"Did you plan this?" he asked.

"No," I said, glad it was the truth. I was a terrible liar.

He relaxed a little as he took in our surroundings. It was like every senior from Burbrook High had suddenly appeared in the house and the underclassmen were filing in the door after them. If he wanted to put a stop to it and kick them all out, it would take him an hour to usher them all out and that was if they were cooperative.

"Where's Macy?" he asked with a sigh.

"Probably the kitchen," I said and led the way.

Music began playing throughout the speakers in the walls, the volume increasing until it was too loud to have a normal conversation over. Macy and Emily were working together to dump a pink drink into a giant glass jar. When they saw us approaching, Emily quickly filled a cup from the spigot and approached Jamie with a smile.

"Have a drink and relax," she said and pressed a kiss to his cheek.

Macy cast me a questioning look and I knew she wanted me to explain what had happened. I shook my head and took a plastic cup from the table and filled it with the mystery drink. It tasted like lemonade, good enough that I took a couple of long sips in the hope that it would make me feel less mortified at nearly throwing myself on Jamie Quinn.

"Have you guys been planning this?" he asked, taking the cup but not drinking.

Emily and Macy exchanged looks. I caught Jamie's eye, which froze me in place. The anger in his expression faltered a little as he stared back.

"Does that really matter now that it's happening?" Macy asked, sending him the same innocent doll eyes I'd seen her use on boys at school to get what she wanted.

That wouldn't work on Jamie.

"Well, you guys can kick them all out then," he said and slammed the cup down on the counter. He nearly slipped past two boys making their way through the kitchen for the growing sea of dancers in the living room. Emily grabbed on to one of his forearms, sliding herself in front of him and moving her hands to his face. He stopped, his lips inches from hers and she said something to him that got lost in the bass of a trendy pop song.

Emily draped her arms around his neck and pulled him back toward us, whispering in his ear. Jamie looked at me over her shoulder. The anger was gone from his face now. My stomach twisted in knots as his eyes flicked over my body before catching my gaze again. His shoulders relaxed and he slipped away from Emily, putting the counter between him and us.

"I think we all need to relax a little," I said.

Jamie nodded slowly. He opened a cabinet and took down a glass and then reached for a half-empty bottle of vodka that sat next to the drink dispenser. He poured a shot of it in the glass and then raised it to his lips, downing the vodka without so much as a grimace.

Emily let out a squeal and grabbed Macy's hand. "Let's all go join in."

They both bounced toward the group of dancers in the living room. Jamie rounded the counter and stepped in front of me. He handed the empty glass to me and drew in close.

"Give me some time." He said the words like a promise, his soft expression confirming it and easing some of the tension in my shoulders. He lifted the red cup from the counter and disappeared into the crowd to join the others.

I walked the first floor, thankfully the only area the party had spread to, while I drank my first cup of spiked lemonade. Everyone was having a great time, and no one was getting too crazy yet.

When I looked up from refilling my cup, Connor Taylor stood next to me with an empty cup.

"Hey," I said. The last time I talked with Connor was at Starbucks when he was going to ask Tasha James out to homecoming. "Are you here with Tasha?"

"Yeah, actually," he said and leaned over to fill his cup. "She's out there somewhere dancing. That girl ... She's too good for me."

The way he smiled was infectious, so wholesome.

"I'm glad things worked out. She's so nice," I said and took a sip of my drink. Emily or Macy must have refilled the jug because this batch tasted much stronger than the first helping.

"So, what about Quinn?" Connor asked with a sly smirk.

"Oh, that's not ... He's with someone," I said, hoping my reply didn't give anything away. I lifted my drink to my lips to hide my face.

Connor snorted. "Maybe not."

I swallowed hard, my throat burning. "What do you mean?"

He smiled. "He was talking with that blonde girl and then he left pretty quick. She looked annoyed with whatever they were talking about."

Oh no.

When Jamie said he needed time, I thought he meant that we would talk later. As in, after the party when it was quiet and private.

I felt my phone vibrate in my back pocket and I pulled it out, telling Connor I'd see him later as I moved from the kitchen to the long hall that led to the garage. I answered the call and put it to my ear.

"Is this about Tori?" Emily's voice exploded through the speaker.

I stuttered into the phone, realizing now that I'd stuck my phone in a different pocket than normal before I'd snagged Jamie's before the party.

"Tori? Why do you have Jamie's phone?"

Finally, I hung up and looked down at the phone in my hand. The screen saver lit up, a photo Emily took in the bathroom mirror of her smiling while Jamie kissed her cheek. This was a disaster. She's a member of our circle. It wasn't like she'd just leave if Jamie broke up with her.

"Tori," he said, sending all the panic from my mind.

Jamie came down the hall to join me among the decades of photos of him and Izzy hanging on the wall.

"Did you break up with her?" I asked, shoving the phone back in my pocket.

He let out a sigh and shook his head. "No."

My heart sank.

"Okay." It was the only word I could muster, and it came out as small as I felt.

"I told her we needed to slow down so I could figure some things out," he said. He snorted and shook his head in disbelief, and he closed the gap between us so we were just a few feet apart. "She already knew why I was asking. Everyone seems to expect it. I can't pretend that I don't feel something pulling us closer together, even though we've put some distance between us."

"I know."

He moved closer and I took a step away, feeling the wall of the hallway behind me. A quick glance toward the party confirmed that we were alone and too far down the hallway for anyone passing by to notice us standing in the dim light.

Jamie stood just in front of me, so close that if I raised my arms just a fraction, I could touch him.

"Do you ever think about that maze?" he asked. "If things would be different now?"

"All the time,"

He hesitated before stepping closer. He didn't touch me, but the bottom of his leather jacket brushed mine.

"If I kissed you right now ..."

"We'd match," I said.

His brow furrowed. "How do you know?"

"Because the ferryman showed it to me," I said.

"What? Why?"

What was I supposed to say? My hesitation must've shown my face, because he backed away.

"You know something, don't you?" he asked, more curious than accusatory.

"Jamie ..."

"Why would the ferryman tell you we're a match? That's something they'd want to prevent."

I had to tell him something or he'd never stop. That didn't mean it had to be all the truth.

"The ferryman was your father. That's why he told me," I said.

Jamie looked even more confused. He opened his mouth to speak, but the shock kept him silent. He turned from me a moment, fingers going to the leather watch strap he always wore around his wrist. After taking a calming breath, he turned to face me again.

"He gave me the pendant for a reason. That's why I didn't think it was dangerous when all of you tried getting me to destroy it." I pulled the necklace from around my neck and showed him the pendant. "He wore that all the time. I saw it in that picture on the mantel. Do you recognize it now?"

Jamie took the pendant in his hand and ran a thumb over the roman numerals stamped in the metal. He nodded, still studying the pendant. When he finally looked up, his mouth parted in awe.

"How did you get that out of the fire?"

"Macy did."

"Macy?" he asked with a laugh.

I nodded. "She triggered her powers that night. She can become invisible."

We both laughed and didn't stop until Jamie moved closer to me. I backed up until I was against the wall again. He pressed his hands to the hallway next to me, inches from my waist.

"If you kissed me right now, we would match and be stronger than anything that comes after us," I said.

Jamie's forehead rested against mine.

"I won't kiss you tonight," he said. "But when I do ..."

My heart fluttered in my chest as a smile spread across his face. He pulled away and left me aching for more.

"Emily and I are going to the meadow tomorrow to exchange Christmas gifts. I will talk to her then," Jamie said.

I followed him back to the party, where I lost him in the crowd again. I went back to the kitchen for a fresh cup of lemonade, turning from the jug to see Macy hurrying toward me with an excited smile on her face.

"We've been looking everywhere for you," she giggled.

We?

She dragged me through the crowd and to a small sitting area in the corner of the living room. Emily scooted over on the couch to make space for me. Macy plopped down on the armrest next to Emily.

"Who wants to play a drinking game?" Macy asked.

"I think you've hit your limit," I told her.

Emily laughed next to me as though we'd never had that awkward phone conversation.

"Are there really limits when you're immortal?" Macy asked. She held her drink out in a toast. "Here's to all of us, one guardian closer to completing our circle."

"To sealing the gate for good," Emily said and lifted her cup.

We pressed out plastic cups together, Macy's spilling over into both of ours. She raised her cup to her lips and realized it was empty.

"I'll be right back," she said and darted into the crowd.

"I'll stop her," I said, but Emily grabbed my cup hard enough that some of the drink spilled onto my pants. Her eyes could've pierced right through me.

"I know that you and had Jamie had this thing between you before, and I know that since we aren't a match you feel like you might have some kind of guardian connection, but remember this," she said and leaned in close. "If you two match, you become mortal. That makes you stronger, but that makes you easier to kill. That makes *Jamie* easier to kill."

She let go of me and stood up, leaning over me to deliver her final warning.

"Stay away from him."

She stormed off. I raised my cup to my lips, noticing that the drink was frozen solid. I set the cup aside and decided to go find Macy before she said or did something she'd regret. I had just reached the kitchen, which was packed with people thanks to a competition between Sean Peterson and some underclassmen to see who could chug their drink the quickest.

Just as Sean finished and spiked his cup on the tile floor, the room erupted in a deafening cheer, and someone wrapped their arms around my waist and pulled me out the back door.

CHAPTER 26

I whirled around to face my attacker, freezing when I recognized Angel.

"What are you doing here?" I asked.

Angel held his hands up, not at all concerned with whether I would unleash my powers on him despite the gesture. "I just want to talk."

"Pretty bold of you to come to the headquarters of a whole circle of guardians who kill beasts like you."

He nodded, too focused on whatever he wanted to ask to react to my insult. It was strange. He wasn't the blood-driven monster that Jamie and Izzy told me that vampires were, stalking and killing just about anything with a pulse. Was he picky?

"What do you want?" I asked.

He snorted as if the answer was obvious. "The cure."

I didn't reply. Why would I know anything about a cure and what kind of cure was he after anyway?

Angel glanced in the windows, the crowd busy prepping

for another round of their drinking game. He motioned for me to follow and for some reason, I did. We moved away from the windows and to the corner of the house where we couldn't be seen.

"What cure?" I asked, rubbing Izzy's boots over the snow to try compacting it in case I needed to fight. At least the heavy boots were coming in handy.

Angel let out a deep breath. He was nervous. This wasn't like him at all. He took everything in stride, not even phased when that woman from out of town threatened to toss a coffee in his face after I'd made her drink wrong.

"Is the cure for you? Like, a cure for vampirism?" I asked. The way his jaw tensed told me I was right, and it was a sore spot.

"You don't know what it's like," he said, voice shaking.

"I know that you have to kill people to survive."

"I don't kill anyone of worth."

I scoffed. "Who are you to decide that?"

"Take your lawyer hat off for a minute and think about the reality of what I'm going to tell you. Can you do that? No judgments? One minute?"

He wasn't demanding but begging me. I had the power here and though I'd never done it before, I was sure that I could hold my own against him if I needed to. I nodded.

"I ended up here after I took out a serial killer in Denver," he started.

"You mean fed on him," I said before I could stop myself. His pleading look had me apologizing. "Sorry. Go on."

"I ended up in Burbrook because of something I heard on the streets. There were demons who had left Burbrook because of a huge power they felt here. They talked about there being a circle of guardians and one of them was something they called an anchor. They didn't explain anything except that no demon would be dumb enough to stick around. So, that's why I came here."

"You need a guardian?"

He nodded.

"It sounded like your circle wouldn't be busy with demons and I thought, not exactly looking like a monster from the Shadowlands, that I could meet with you and talk."

How diplomatic. It was exactly what the Angel I knew from work would do, the man who enjoyed creating different drinks, the man who told me he'd cover my shift while I cried in the back. The more I studied his face, the more I wanted to believe every word he said. I didn't have a reason not to trust him other than the fact that he was a vampire—and that was just what I had heard of vampires from Izzy and Jamie.

Was it possible that vampires, like that witch girl I met on the dock of the Shadowlands, were not monsters bound by their instincts the way other demons were?

"So, what exactly do you need from our circle?" I asked, the words coming out slowly.

He hesitated before speaking. "I need the blood of a guardian."

My heart skipped. *Blood.* Why did everything come down to that? What made my blood gold to the Shadowlands?

"No," I said and moved toward the backyard.

"Wait!"

I felt a hand grip my bicep like iron, instantly making everything from the elbow down go numb. I knew his hold was too strong to break, so I used his pull to my advantage. With my free hand, I pulled the demon dagger free from my waist and I let it sink into his abdomen when he pulled me to his chest.

I heard him gasp in my left ear, but he didn't let go. I twisted the knife, ignoring the sick feeling rising into my throat. An annoyed groan rumbled within him, and he placed a hand over mine, pulling the knife in my grip from his gut and gently pushing me away until I stood a few feet back with the dripping blade.

I stared back at him, shocked that despite the pained expression on his face, he wasn't more alarmed. He raised his shirt to reveal the wound. It was already knitted together in a pink line, fresh blood still dripping over his waistband from a nonexistent gash.

"Those magic blades don't work on vampires," he said.

I thought back to the blonde vampire who attacked me in Holston. Izzy kept yelling for me to stake her.

"Why *my* blood?" I asked.

He looked at me as though it was obvious. "I planned to locate your circle's headquarters, but I met you first. It was easy. Why try finding the entire circle when you were already right there and trusted me?"

I watched for any sign that he was lying or hiding part of the truth. He was either very good, or he didn't know a thing about me.

"So, it could've been any of us?"

"Yes," he said. "I need the blood of a guardian. It doesn't have to be much. From what I was told, a single drop would be enough. All I need is a guardian willing to give it."

I looked down at the demon dagger in my hand, blood still dripping into a small pool at my feet. Izzy would be pissed about the stains on the toes of these boots, but if she knew what I was doing in them ...

"Why should I trust you?" I asked.

He sucked in a deep breath. His eyes went to the stars for a moment before he looked back at me. "I saved you from that demon chasing you in the national park."

I thought the dark shape seemed strange. I knew it wasn't a guardian.

"I couldn't give you my blood if it was all over the snow," I said.

He opened his mouth to speak but closed it a second later. He nodded.

"I'm leaving Burbrook for New York, but I thought I would ask for your help one more time. I know I don't deserve it, but I am a man of my word. I'm gone. This is the last that you will ever see of me. If you don't want to give me your blood, I'll continue my search for another guardian. For what it's worth, I didn't just save you to earn your trust. I consider you a friend too."

Again, I saw nothing but sincerity in his eyes.

I cleaned the demon dagger with a scoop of snow and my dark pants. I placed the edge of the knife to my palm and made the cut, holding my breath against the sting. He'd moved so quickly and so silently that I hadn't realized he was there until he held a small vial to my hand. I turned my palm so a stream of blood could flow into the tube until it was nearly full, the cut already healing.

Angel pressed a cork into the top and put the vial in his pocket, relief washing over his face.

"Thank you," he said.

I didn't say a word. Angel looked away from the house and I followed his gaze, ready for whatever was approaching. Nothing was there except for a stretch of untouched snow and an evergreen tree. When I looked back, Angel was gone.

When I rejoined the party, it was half the size as when I'd left. Jamie and Emily were standing across the living room and near the entryway where more partygoers were on their way out for the night.

"Where have you been?" Macy asked.

I was glad to see that she was holding a glass of water instead of more punch.

I almost lied and said I was in the bathroom, but Macy was the only person I'd told about Angel, and I'd already told her so many other secrets. What was one more?

"Angel was here."

She gasped. "That hot vampire from work? What did he want?"

This time, I did lie.

"He just wanted to apologize and say he was leaving. He's probably out of town now. Did you know, vampires can fly?"

Macy smiled and took a sip of her water. "Probably better this way. Everyone else would hunt him down if you told them what he was. He is a vampire, a hot one, but still..."

I nodded and looked toward the entryway. Jamie and Emily were gone and so was the crowd of people who had been chatting there before. The glow of a pair of headlights fell over the frosted glass of the front door.

"I would say that was a pretty successful party," I said and turned back to Macy.

She shook her head with a laugh. "It's so obvious that you don't go to parties. This was tame."

It had been more relaxed than I anticipated. Now that the room was empty, I could see that not a single piece of furniture was out of place and most of the mess was contained to the kitchen where the worst of it was the red Solo cups scattered over the countertops.

My phone buzzed in my back pocket. I pulled it out and stared as a text message popped up on my phone. I stared at the name of the sender until the screen went dark.

"Who's that?" Macy asked, voice full of concern.

I unlocked my phone and opened the message app. Angel's name with an emoji of a mug of coffee was lit up like a beacon. So much for the whole leaving and never hearing from him again.

I opened the text message and instantly felt my body go cold.

That soldier bitch from the forest is at the party.

His text threw me back in time to that afternoon. My first thought was how he would know. She dressed in armor from head to toe, but as the attack replayed in my mind I remembered. I'd knocked off her helmet. Angel might be the only person who knew what the shade looked like.

What did she look like?

"Tori, say something. I'm starting to freak out a bit," Macy said.

I looked up from my phone, making sure no one else was around to overhear. Jamie had just shut the front door and Emily walked toward the kitchen.

My phone vibrated in my hand, and I glanced down at the message.

. . .

She's blonde. I'm sorry. I'd know her if I saw her.

I handed my phone to Macy so she could read it. Telling Jamie and Emily would mean explaining what Angel was and I didn't want to distract from the real problem.

"Is everyone gone?" I asked Jamie and Emily.

Emily stacked the used cups into a single tower.

"Yes," she said. "Not a single car left and since we had to manually open the gate, we could make sure that no one was driving who shouldn't be."

"Well, I had a great time," Macy declared, sliding my phone into my back pocket as she passed for the living room. A second had barely passed before I felt it vibrate. This time it was Macy who'd texted.

I'm going to use my powers to do a sweep of the house. If she's here, we'll find her.

I had a feeling that she left with the guests. She'd probably come to scope out our headquarters. A party didn't make for a good location for an attack, especially considering our powers.

"I'm glad that's over. Things could've gone south fast," Jamie said, sending an annoyed look my way.

"I was in the dark almost as long as you were. I didn't have anything to do with planning this," I said, feeling the tension settle in the air as soon as the words fell from my lips. Emily's expression darkened, changing to a sweet smile the minute Jamie looked at her.

"I just thought we all needed to relax and celebrate. Christmas is supposed to be spent with friends," she said.

Wow, the whiplash!

Jamie relaxed, the fact that he let her wrap both arms around his bicep causing a pit to form in my stomach. Emily rose onto her toes to press a kiss to his cheek.

"I'm going to bed," he said and pulled his arm free, not giving us a second glance as he started toward the stairs. The cold response eased my nerves. It was funny now that I could see the frustration in Emily's eyes.

I held a hand toward the counter and used my powers to sweep the mess of plastic cups into a single pile. I pulled a trash bag from under the sink and held it open at the end of the counter, letting my powers do the work of pushing the pile into the bag. I propped the bag against the counter and started toward the stairs, ignoring the daggers Emily was sending my way from the dining room table.

I nearly reached the staircase when my feet flew from underneath me. I saw stars and the back of my head throbbed. The ground under me was slick and cold. It took me a second to realize I was lying on a patch of ice. My blurry vision slowly stabilized until I was staring up at the giant chandelier, Emily coming into view a moment later.

She crossed her arms, a sideways smirk on her face.

"You'd give me a concussion over a boy?" I asked her, propping myself up on my forearms.

She shrugged. "Guardians can't die."

"Not unless they have a match," I said. Her smile faded. "I guess it's not your fault. I'd be a petty bitch too if I was stuck forever in the Shadowlands after the boy I loved rejected me."

I knew I hit a nerve with the revelation. With a much fire in her eyes as I could see now, I wouldn't have put it past her to kick me in the ribs. She uncrossed her arms and leaned down, stopping a foot away from my face.

"You might think you and Jamie have something special, but if he really thought you were his match, then would he give me this?" she said the words like a whisper and raised her arm to show off the bracelet.

"What's so special about a Christmas gift between friends? He probably has a gift for all of us."

She laughed. "Has he professed his love for you?" she asked and straightened up, admiring her bracelet before smiling back at me. "Because he *engraved* his love for me."

She stepped over my legs and went up the stairs. Emily was a snake. You'd never see her coming and I had not expected the girl who spoke with that lilting tone and acted sweet as cotton candy to stand over me like a mountain lion over a deer.

I slid over the ice on the entryway until I found dry ground. I pulled off Izzy's boots, deciding to leave them by the door instead of replacing them in her closet. They were stained with blood, mine and Angel's.

My heart nearly left my body when I looked up from the floor and saw Macy standing in front of me, extending her hand to help me up.

"Geez. You scared me," I said and took her hand.

"There's no one in the house that shouldn't be," she said as she helped me up. "Did Angel text you anything else? Tell me we have more to go off than just some blonde girl."

I shook my head. "I wonder how many blonde girls go to Burbrook High."

"This is stupid," Macy said under her breath. "Maybe we should tell the others."

I grabbed her arm. "We aren't telling anyone, especially Emily."

"What's wrong with Emily?" Macy asked.

I groaned. How was it that the mean girls somehow always

ended up being Macy's friends? Alison had managed to be Macy's friend while also making fun of me behind her back all of high school. I wouldn't let Emily do the same.

"She found out that Jamie and I have a thing and she was able to piece everything together about tonight. Like, Jamie and I were together. She called him and I thought it was my phone ..."

Macy let out a low hum. "Yikes."

"Pretty much."

"So, what's the status now? Are they ..."

I shrugged and then shook my head. "He said he was going to talk to her tomorrow when they exchange Christmas gifts."

"Well, even if she's been rude to you, she deserves the private conversation," Macy said.

I was sure I'd rolled my eyes.

"I know but, it's just annoying," I said and started for the stairs. I was exhausted and wanted the whole day to just end. "And Emily said Jamie already gave her a Christmas gift tonight, so it's not like they have any reason to go out tomorrow."

That part felt like a hole in my chest. Why would he give her that kind of gift if he planned on breaking up with her? It wasn't like it was just any bracelet. If it really was engraved, then that message couldn't be removed. It would be there every time she wore it.

"I'm crashing in Izzy's room. I'm tired," I said once we'd reached the top of the stairs. Instead of leaving me, Macy followed me into the room and shut the door. Her face was full of empathy as she looked back at me as I stripped off the leather jacket and got under Izzy's thick comforter.

After a moment, I threw back the comforter next to me and slid to one side. With a smile, she climbed in and pulled the comforter over both of us.

"If there's anything I've learned after everything we've been through in the last few months, it's that you really are my number one," she said.

I felt the smile pull at my lips. "Same to you."

CHAPTER 27

T dreamt that I was drowning, except each time my vision went dark I woke up again and started the process over. I was a yard under the surface of the lake, close enough to see the sunlight overhead but far enough under to be surrounded by the dark water.

I heard the soft voice speak to me, the same one that told me to go to the lake whenever I wore the pendant. This time, it had new instructions. It was a distant chant telling me to run. The scene changed and I was in that cold jail cell in the Shadowlands. The witch stood behind the bars of the cell across from me, telling me to run. She chanted the words almost like a spell. The door opened, and I ran through the halls, past the tapestry of the three figures, and I was out the door and across the lawn. I reached the end of the dock where I slipped and hit the back of my head.

I opened my eyes, and I was staring at the ceiling of Izzy's bedroom. I looked to my right and Macy sat on the bed watching me with a worried expression.

"Are you okay? You were tossing," she said.

Before I could reply, the voice returned in my head.

Keep away.

Away from what? All this time the voice had been directing me toward the lake. It wanted me to go to the gate. As if reading my mind, the voice spoke again. This time, it was even softer, as if our connection was dying out.

Him.

"Tori?" Macy asked again, tapping my shoulder.

"Something's bugging me," I said and got out of the bed. "It's like my brain is trying to tell me something and it's just not fully clicking."

More like the voices. I was sure there was some kind of connection through the necklace. I didn't think these were demons. They had to be other guardians and if they were speaking to me, then maybe they were just like me. It made me sort through all the dreams and images that had floated through my brain the last few weeks.

"About last night?" she asked, watching as I moved around the room. My clothes were bloodstained from my encounter with Angel, so I pulled open the door to Izzy's closet and started looking for a comfortable outfit.

"This whole thing," I told her and turned from the closet with a pair of leggings and a T-shirt in my hands. "Everything since the shade arrived has been weird. We know she's been stalking me, so the fact that I kept seeing Alison in my dreams before she body-jumped isn't all the weird, but I keep … I think the voices speaking through the pendant have been trying to warn me whenever she's about to make a move."

"Did they just say something to you?" Macy asked, following my lead, and going to Izzy's closet for clean clothes.

I slid my feet into my boots, the only item in my outfit that was my own. "Yes."

"Okay. What did they say?"

"A voice told me to keep away," I said. I straightened up from tying my boots, thinking through everything that had happened since homecoming while Macy pulled a pair of leggings up her thighs.

First, it was seeing Alison. Then, it was the shadow demons in the corn maze. There were the voices telling me to go to the lake, which were now warning me to stay away. We know that the shade had been using Alison's body and left her body for another. She was a blonde, according to Angel.

"Keep away from what? Keep away from the shade? Yeah, that's easy to do when we don't even know what she looks like," Macy said and flattened a shirt over her stomach.

I ignored her and continued sorting through what we knew. I was sure she was the witch who helped me escape the Shadowlands. That made her blonde. We didn't know much about the shade, but I did have a theory about how she was here and not in the Shadowlands. When I visited CU Boulder and saw those students rehearsing, it sent me down a rabbit hole filled with Greek myths. According to the stories, shades were like ghosts. They were here because something was anchoring them to our world. If that was the case, then the shade had somehow left a part of herself behind. It was something that Alison had. It was the only reason why she would've ended up in her body first.

"The shade is only here because some kind of personal

object is keeping her here," I said aloud, tightening my fist around the pendant as if I could summon the voices.

"Like your necklace?" Macy asked as she finished tying her boots. "You think she had some kind of talisman? How would she have even gotten it here?"

I opened my mouth to say that it didn't have to be jewelry, just a personal object that held deep significance to the shade. But maybe it was a piece of jewelry. The idea of getting something through the gate and into the mortal world jogged my memory to that night I woke up on the dock of the Shallows.

It started with me helping a witch to cross the Shallows. I was able to open the gate at the end and let us both into the Shadowlands. That's when everything fell apart. We wound up in a dungeon and I only escaped because of her. The witch used an ice spell to knock out the guard and take his keys. Instead of freeing herself, she helped me escape and gave me a gift I could use to pay off the ferryman into letting me cross back to the mortal world. Only, he didn't accept it. He let me keep it.

I had only worn that bracelet a few times before Alison stole it off me at the homecoming game. I got so used to putting it on that I forgot about the initials engraved on the gold band. *E. L. M.* I only now remembered reading the words engraved on the inside of the bracelet.

I love you forever- Jay

My breath caught in my chest. I left Macy standing in the middle of the room and went back to the bed, rummaging through the sheets to find my phone. When I opened it, I got a low battery warning. I dismissed it and opened Angel's text message from last night. I searched for through my phone until I found a photo of all the girls in our circle that day we met at Starbucks. I attached the photo to a text and sent it to Angel, sending another text asking if he could identify anyone in the photo.

"What just happened?" Macy asked, coming to my side of the bed. I moved past her with my phone in my hand, hoping it didn't die before I got a response.

"I think that the object anchoring the shade here is a bracelet," I told her.

My phone vibrated and I opened the message.

The one in front. I didn't see the color in her hair until now, but that's her.

My stomach burned with anger. It all made sense now. The bracelet. The ice powers. She even used the same move on me last night that she'd used on that guard in the castle.

"Emily said Jamie gave her a bracelet, but it didn't make any sense. He said he was giving her a gift today," I said, letting Macy take my phone and look through the messages.

"The shade is possessing Emily's body?" she asked.

I shook my head. "No, Emily *is* the shade. That witch that helped me out of the Shadowlands, she used ice powers. She was blonde. I knew Emily looked familiar. That's why Jamie was so surprised by her appearance. She tried changing the way she looked so I wouldn't remember."

"Holy shit," Macy said. "You were right about those voices. They want you to keep away. We've got to go. *Now.*"

As if on cue, I heard the faint voice again.

Him.

My heart was pounding in my chest now. I threw the door open and went down the hall to Jamie's room. The room was empty. Bed made. There wasn't a sign that anyone was here at all. I opened my phone and dialed Jamie's number as I walked back to Izzy's room.

I could hear a distant buzzing and I felt my stomach drop when Macy lifted Jamie's phone from under the comforter.

Shit. Shit. Shit.

"The voices weren't telling me to keep away. They were telling me to keep Jamie away," I said, pulling on my leather jacket and leading the way toward the stairs.

"Emily said they were going to the meadow at the national park to exchange Christmas gifts this morning," Macy called out as I went out the front door.

"We have to get there fast," I said and ran toward her car in the driveway. "The voices weren't trying to lead me into the lake. They were telling me that someone else is trying to. Emily is using Jamie. She's going to take him through the gate to lure me there."

"Why not just take your blood in your sleep?" Macy asked as we both climbed into our seats. I had barely clicked my seatbelt into place when she threw the car in reverse, and we were backing into a very jerky two-point turn.

"Why take my blood to the Shadow Mistress when you could deliver me alive?" I asked.

Macy put the car in drive and took a deep breath. "I'm going to need you to do your telekinesis thing."

Before I realized what she meant, the tires screeched on the pavement and we were flying toward the main gate. I held both my hands out and the gate flew off the hinges and across the road, settling against the trees in the ditch.

We drove so fast down the mountain that I worried we might get pulled over. We were lucky. We didn't pass a single car on the way through town and the road to the national park was so free from traffic that a dusting of snow lay across the pavement.

"I'm calling Izzy and Puck," I said, the phone already ringing in my ear. I held my breath with each ring, hoping it wasn't so early in the morning that they were still asleep.

Please be awake. Please be ready to come help.

"Izzy," I said.

"Damn. Why are you yelling?"

"You guys have to get to the meadow at the national park. Jamie's in trouble. Emily's the shade." The words tumbled out of my mouth so quickly that I wasn't sure she'd heard me. It was so silent that I checked to make sure the call hadn't dropped.

"What? What do you mean?" she asked.

"Emily is the shade. I'll explain how I know later, but you have to get here. She's going to pull Jamie into the gate." I barely got the words out before I heard a beep in my ear. When I looked at my phone, the screen was black. No amount of button mashing would make it light up.

"Don't worry. We're at the lot," Macy said as turned onto the main road of the national park. The car fishtailed as she made it to the parking lot of the community building. She stopped the car parallel with a parking spot. I threw my door open and stepped right into a snowbank that went up to my knee.

"The meadow!" I yelled and tried my best to run through the thick snow. It was an exhausting effort. I could hear Macy panting just behind me.

"There has to be a faster way," Macy said.

Maybe there was.

I thrust my arms out, a grunt coming out with it that surprised me. The snow ahead of us parted in a shower of white dust, creating a nearly clear path of brown grass. Macy cheered me on as I kept the pace. I used my powers every couple of yards until we had moved far enough into the forest that the snow was easier to run over.

I wondered if I could run faster if I'd taken a pair of Izzy's sneakers or if they would've just contributed to how cold I was. I could feel sweat building under the sleeves of my jacket. My feet ached in my snow boots and just as I began to panic that we wouldn't make it in time, I saw the clearing ahead.

"Go! Go! Go!" I yelled, more for my own motivation than for Macy.

"Tori?" Jamie called out.

They were standing near the edge of the meadow, too close together for my comfort.

"Jamie, get away from her!" I yelled as I ran closer.

He looked back at me like I'd lost my mind.

"Why are you here?"

"She's the shade," I said and stopped running.

Emily glared back at me and moved a step closer to Jamie. Just as he started to ask why I would accuse her, I used my powers to knock him off his feet. He stumbled away from her and fell into the snow, staring back at me in shock.

"She's the witch from the Shadowlands—at least she pretended to be. She gave me a bracelet to get back through the gate," I told him.

"What is wrong with you?" Emily said, feigning her usual innocent expression.

"Jamie, you gave her a bracelet the last time she was here, one that said you would love her forever. It had her nickname for you. Jay. I'm right, aren't I?" I asked.

"How could you ..." He stopped mid-sentence, getting to his feet and looking back at Emily. Panic flashed through her eyes before the anger returned.

"You would've taken her deal, if it had been you," Emily told me. "All I had to do was bring you to her. She made my powers stronger. She promised to let me leave the Shadowlands for good if I did that one thing."

"Emily," Jamie said, still recovering from the betrayal.

"You're a guardian. You've sold your soul to the Shadowlands for what—immortality and power?" I asked.

Emily shrugged, a smirk spreading on her face.

"I've lived longer than any of you. I've seen decades go by and cultures shift. I am our entire history." She laughed as if me discovering her secret was the most insignificant part.

"History is exactly what you'll be," I told her and dug my heel into the snow.

I tried using my powers to throw her into the trees, but she conjured a sheet of ice between us. It shattered from the force of my powers, raining shards of ice over us. I felt them tugging at my jacket sleeves, one leaving a stinging cut across my right cheek. When I lowered my arms to face her again, she was standing behind Jamie with a knife at his throat.

Before I could raise a hand, something pulled her from behind. She stumbled backward, arms flailing at the unseen force holding her by her ponytail. With a scream of frustration, she held an arm out and an icy spear came up from the ground. She grabbed ahold of it and thrust it over her shoulder, Macy's scream echoing off the trees.

Macy appeared just behind her, clutching the spear that stuck through her left shoulder and out her back.

Jamie reached over his shoulder and grabbed Emily by the back of her head. He doubled over, flipping her over his back and slamming her to the ground. Just as he bent over to grab her, I saw the flash of metal and Jamie let out a yell.

Emily pointed a finger toward the trees and a slab of ice appeared over the snow. She gave Jamie a shove and he fell onto it, hands pressed to his stomach where a dark pool of blood was seeping into his shirt. Emily climbed on top of him and kicked at the snow. They began sliding away from the meadow and with a final triumphant smile, they disappeared into the trees.

CHAPTER 28

"Macy?" I asked, looking back at her. She managed to pull the spear free, blood leaking down her shoulder.

"Go! I'll catch up," she said past her wince.

I didn't wait. I ran through the trees, using my power to plow through the snow the way I had earlier. I could hear the ice sled skidding over the snow, but I couldn't see them. I knew where we were heading though, so I pushed the pace. I ran as fast as I could. It got easier as the ground sloped downward.

"Tori, watch out!" Macy yelled.

I heard the howl of the wind through the trees. No, not the wind.

I was tumbling down the slope, the razor claws of a shadow demon on my right arm as we came to a stop at the base of a tree. I raised my left hand, and the demon was ripped from my arm, taking with it a handful of leather and piece of flesh. My scream burst from my lungs before I recognized it as my own.

Blood poured from the gash in my jacket and onto the

snow. I tried to ignore the pain and got to my feet, running through the last of the trees.

"Jamie!" I yelled. I could see them at the bank. The shallow edge of the water was iced over, but a few yards away the freezing water was hauntingly still. Jamie lay on the ice, unconscious. Emily stood over him, looking up at me as I raced for the bank.

"Looks like I'm bringing the mistress two guardians for the price of one," she said, grabbing onto Jamie's ankle and pulling him closer to the edge of the ice.

If Jamie went into the gate without a match, he wouldn't be leaving no matter what I did. I ran as hard as I could toward the frozen lake, throwing my body onto the ice as Emily sank into the water. Jamie began to slide into the lake, his eyes flying open once he was the water lapped over his knees. He flipped onto his stomach and reached out to me.

I grabbed his hand just as his chest slipped into the water. He pulled me in after him. The cold water felt like knives, sharp and nearly took my breath away as it swirled around us. I focused on the task at hand as we sank, Emily our anchor.

I wrapped my arms around his neck and my legs around his hips. I brought my lips to his and suddenly everything felt warm. It was radiating from my chest all the way to the tips of my fingers and toes. I felt like I'd woken from the longest night of sleep on the most comfortable mattress. The water felt warm around us as we moved. I wrapped my arms tighter around him, running my thumb along his jaw. My heart skipped in my chest as he cinched his arms around my waist, locking me in place too tightly for anything to break us free. And I didn't want to break free, but the feel of something firm around us and the flicker of candlelight over my face brought me out of the trance and into the boat on the Shallows.

"What the hell," Jamie breathed next to me.

"Where is she?" I asked, looking toward the dock. It was empty, not even the new ferryman there to help.

My heart leaped into my throat as our boat rocked, the only thing keeping me from going overboard was Jamie's firm grip on my jacket.

"Things keep getting better," Emily said from the boat beside us. "You're easier to kill now."

Jamie leaned out of our boat and grabbed onto the front of hers. Emily nearly lost her balance when he pulled the boats together. With a single hand and a quick twist, a crack split the front of her boat, so the blue water began pouring in.

Emily stepped into our boat as hers slipped under the water, fear in her eyes for the first time. The power burst so easily from me that it felt like breathing. Emily was launched from our boat and at least five feet into the air. Before she landed on the water, the entire pool iced over. She slid feet from the dock and turned to launch shards of ice at us.

Jamie shielded me with his body. I heard him groan in my ear before straightening up again. One of the shards had caught his shoulder, ripping opening the fabric of his jacket.

"What happened to you, Emily?" Jamie asked, his voice a roar in the cave. Emily smiled back at him, standing on the ice with her head held high. "What happened to the Emily Mason I fell in love with?"

The words pierced, but I know that knife wasn't meant for me. Still, it didn't seem to affect Emily, who laughed back at him.

"I thought I loved you once, but we weren't a match," she said as though it was all the explanation he needed.

Jamie was stunned.

"Did you ever love me?" he asked, his voice more curious than hurt.

Emily's expression softened. Her eyes went to Jamie, and I

could see the pain in her face. I thought for a moment that their connection would save us, but when she looked at me, I knew there was no coming back. She straightened up and held her head high.

Emily shrugged. "If I did, would I be able to do this?"

She pointed at Jamie and a spear of ice rocketed toward him. I used my powers to stop it a few feet away so that it burst into tiny fragments. I hadn't seen Emily running at us until it was too late. She tackled me, sending me to my back on the boat. I backhanded her across the face before I felt her fist connect with my cheek.

Her weight lifted off me and once my vision recovered, I saw Jamie toss her over the frozen Shallows like a doll. She slid away from us. Jamie leaped out of the boat after her. At first, he seemed in control of his momentum. Then, Emily added another layer of ice before him. It sent him off balance, just enough that she was able to give him a push that sent him crashing.

"Don't," Emily warned as I raised a hand. She stepped over Jamie's back, pulling him into a kneeling position by his hair. Her silver dagger was just under his chin. The memory of our kiss filled me with terror. I lowered my arm.

Emily reached into her pocket with her free hand and pulled out a vial. She held it up so I could see it before she tossed it at me. I caught it in my right hand and looked down at it in my palm. A few drops of blood for the sake of Jamie's life.

"Tori, don't," Jamie said.

I looked up at him. He winced as Emily tugged his hair, so he was staring at the darkness above us. Emily smirked my way before pressing a kiss to Jamie's throat just above the blade of her dagger.

"Your choice," she told me.

I ignored Jamie's protests as I pulled my demon dagger free from my waist. Just as I had the day before for Angel, I sliced my palm and let the blood flow into the vial. Instead of beginning to heal, the cut ached as I stoppered the vial and tossed it to Jamie. He caught it, sending me a somber expression.

"You have what you need. Your mistress will be happy. Let him go," I told Emily.

She smiled. "That was before I realized you'd matched. Just a few inches and I can cut your strength in half. What's a mortal guardian without their match?"

My scream vanished in the earsplitting sound of shattering ice. Jamie had used her hesitation to smash his fist against the Shallows. A deep crack grew between his legs before the entire pool broke apart and they both went under.

"Jamie!" The echo of my voice was the only sound before Emily and Jamie broke the surface, both gasping. They swam franticly toward the boat, and I scrambled to the edge, arms outstretched toward Jamie.

"Hurry. Hurry up!" I told him.

Emily let out a scream so terrifying that it iced my veins. She was gone in seconds, slipping farther and farther away until it was hard to distinguish her writhing body from the dark souls swirling around her.

"It's fine. I'm fine," Jamie said, his fingers reaching mine for just moments before he was pulled under. I tried grabbing for his arms, but the water was slimy.

"No. No. No." I stood up and did the only thing I could. I held a hand over the water and focused my power on the spot under me. I could feel the resistance for a second and then a pulling sensation. Jamie erupted from the surface, enough force behind my power that he was able to grab onto the edge of our boat.

"I got you," I said and helped tow him onboard. He lay flat

on the floor, panting. The water slid off him in thick pieces. I leaned over his chest and cupped his face, looking for any sign of injury as he caught his breath.

"I thought my blood would be enough. I thought she would let you go," I said, feeling the sting of tears in my eyes.

Jamie nodded and slowly sat up. He held up a hand, showing me the vial of blood. I couldn't contain my relief. A laugh burst from my chest, and I was so glad to see that he was smiling too. He put the vial in his pocket, and he reached out to cup my face the same moment the boat lurched under us.

I turned to see the ferryman standing at the edge of the dock with a hand fully extended toward us. Jamie slipped his hand in mine as we were towed in. We stopped at the edge of the dock before the dark figure.

"Dad?" Jamie asked, getting to his feet. I stopped him with a hand over his chest.

"Your dad moved on after homecoming," I told him. I could sense it. When he betrayed the Shadow Mistress, it broke whatever had imprisoned him and he turned to ash. He was gone.

I turned back to the new ferryman. He held both hands out to us now. He held one hand with his palm skyward, as though waiting for me to place something in his hand. With the other he rubbed his index finger and thumb together.

Payment.

"We aren't giving him the vial," Jamie said.

"If we don't give him something, he won't let us back through the gate," I said. I thought for a moment about what I could possibly have that would be worth anything.

I did have one thing.

I pulled the necklace over my head and held it out to him, the pendant catching the candlelight at the bow of our boat so I could see the Roman numerals for six etched into it. I was glad that Jamie stayed quiet. The ferryman stood perfectly still as though assessing the necklace for its worth.

In one quick move, he wrapped a hand around my wrist, and I was inches away from his dark hood. Jamie let out a string of curses behind me, hands fighting to take mine. I used my power to give him just enough of a push so that he was forced to sit in the boat. The ferryman raised his hood to my face, watching me from within the darkness.

"Take it," I told him.

His free hand pulled the necklace from my grasp. He let go of me roughly, so I fell backward into Jamie. The ferryman stepped to the very edge of the dock and held both hands over us. When he lowered them in a quick movement, the boat tipped to the right and we were both tossed into the water.

I opened my mouth to scream, but the freezing water stole the air from my lungs. The clear water of the Shallows darkened until we were back in the icy lake in the national park. I looked around for Jamie as I kicked for the surface, seeing him several feet away.

We broke the surface of the lake at the same time, our eyes meeting. We closed the space between us in seconds, his hands on my face and mine on his.

"You're hurt," I said, remembering the cut at his shoulder.

"It's not bad," he said, eyes roving the cut on my cheek.

"I'm fine," I told him and for once, instead of obsessing over my wellbeing, he pulled my face to his. Our legs knocked against each other as we kissed, our chattering teeth interrupting the moment not long after.

I turned to swim ahead of him and noticed two figures emerging from the trees. One was a man and the other a young girl. They leaned into each other in conversation, never taking their eyes off us.

"Jamie," I said, slowing my pace so he could join me. The

frozen bank was just a few yards away, putting us close enough now to get a better look at the approaching figures. The boy had short, dark hair and was dressed in jeans and a sweatshirt. The girl next to him looked maybe seven or eight. Her dark hair was cut short around her face, and she had blunt bangs that were straight across her brow. After a moment I recognized her as the girl from the photo Jamie's mom had taped in her diary.

Suri.

"No way," Jamie said as he stared at them. Before I could ask if he knew them, he swam toward the bank. He pulled himself onto the ice and carefully got to his feet. He waited for me, helping me navigate the ice so we didn't fall through. Once we made it to the bank, he approached the man, not even looking at the peculiar girl next to him.

"Jamie," the man said with a smile.

"Ahmad? Is it really you?" Jamie asked.

Ahmad opened his arms in invitation and Jamie pulled him into a hug, tight enough that Ahmad grunted from the force of it. The girl approached me and stopped just a few feet away, staring up at me curiously the way you might stare at a painting in a museum.

"You're the other anchor," she said. My body recognized her voice before I did, chills running up my back. The ghostly voice I'd been hearing had been hers this whole time.

"Suri," I said.

She didn't seem surprised that I knew her name. Her expression remained neutral.

"I was worried," she said and looked over the lake. "I couldn't sense you the last twenty minutes."

She looked at my chest and I knew she was looking for the necklace.

"I took off the necklace," I told her.

Her brow furrowed. "Took it off? Why?"

"It's complicated."

Jamie approached us now with an arm around Ahmad, both smiling like it was the best day ever.

"This is Tori, my match," he said.

The words made me feel light. I caught his eye for a second, just long enough to feel the longing. That would have to wait for later.

"Hi," I said and shook his hand.

"This is Ahmad. I told you about him when I asked you to homecoming," Jamie said. It took me a moment to remember the story. Ahmad was the only other guardian with telekinesis he and Izzy had ever met. He said Ahmad could do some amazing things. Jamie told me telekinesis was rare and here we were, three of us in tiny Burbrook.

"It's good to meet you. Jamie told me you just disappeared one day," I said, hoping I wasn't ruining the moment.

Ahmad's smile faded a little and he looked at Suri.

"She took off the necklace," Suri said. "That's why I couldn't sense her."

"Took it off?" Ahmad asked and looked at me with the same confusion that she had. "Why?"

Something told me that the necklace was more important that I thought.

"We used it to buy off the ferryman," Jamie said. "It was that or her blood."

Suri and Ahmad looked horrified.

"In all my years, I've never found an anchor who gave away their talisman," Suri said. She turned her blank expression on me and let out a long sigh. Then, she started walking back into the trees.

Ahmad looked from her to us as though deciding what to do.

"Suri? Suri, wait," he called to her, following a moment later.

"I knew that pendant was important," I said.

Jamie gave my hand a squeeze. "It was all we could do to get back here. They need your blood."

"What if they need that pendant, too?" I asked, looking straight at him. Worry crossed his face. He never was good at hiding his emotions.

"We'll figure it out," he said, lifting my hand and pressing his lips to my knuckles.

We looked up when we heard Ahmad approaching. He looked frustrated, like whatever Suri said had been scathing enough that he was having a hard time deciding how to relay the message to us.

"Is there somewhere private where we could talk?" he asked.

I was glad he was ready to move somewhere warmer. I could barely contain my shivering. Jamie nodded.

"Ahmad," he started before his friend could take more than a few steps back toward the trees. "Why are you here?"

Ahmad's face said it all. He was sorry for vanishing without a word. They had been good friends and he left them.

"We know how to close the gate," he said. He glanced toward the trees where I was sure Suri was. "We've done it twice before."

Ahmad glanced my way, as though he understood something about me that I hadn't yet realized. He left us standing together on the bank while he went to talk with Suri again. It was my turn to give Jamie's hand a squeeze.

"Do you trust him?" I asked.

Jamie nodded. "With my life."

That made me feel a fraction better. If there was a way to close the gate without finishing our circle and without all our members finding their match, then we could all move on with our lives sooner rather than later. College wasn't the far-off dream I feared. Still, something about the way Ahmad and Suri looked at me told me the worst was ahead.

"They're here to help. More guardians means less demons and more manpower, should we need it. This is the best thing that's happened to our circle in a very long time," Jamie said and pressed a kiss to my temple. "I have you and you have me. Everything is going to be fine."

I thought about the vision the ferryman showed me on homecoming night. As much as I wish I could forget, or pretend it wasn't real, that vision ended with Jamie face down in the lake at the Shadow Mistress's feet.

"Yeah," I said, more aware than ever of how cold I was. "Fine."

ACKNOWLEDGMENTS

These characters have been so much fun to write, and I am so thankful for all the people who helped me make them come to life. This book is dedicated to my college roommate, someone who always encouraged me in my writing and never saw the mistakes in my work (even the really bad grammar mistakes) but was always the first person to explain all the good parts. Malory, you may not have read the early draft first, but having read my first drafts before, you've taught me to always see the good first (in my books and life) before I start to address the not-so-good. I think everyone needs someone like that, a little ray of sunshine between the clouds. Malory, you showed me how to find the sunlight in a time when my world was nothing but clouds. I am a better person thanks to our friendship.

Of course, none of the things I have accomplished would have been possible without the support and encouragement of my family. Alex, you are always the first to give me the push I need to get started and always the voice of reason. If I have a problem, you seem to know each time how to find the answer. You're amazing. I love you. You have helped me and given me the support I needed to grow into the best version of myself. Again, I love you.

I couldn't create the books like I do without a team of professionals to help along the way. I may have created the story, but my wonderful editor is the one who helps make sure the story is as strong as it can be. Lucia Ferrara, thank you for all of your hard work and honest feedback. I promise I'll remember it's "toward" and not "towards" in the next book. I can't wait to continue writing stories with you to tell me when they suck. You do great work and I've become a better writer with each book you've edited.

Becoming the best writer that I can be and transforming my stories into the most polished version is only part of what makes a book stand out. Lena Yang, your beautiful cover designs help these stories stand out on the shelves and I always make sure to mention your name each time I get a compliment on how beautiful they are. I'm amazed each time by how you can take my disorganized ideas and turn them into these masterpieces. I can't wait to work with you on the conclusion to this series and the many other stories I have planned.

Of course, I have to thank you, the reader. Thank you for reading my stories and for all of the support you've shown me. It means the world to me. My wonderful readers are the reason I can continue to write the stories that I do, and I could never thank them enough. Thank you. Thank you.

ABOUT THE AUTHOR

Amy Prokopis is a fiction author from Oklahoma who writes books for young adults. She loves writing everything from science fiction and fantasy to contemporary romance. She graduated from Oklahoma State University with a bachelor's degree in English and a minor in German before obtaining a master's degree in school counseling. Besides writing, Amy enjoys distance running and spending time with her husband, their son, and their Havanese, June.

ALSO BY AMY PROKOPIS

The Arena

Kenna Riley is Aldierian, but no one but her adoptive father knows and no one else can. All she wants is to escape poverty in her village. All that changes when her identity is outed, she's branded a terrorist, and is sentenced to death in the arena.

Kieran Grace wants to leave the capital of Gallaterra and get as far away from his father as he can. After speaking out against the war with the Aldierans one too many times, he's ordered to live up to his family's legacy by killing an Aldierian in the arena.

Together they do something no one else has, escape the arena and learn a Gallaterran secret along the way. In their search for help from the Aldierians, they find adventure and opportunity that they never thought they'd be allowed. It makes their mission even more dangerous. Despite fighting together, they both must decide what is worth sacrificing alone.

Guardians of the Sixth Gate

Guardians of the Sixth Gate. Complete the circle. Find your match.

Victoria "Tori" Johnson wants senior year to be different. Tired of being the straight-laced brainiac living in the shadow of her best friend, she agrees to go to her first high school party where she gets in an accident that should've killed her. Instead, she wakes up to discover that boring Burbrook isn't as quiet as it seems.

Jamie Quinn, and his mysterious sister, Izzy, introduce her to their circle of guardians and an underground world where supernatural abilities and dark creatures run rampant. Without a complete circle of guardians, the trio are left to destroy the evil that finds its way through the gate.

As if fighting demons wasn't hard enough, the Ferryman from the Shadowlands launches a hunt for Tori's blood. The trio search for ways to protect her and the reason why her blood is so important. Tori worries that there may be more to Jamie Quinn than leather jackets and straight-A's. He might be her match. A match would strengthen their circle and render them both mortal, but it would come at a devastating price. Is it possible to outrun fate or will resisting destroy any chance they have of sealing the gate for good?

TURN THE PAGE FOR A
SNEAK PEEK OF BOOK 2

CHAPTER 1

The Audi was already running. I felt the warmth the moment I opened the door and couldn't help the sigh of relief from slipping past my chattering teeth. I was still dripping from swimming in the freezing lake and Jamie and I had walked a painful fifteen minutes to make it to his car, Ahmad and Suri following close behind.

"I wish Izzy was with us," I said. I was sure her powers would make her the perfect human hairdryer right now. Thinking of her made me remember Macy on the other side of the lake. We told Macy and Puck to find us at the national park, but they didn't get there in time before everything unfolded.

"Damn," Jamie said under his breath. He held his iPhone in his right hand, the screen dark. If I wasn't shivering so much, I might've been more concerned by the fact that mine had gone through the watery gate and back out again in the confine of my jacket.

Ahmad and Suri closed the back doors, and I glanced in the rearview mirror at them. Ahmad looked as if this was the best day in his life. It was a little annoying, but also endearing. He was an old friend of Jamie's. He also said he knew how to close the gate and had done it twice. Those words changed everything. If they could help us, and fast, then I didn't have to worry so much about the ferryman's vision of Jamie drowning in the lake. All I had to do was keep him close and adjust to the change in my powers now that we're matched. We were stronger now together than we were apart, despite our immortality leaving.

I caught a pair of dark eyes, laser-focused on me in the mirror. Suri didn't move. Unlike me, she wasn't at all shocked to catch my attention. The girl was so short that all I could see of her was her eyes and the top of her head, but even that was enough for me to feel the scrutiny. If I hadn't been there when Ahmad introduced us, I would've thought I'd offended her. Maybe I had, somehow. Or maybe, I was a disappointment. Something about what had happened at the lake seemed to set her off. It's the reason she'd gone back into the trees and Ahmad had to chase after her. Something hadn't gone the way she'd hoped.

A shiver ran up my spine.

My attention went back to the road as Jamie put the car in reverse and the tires crunched over snow. Once we made our way through the entrance to the park and were back on the highway toward Burbrook, he reached his hand over his shoulder.

"I need to call our circle," he said.

Ahmad fished his phone from his pocket and handed it to Jamie who then held it to me. I took it and looked down at the unlocked screen. The photo behind all the apps was of Ahmad. His arms were wrapped around a girl who was laughing, his lips pressed to her neck while her head was tossed back in laughter. She had dark hair with caramel highlights throughout that shimmered in the sunlight.

"Nine, eight, three..."

I quickly opened the right app and began to type in the number, putting the phone on speaker as soon as it started to ring. It wasn't long before someone picked up. I could hear a car door slamming shut and then the hard crunch of snow underfoot.

"Jamie? Tori?" Izzy asked, breathless.

"We're both here and we have guests," Jamie said.

There was a second of silence. "What? Who?"

"Tori and I don't have working phones, so you'll have to tell everyone to meet us at the estate. We'll explain when we get there." Jamie said.

Izzy was in the middle of asking what had happened when Jamie took the phone from my hand and ended the call. He held it over his shoulder for Ahmad.